A Canadian Professor escapes suicide only to have his sister disappear without a trace...

A computer-linked burglar rescues a young woman from the terminal ecstasy of "wire-heading..."

Two men and one woman search for—and find—the ultimate frontier of experience, in a major new novel by one of today's most acclaimed science fiction talents.

Spider Robinson's
MINDKILLER

"Spider Robinson gives you the computerized world of tomorrow... This is a good one!"

—Robert Sheckley

"Full of action and suspense..."

—*Publishers Weekly*

MINDKILLER

A NOVEL OF THE NEAR FUTURE

SPIDER ROBINSON

BERKLEY BOOKS, NEW YORK

MINDKILLER

A Berkley Book/published by arrangement with
Holt, Rinehart and Winston

PRINTING HISTORY
Holt, Rinehart edition/September 1982
Berkley edition/November 1983

This book is dedicated
to Psyche
and to Allison.

ACKNOWLEDGMENTS

In writing this novel I have borrowed from the ideas, insights, and observations of many people. In no particular order, they are:

Dr. Jim Lynch, my oldest friend, who first put me onto brain reward; Larry Niven, whose novella "Death by Ecstasy" is probably the definitive story on the subject; Dr. Jerry Pournelle; Dr. Adam Reed of Rockefeller University; Bob Shaw; Aryeh Routtenberg, whose article in the November 1978 *Scientific American* was the final spark for the creation of this book; John D. MacDonald; Robert A. Heinlein; and of course Olds and Milner, who started the whole thing by poking electrodes into rat brains at McGill University in the 1950s. None of these gentlemen is to blame for what I have done with their ideas; as I write, only two are even aware that I have borrowed from them.

Research assistance was given me by Bob Atkinson, Bill

Jones, John Bell, George Allanson, and Andrew Gilbert; Bob Atkinson typed more than half the manuscript while my arm was in a cast. Invaluable suggestions were made by my editor, Donald Hutter of Holt, Rinehart and Winston, and by my agent, Kirby McCauley. Jeanne, my other leg, read the whole thing in progress, called me back from the blind alleys, and helped me patch the leaks. Heartfelt thanks to them all. Oh, and thanks to the Gunner in Brattleboro for the Atcheson Assault Twelve and to the Sea Breeze Inn in St. Margaret's Bay for the hospitality.

Any resemblance between characters in this book and real people, living or dead, is unintentional. A character's opinions should *never* necessarily be taken to be those of the author, but I would like at this time to specifically repudiate any derogatory opinions about the city of Halifax expressed by characters hereinafter. It is the nicest city I have ever inhabited. But try persuading a New Yorker of that!

For those interested in influences, this book was written on a steady diet of Charlie Parker, Jon Hendricks, Frank Zappa, John Lennon, Tom Waits, and the Dixie Dregs.

—HALIFAX, 1981

1

1994   Halifax Harbor at night is a beautiful sight, and June usually finds the MacDonald Bridge lined with lovers and other appreciators. But in Halifax even June can turn on one with icy claws.

A thermometer sheltered from the brisk wind would have shown a little below Centigrade zero. Norman Kent had the magnificent scenery all to himself.

He was aware of the view; it was before his face, and his eyes were not closed. He was aware of the cold too, because occasionally when he worked his face frozen tears would break and fall from his cheeks. Neither meant anything to him. He was even vaguely aware of the sound of steady traffic behind him, successive dopplers like the rhythmic moaning of some wounded giant. They meant nothing to him either. On careful reflection Norman could think of nothing that *did* mean anything to him, and so he put one leg over the outer rail.

A voice came out of the night. "Hey, Cap, *don't!*"

He froze for a long moment. Running footsteps approached from the Dartmouth end of the bridge. Norman turned and saw the man coming up fast in the wash of passing headlights, and that decided him. He got the other leg over and stood teetering on the narrow ledge, the wind full in his face. His hat blew off, and insanely he spun around after it and incredibly he caught it, and was caught himself at wrist and forearm by two very strong hands. They dragged him bodily back over the rail again, nearly breaking his arm, and deposited him hard on his back on the pedestrian walkway. His breath left him, and he lay there blinking up at bridge structure and midnight sky for perhaps half a minute.

He became aware that his unwanted rescuer was sitting beside him, back against the rail and to the wind, breathing heavily. Norman rolled his head, felt cold stone bite his cheek, saw a large man in a shabby coat, silhouetted against a pool of light. From the frosted breath he knew that the large man was shaking his head.

Norman lifted himself on his elbows and sat beside the other, lifting his collar against the cold. He fumbled out a pack of Players Light and lit one with a flameless lighter. He held it out to the man, who accepted it silently, and lit another for himself.

"My wife left me," Norman said. "Six years this August, and she left me. Six *years!* Said she married too soon, she had to 'find herself.' And the semester's almost over, I've bitched it all up, nothing at all lined up for the summer, and there's a really good chance I won't be hired back in September. Old MacLeod with his hoary hints about austerity and sacrifices and a department chairman's heavy responsibility, he wouldn't even come right out and tell me! *Find* herself, for Christ's stinking sake! Got herself a nineteen-year-old plumbing student, he's going to help her *find* herself." He broke off and smoked for a while. When he could speak again he said, "Perhaps I could have handled either one, but the two together is . . . it's only fair to tell you, I'm going to try again, and you can't stop me forever."

The other spoke for the first time. His voice was deep and

gravelly and dispassionate. "Don't let me stop you."

Norman turned to stare. "Then why—?" He stopped then, for the knife picked up the oncoming headlights very well.

"I never meant to *stop* you, Cap," the large man said calmly. "Just, uh—heh, heh—hold you up a little."

He was not even troubling to keep the knife hidden from the traffic. Norman glanced briefly at the oncoming cars; as in a slapstick movie sequence he saw four drivers, one after the other, do the identical single-take and then return their eyes grimly to the road. He yanked his own eyes back to the knife. It was quite large and looked sharp. The large man held it as though he knew how, and all at once it came to Norman that he had cashed a check today, and had two hundred New dollars in twenties in his wallet.

He let go of his cigarette and the wind took it. He put his gloved left hand palm up on his lap. On it he placed his wallet, his cigarettes, a half-empty pack of joints, and the small lighter. As he peeled the watch from the inside of his wrist he noticed that both hands were shaking badly. Oh, yes, he told himself, that's right, it is very cold. He added the watch to the pile, worked the right glove off against his hip, and took his pocket change in that hand.

"On my lap, brother," the large man directed. "Then go. Back to town or over the side, it's all the same to me."

Norman sighed deeply, and flung everything high and to his right. Nearly all of it went over the rail and into the harbor; a few bills were blown into traffic and toward the other rail.

The large man sat motionless. His eyes did not follow the loot but remained fixed on Norman, who stared back.

At last the large man got to his feet. "Cap," he said, shaking his head again, "you got a lot of hard bark on you." The knife disappeared. "Sorry I bothered you." He turned and began walking back toward Dartmouth, hunching against the wind, still smoking Norman's cigarette.

"You gutless bastard," Norman whispered, and wondered who he was talking to.

Norman Kent was thirty years old. He was one hundred and sixty-five centimeters tall and weighed fifty-five kilograms—

although, having been born in America in 1965, he habitually thought of himself as five-five and a hundred and twenty pounds. Despite his actual stature, people usually remembered him as being of average height: there was a solidity to his body and movements. It implied a strength and physical conditioning he had not actually possessed since leaving the United States Army six years before. His face was passable, with wide-set grey eyes, a perfect aquiline nose, and a chin that would have seemed strong if it had not been topped by a mouth a fraction too wide. Overdeveloped folds at each corner of the mouth made it seem, when at rest, to be a faint, smug smile.

One could have flattered him most by calling him elegant. He had shaved for his suicide. The suit was tasteful enough to befit an assistant professor of English—it was his best suit—and the topcoat was pure quality. At thirty his hairline had not yet receded visibly. He wore his hair moderately long; the wind had whipped it into a fantastic sculpture and kept revising the design. The only nonconformist indulgence he permitted himself was his necktie, which looked like a riot in a paint shop.

After a time he put his glove back on, got stiffly to his feet, and left the bridge at the Halifax end, stamping his feet to restore circulation. He had not known genuine physical fear in six years, and he had forgotten the exhilaration that comes with survival. It was a twenty-minute walk home, and he savored every step. The smell of the harbor, the seedy waterfront squalor of Hollis Street, the brave, forlorn hookers too frozen to display their wares, the fake stained glass in the front windows of Skipper's Lounge, the special and inimitable color of leaves backlit by a street light, the clacking sounds of traffic lights and the laboring power plant of Victoria General Hospital—all were brand new again, treasures to be appreciated for the first time. He walked happily, mindless as a child. When he reached his apartment tower on Wellington Street, he was whistling. On the way up in the elevator, he graduated to humming, and by the time he reached his floor he was singing the words too, whereupon he was amused to discover that the tune he had been humming so merrily was the old Tom Lehrer song, "Poisoning Pigeons in the Park."

Half the lights were out in the hall, as usual, including the one by his door, but he did not care. He felt preternaturally observant, as though all his organs of perception had been recently fine-tuned and the gain stepped up, and along with this came such a feeling of euphoria that when he reached his apartment door and perceived coming out from under it not the sounds of the tuner, which he had left on, but the soft light of the lamp, which he had not, the implications failed to disturb him in the slightest. Got to be junkies, he thought calmly, Lois is off on the Mountain for the weekend. Ho ho. Ought to go right back downshaft and wake up old Julius, have him phone this in. Yes indeed.

As recently as the night before, he would have done precisely that, while congratulating himself on being too much of an old soldier to walk unheeding into danger.

Still singing, he took his keys from his pocket, making a noisy production of it. He was heartened to notice that the security camera over his door was intact, as were the ones at either end of the hall—his antagonists must be idiots. The cameras did not depend on visible light. Let's see, he thought, the gun is in the bottom left-hand drawer of the desk: one long run and I'm there, claw it open from underneath, kick the legs out from under the bookcase to spoil their aim, and roll behind the corner sofa—it'll stop bullets. Then try to negotiate.

A part of his mind was startled to learn that a mild-mannered assistant professor could undertake anything like this so cheerily—it had been a long time—but he was in no wise afraid. It was not fear that made time slow so drastically for him now, but something more like joy. He shucked off topcoat, jacket, tie, and gloves. He unlocked the door, dropped into a sprinter's crouch so as to convey his head into the room at an unexpected height, and threw the door open—hard, but not so hard that it would rebound into him. He got a good start, clearing the frame just as the door got out of his way, staying low and gaining speed with every step, still singing lustily about poisoning pigeons in the park.

The room was poorly lit by the lamp, but he saw the desk at once, unrifled, drawers all closed, gun presumably undiscovered. Glance left: no hostiles visible. Glance right: one in deep shadow, very long hair, half hidden by the couch, possibly more in the hall or other rooms. He wanted to study the one he could see for at least another tenth of a second, because both hands were beginning to come up and he wanted to know what was in them, but his subconscious insisted on yanking his gaze back in front of him again. It was very nearly in time, but by the time he saw the *Village Voice* lying where he had left it on the floor, he was committed to stepping on it. His feet went out from under him and he went airborne. He lowered his head automatically, and even managed to get both hands up in front of him, with the net result that the top of his skull impacted with great force against both fists. He dropped heavily on his face on the carpet.

Remarkably, he was unstunned. He sprang to his knees at once and yanked the drawer open, expecting at any second to experience some kind of impact. The gun seemed to spring into his hand; he whirled on one knee and located the long-haired one, frozen in an attitude of shock. "Hold it right there," Norman rapped.

The other burst into sudden, uproarious, unmistakably feminine laughter.

Now he was stunned. He lowered the gun involuntarily, then simply let go. It landed unheeded and safely, the safety still locked. He fell off his heels and sat down hard on the carpet.

"Jesus Christ in rhinestones," he said hoarsely. "Maddy. What are *you* doing here?"

She could not stop laughing. "Don't . . . don't kill me, brother," she managed, and doubled over.

He found that he was giggling himself, and it felt very good, so he let it build into deep laughter until he too was doubled over. The aching of his hands and the throbbing of his head were hilarious. The shared laughter went on for a long time, and when it might have stopped she said, "Poisoning pigeons," and they were off again. It was one of the great laughs.

At last she came around from behind the couch and sat in front of him, taking both his hands. "Hello, old younger brother," she said in a Swiss French accent. "It is very good to see you again."

"It is *incredibly* good to see you," he responded enthusiastically, and hugged her close.

Madeleine Kent was four years older than her brother, and a good eight centimeters taller. The resemblance was fairly pronounced: she had his audiotape-colored hair, his perfect nose and perfect teeth, and on her the overwide mouth looked good. But a different character had built on those features; a polite stranger would have called her not elegant but bold. Or possibly daring . . . but not quite reckless, there was too much wry wisdom in the eyes for that. The facial difference between the siblings was subtle but unmistakable. Norman looked like a man who had been around; Madeleine looked like a woman who had been around and still was. Her voice was deeper than he remembered, a throaty contralto that was quite sexy. Her clothes were impeccable and expensive. Her arms were strong.

The hug stretched out, and then they both became self-conscious and disengaged. Madeleine smiled uneasily, then got to her feet and stepped back a few paces. She turned away and put both hands on a bookcase.

"I'm a little bit embarrassed at how good it is to see you," she said.

"You speak English like a Swiss," he said, getting up.

She started. "Do I? Why, I *do*." She made an effort and dropped the accent. "Habit, I guess. An American is not a good thing to be in Switzerland these days."

"Why is it that I'm embarrassed too? At how good it is to see you."

She pulled a volume at random from the bookcase and appeared to examine it closely. "Why *I* am embarrassed is that you and I have never been the very best of friends."

"Maddy—"

"Let me say it, no? It's been ten years, I don't write many letters. I'll be honest, in that ten years I might have thought of you ten times. Well, give or take five."

He had to smile. "Much the same with me."

She turned to face him, and smiled when she saw his smile. But hers was tight, unconvincing. "Now here I am on your doorstep. *Past* your doorstep, there are four suitcases in your bedroom. I needed a place to be, and it came to me that you are the only close family I have left in all the world, and Norman, I need close family very badly right now. Can I stay here for a while?"

Norman was still smiling, but his eyes glistened in the lamp-light. "Maddy, if you haven't written much in ten years, you haven't left any letters unanswered either. I have this crazy impulse to apologize because I didn't pop up and see you when I was in Africa. I will confess here and now that if you had called ahead first, I would have tried to put you off. But the moment I recognized you, it came to me that you are all the family I have left in the world. As you speak, I realize that I need close family very badly now too. Please stay."

Relief showed in her face, and they hugged again, without reservation this time.

"Have you eaten?" he asked, fetching his outer clothes from the hallway.

"No. I showed the security guard downstairs—Julius, is it?—my identification and got him to let me in, but I didn't feel right prowling around in your home while you—"

"Our home. Let's eat."

"Well—coffee? Black and sweet?"

"And toasted English, lots of jam, Irish in the coffee."

"*Merveilleux*. Go ahead, I'll join you in a minute."

She was true to her word; he had only just finished producing two cups of fresh coffee and toast, a sixty-second job, when she came into the kitchen, carrying a package of unmistakable shape: a disc.

"A present for you," she said. "It was quite a job getting it past customs."

Norman finished pouring hastily and unwrapped his present, wondering what program she had brought him. But it was not a floppy disc, but an old-fashioned vinyl audio-only record.

It was a copy of Lambert, Hendricks, and Ross's first Columbia recording, "The Hottest New Group in Jazz." Not the 1974 reissue, the original. It was older than he was, one of the first stereo jazz albums. The cardboard jacket was also original, in impeccable condition.

"Holy God," he breathed.

The inner sleeve was new, a paper-and-plastic disc pre-server. He took it from the jacket and slid the record out with a practiced hand, touching it only at the rim and label. The disc was immaculate. It did not appear ever to have been played, it had that special sheen. He could not guess at its worth in dollars. Not many people bothered with the obsolete disc format for their music these days; simply as an artifact, the thing was priceless.

She saw his awe. "I chose wisely, then?"

"Dear God, Maddy, it's—" Words failed him. "Thank you. Thank you. God, if they'd caught you at customs, they'd have had your bloody *head*."

"I remembered that you liked their music, and I didn't think you had this one in your collection. I was certain you didn't have it in disc form."

"I've heard it through twice in my life. It's never been accessed. There might be half a dozen copies in North America, and none of them would be virgin. Maddy, where did you *get* it? *How* did you get it?"

"A present from—from a friend. Forget it. Where do I sleep tonight, the couch?" She picked up her coffee and looked for sugar.

He fetched it, and found that he was terrified of dropping his new treasure but could not bear to set it down anywhere in the kitchen. "Nonsense, I've got a bed set up in the den, I'll doss there and you take the queen-size." He went to the living room, stored the record safely by the antique turntable, looked at it and sighed, and returned to the kitchen. She had already demolished her English muffin and finished half her coffee. He thought: She was really hungry and she waited for me to get back home. Maybe this is going to work out okay.

"Listen," he said, "I don't know how to thank you."

She smiled. "I'm glad you're pleased."

Her smile seemed to fade a bit too quickly. "Hey, I'm sorry. You spoke of bed."

"Oh, I didn't mean right now, necessarily . . . unless *you*—"

"Wait a minute now, let me get the chronology straight. It's—" He tried to look at his watch, but it was not there.

"Ten o'clock," she supplied.

"Then it must be the middle of the morning by your internal clock. You must be dead on your feet . . . or have I got it backwards?"

"Here, it's simple. I left my apartment in Zurich at 4:30

P.M., flew straight to London, and caught an Air Canada flight to here. Total transit time, ten hours, eight of that in the air. I got here half an hour ago, at 9:30 Atlantic Standard Time. By my 'clock' it's 3:00 A.M."

"Then let's get you to bed—"

"Hold it. First of all, my customary bedtime is about 2:00 A.M."

"But jet lag—"

"—is not so bad traveling west as it is traveling east. I chased the sun all day, so for me it has only been a few hours since sunset. I'm not sleepy yet." She finished her coffee. "But that's not it. *You* don't look at all sleepy . . ."

He considered it. "No. Not at all."

". . . and somehow I get the impression that you have a good deal on your mind that you want very much to talk about."

He considered that. "Yes, I do. How did you know?"

She hesitated. "Well, partly from the fact that Lois isn't here and there's no trace of her in the apartment and you haven't said a word about her."

He winced. "Ah, yes," he said, in halfhearted imitation of W. C. Fields, but dropped it at once. "And there would, I suppose, be a general overall spoor of the bachelor male in his anguish about the place, wouldn't there? Laundry all about, bed unmade, ashtrays full—"

"—bottles empty," she agreed. "If you've been having any fun lately, it hasn't been here."

"It hasn't been anywhere. Till you showed up."

"Norman, if . . . look, if you need any money, just to tide you over, I can—"

"Money? What gave you the idea I needed money? That's the only problem I don't have."

"Well, you've no hat—your hair looks like something out of Dali. And I know you pawned your watch—I can see the little stickum patch where it used to be on your wrist."

He looked blank for a second, and then suddenly burst into laughter. "I will be go to hell!"

She looked politely puzzled.

"That's just too perfect." He gave himself to his laughter for a moment. "No, it's all right, I'll tell you. Look, let's go into the living room; this is going to take a while."

They took freshened cups of coffee relaced with Bushmill's. It was excellent coffee, and he was faintly miffed that she had not commented on it. Perhaps in the circles she'd been traveling in, first-rate coffee was taken for granted.

"Now, what's so funny?" she said when they were seated.

"The watch and the hat. The watch is at this moment lying on the bottom of Halifax Harbor, and the hat is almost certainly floating somewhere in the selfsame harbor. That's the funny part. If it wasn't for that hat, I'd undoubtedly be down there with the watch—do you know I simply never gave it a thought until you mentioned it?" He chuckled again.

"What do you mean?" she said, and being self-involved he missed the urgency in her tone.

"Well, it's kind of embarrassing. What I was doing—about the time you were talking Julius into letting you in here, I think—I was committing suicide."

He glanced down at his coffee, and so he failed to notice that at that last word she actually relaxed slightly.

"Seems silly now, but it made sense at the time. I wasn't toying with the idea, I was fucking well *doing* it—until I was stopped by a Bad Samaritan."

He narrated the story of his interrupted suicide, cheerily and in some detail.

"You see?" he finished. "If I hadn't tried to save that idiot hat, he'd never have gotten me, I'd have been over the side and gone The damned thing was important enough to give up dying for, and from that instant until the time you mentioned it, I never gave it another thought. It must have blown off the bridge while I was being mugged!"

He began to laugh again, and to his utter astonishment the fourth "ha" came out *"oh!"* as did the fifth and sixth, each harsher and louder than the last, by which time he was jack-knifed so drastically that he fell forward between his own knees. She had begun to move on the second *"oh!"*; her knees hit the carpet at the same instant as his, and she caught him before he could land on his face. With unsuspected strength she heaved him up into a kneeling position and wrapped her arms around him. It broke the stuttering rhythm of his diaphragm, and like an engine catching he settled into great cyclic sobs that filled and emptied his chest.

They rocked together on their knees, clutching like a pair of drowners, and his sorrow was a long time draining. Well before awareness returned to him, his hips began to move against her in the unconscious instinct of one who has been too near death, but she did something neither verbal nor physical, that was neither acceptance nor rejection, and something in him understood and he stopped. It did not come to his conscious attention because he had none then; his memory banks were in playback mode. Firmly but not suddenly, she moved so that she was sitting on the rug and he was lying across her lap, and he flowed like quicksilver into the new embrace without knowing it. Something about the position changed his weeping, or perhaps it was sheer lack of air; the sobs came shorter and closer together, the pitch rose and fell wildly. He had been weeping as a man does; now he wept as a child. It might have been neither the position nor anoxia, just childhood imprinting of the smell of Big Sister, who has time for your smashed toe when Mother is at work and Dad is drinking. More than one species of pain left him in that weeping, more than one wound or one kind of wound closed over and began to scab. After a time his sobs trailed off into deep slow breathing, and she stroked his hair.

His first conscious thought was that something was hurting his cheek. It was one of the silver cashew-shaped buttons of her blouse, and when he moved he knew it had left an imprint that would last an hour or more. With that, reality came back in a rush, and he rolled away and sat up. Her arms, which had been so strong a moment ago, fell away at once when he moved, and she met a searching gaze squarely. He looked for scorn or amusement or pity, and found none of them. As an afterthought he looked within himself for scorn or shame or self-pity, and again came up empty.

"Lord have mercy," he said shakily. "I thought I got it all out in that laugh before." He grinned experimentally. "Thanks, sis."

She had found Kleenex. "Sure. Here."

Why do people always roll up their eyes when they wipe

away tears? he wondered, and thought at once of the last time he had wondered that. "God, I missed you at the funeral, Mad."

She smiled briefly.

"I'm sorry, stupid thing to say, of course you couldn't come. I just meant—"

"It's all right, Norman. Really." She patted his hand. "I said goodbye to both of them in my heart before I left for Europe, and they to me."

"Yes." They both smiled now.

"Can you tell me about it now?" she asked.

"Why I was trying to do myself in tonight? I think so."

He sat on the couch again and lit a cigarette. Seeing this, she produced a pack of Gauloise from her vest and raised an inquiring eyebrow. This surprised and pleased him. To a smoker of North American cigarettes, Gauloise smell like a burning outhouse—a fact of which most Gauloise smokers are sublimely unaware. She had not smoked since she arrived, had not even asked until she was sure that he smoked himself.

He nodded permission at once, and she lit up gratefully. *"Now* we're even," he said, making them both grin.

"All right," he went on. "Lois. I suppose I should start from the beginning. I'm just not certain where that is."

"Then do it backwards. Where does she live now?"

Norman pointed toward the living room window. "About a thousand meters that way and eight floors down. A second-and-third-story duplex apartment across the street. They're away for the moment, at Lois's place in the Valley. She's living with a third-year plumbing student named, God help us all, Rock, and she's still working at the V.G. Hospital up the street from here. She's got a floor now, Neurosurgery."

"How long has she been gone?"

He smiled. "That's another of those difficult questions."

"When did she move out?" she amended patiently.

"Well, over a period of several months, but she took her TV six months ago. I've always sort of considered that conclusive. After that she came by about twice a week for a while, to pick up something or other or share some new insight, and since then she seems to find some reason to drop by on the average of every other week. Her appearances are always unannounced and usually inconvenient for me, and I always let her in. I would estimate that we fuck two visits out of three. She is always gone in the morning. It's a lot like having a leg rebroken every time it's begun to knit." His voice was calm, unemotional.

"What is this Rock like?"

"Aside from biographical trivia, location of aunts and so forth, all Lois has ever seen fit to tell me is that he is nineteen, that he lets her be herself, and that he is a better lover than me. From my own experience I can report only that he is very large and very fast and all over hair and has knuckles like pig iron."

"You fought with him?"

"Oh, yes. As you saw from my entrance tonight, I haven't lost that fine edge of physical conditioning I had in the army. The trained killing machine. I lost a tooth I was fond of, and a suit I wasn't. So I sucker-punched him. Lois gave me hell, and carried him offstage cooing sympathetically."

"Why did she leave you?"

He made no answer, did not move a muscle.

"Why did she say she was leaving?"

The answer was slow in coming. "As nearly as I can understand it, her gist was that in living with her for six years I have acquired some sense of who she is and what she's like. This, to her way of thinking, limits her. Makes it impossible for her to become something new."

"You disagree."

"Not at all. I see and concede the point. People tend to behave the way you expect them to, in direct ratio to your certainty and their own insecurity. It is why marriages often require extended solo vacations. I would happily have given her one if she'd asked for it. Instead she—"

"Perhaps she didn't want to ask."

"—had to go and—what?"

"Nothing."

"—to go and throw *every*thing away, smash the whole business. I came home one night at the usual time and found her in bed with another man. Absolutely the first I knew of any serious discontent, and my God, the blowup we had. You know, she had never once yelled at me before, never once lost her temper and told me to—I—she walked out and didn't come back for a week. I—this is only my perspective, my biased— I don't believe that I ever got a single opening, from that day on. She never gave me a chance. You should smoke the new ashless kind."

She carefully conveyed her hand to the ashtray beside her chair, flicked ash into it.

"I know," he went on, "to be surprised by the whole thing implies that I had blinders on for years. How well could I have known her, to be so stunned? Well, I've run that mental loop about six million times, and I can't buy it. Oh, to some extent, of course—you can't be fooled that well for that long without wanting to be fooled. But *God*, Maddy, I swear there were no clues to be seen, no hints to be picked up. She never paid me the compliment of telling me what she disliked about me and our life, never trusted me to help anything. *I could have tried.*" He stubbed out his cigarette angrily. "I would have."

She sat perfectly still. He lit another cigarette, drew on it harshly, and during this she was motionless and silent. Norman felt that his relationship with his sister had come to another crux. For all of his life Madeleine had been four years older, smarter, stronger, more knowledgeable, and by the time he was twenty and the age difference would have begun to mean less, she was gone to Europe. At the time of her departure they had been on friendly terms, but not friends. He had not seen her since, had seldom heard from or of her, had never had an occasion or an opportunity to put aside a lifetime of subconscious resentment. And from the moment of her reentry into his life he had behaved like an idiot, blundering into his own fists, waving a safetied gun like a spastic desperado, weeping in her lap. Norman perceived his resentment now, to which he had not given a conscious thought in years, tasted it afresh and in full. Against it he balanced the fact that she was an extremely well-mannered house guest who had brought him an extremely valuable guest's gift.

No. It was more than that. It was valuable *to him*. She had remembered his tastes in music, picked one that would have endured for the decade she had been gone.

He hadn't the remotest idea what her tastes in music were.

"That came out rather glibly, didn't it?" His decision process had lasted the span of a deep drag on his new cigarette.

"She's been gone for six months," she said at once. "The story gets polished with repetition."

He smiled. "Almost enough to be really convincing. Thanks, Maddy, but I'm a liar. The signs *were* there. Some of them were there the day I met her. I chose not to see them."

"And she chose to let you."

He nodded. "That's true." He got a thoughtful look, and she left him with it, finishing her coffee. Presently he said, "And ever since she left I've been behaving like a perfect jackass. It hasn't *seemed* like it. I haven't felt as though I've even had any choices—more as if I were on tracks. But what I've been doing is systematically harvesting every opportunity for pain that the situation affords. Because... because she enjoys it, and I—I seem to feel I *owe* it to her. I've known this all along. Why didn't I know I knew it?"

"You weren't ready yet."

"It has been harder saying this—to you—than it was weeping on your collar. Why is that, I wonder?"

She thought about it. "It is hard for a person, especially a man perhaps, to admit to being in pain. But I think for you it has always been even harder to admit stupidity. I think you got that from me."

At the last sentence he sat up straighter. He remembered for the first time that upon her arrival she had tacitly admitted to being in pain herself. "I could certainly have used you, these ten years past," he said suddenly. "You're a good sister, Madeleine. And after thirty years I think it is past time I became your friend. You've helped me to see clearer. Perhaps it's time I looked past my own nose. What brings you to Halifax?"

It was not quite a bodily flinch. Her face acquired the expression of one suppressing a sneeze. "Norman..." She paused. "Look, the bare outline is easy. I loved—I love—a man. I've given him half a year of my life. And then I found out... things that make me suspect he is not... not who I thought him to be, not what I thought him to be. I found out that I had been closing my eyes too, like you. I *think* I have. It's hard to be certain. But if I'm right, I've been giving my love to—to a—to someone unworthy." She hesitated. "But that's just the bare outline. And I'm afraid it's all I can tell you now, Norman." She held up a hand. "Wait. I'm not trying to cheat you, honestly I'm not. I'm not too proud to swap stupidity stories with you—and if what I fear is true, I've made you look like a genius. But I *mustn't* speak about it yet. Will you trust me, brother? For perhaps as long as a week or two?"

But maybe I can help! was what he started to say, but something in her face stopped him. "Are you sure that's what you want?"

"I'm sure."

"You know," he said cheerfully and at once, "ever since you got here I've been trying to put my finger on exactly what the hell the 'continental look' is. Because you've got it—I'd never have taken you for an American. It's more than just the accent. Something about the way you carry yourself."

It was her first smile of its kind, unplanned and soft at the edges; it destroyed temporarily the "look" to which he had just alluded. For the first time she reminded him powerfully of the Maddy he had known as a child. "A friend of mine said something very like that once," she murmured wistfully. "His theory was that Americans make a fetish of appearing strong, and Europeans just naturally are." Norman saw her pursue that line of thought and find something that made her hastily retrace her steps. "I'm not sure about Canadians."

"Oh, Canadians are insecure and don't care who knows about it," Norman said with a grin. "Look at Halifax, capital of this great province. No Sunday news programming, no Saturday postal service, and within fifteen minutes' drive you can find whole communities with outdoor plumbing, sound-only phones, and one communal terminal in the general store. There's no opera, next to no dance, a shocking amount of fake country music, and from one end of the city to the other there might be two hundred people who have ever heard of Miles Davis. You can draw a blank with Ray Charles.

"And do you know what? I love this town. I've been walking the streets unarmed for over five years, and tonight was only the second time I've been hit on—it *almost* made me homesick

for New York, but not quite. Ordinary glass is good enough
for windows here, and you can drink tap water with the right
filter. Police service is still voluntary; you can enter a mall
without having to go through a god damned metal detector.
You never have to wait for computer time. Even though a
goodly amount of North America's heroin enters at this port,
none of it stays—you could fit all the junkies in town into
three or four squad cars. For a city it's pretty pleasant, in other
words."

"Compared to Zurich, it sounds like paradise. I can live
without opera."

"Well, at least we've got good music here—thanks to you.
What say we heat up the old turntable, if the drive band hasn't
rotted by now? I keep having this feeling that I should get that
record on tape before lightning strikes it."

"That sounds wonderful. They *are* the ones who wrote 'Shiny
Stockings,' aren't they?"

"Jon Hendricks did, yes," he said, getting up and retrieving
both their empties. "With a guy named..." He stopped. He
stood as if listening for a moment, then cleared his throat and
met her eyes. "Madeleine, I know I said this already, but it's
awfully good to have you here."

"It's good to have here to be."

It was 4:00 A.M. for him, and 9:00 A.M. for her, when they
finally broke it up and went to bed; fortunately it was Saturday.
That set the pattern for the next week: every hour not occupied
by mundane necessities they spent talking together. Some of
the talk was catching up on the ten years they had spent apart,
essentially a swapping of accumulated anecdotes. Another, perhaps larger part of the talk involved reliving their respective
childhoods, each giving their own perspective on the formative
years of the other, and comparing their memories of shared
experiences. By the end of the week, Norman felt that he knew
himself better than he ever had, and knew that Madeleine felt
something similar. A kind of tension went out of both of them
as they talked, to be replaced by something like peace.

This mutual spiritual progression was not accomplished
smoothly in tandem, but more the way a tractor operator works

his way out of deep mud, feeding power to alternate wheels in fits and starts. It was their firm connection that made any progress possible.

By the second week, conversation had achieved about all it could on its own. He began introducing her, carefully and thoughtfully, to certain of his friends, and was satisfied with the results. The end-of-term madness was beginning to snowball at the University, and he was startled to discover how little it troubled him. Dr. MacLeod, the department chairman, actually paid him a grudging compliment. Norman met an attractive and interesting woman, a single parent who had come to his office to discuss her son's prospects of passing his course, and saw small signs that his interest was returned. One night he dug out the half-forgotten, half-finished manuscript of The Book and read it through; he threw out half the chapters and made extensive notes for the replacement.

Madeleine fit right into the rhythms of his home life, enhancing it in many small ways and disrupting nothing he cared about. She had a fanatic neatness learned in a country where living space was at a premium, and an easy tolerance of his own looser standards. She was seriously impressed by parts of his music library, which flattered him; and one day she came home with an armful of tapes that startled him just as pleasurably. They swapped favorite books and videotapes, favorite recipes and jokes. She displayed no inclination to look for work, but she used her free time to do household maintenance chores he had been forced to neglect. And she did not appear to lack for money—indeed, he had to be quite firm before she would let him reimburse her for half of the groceries and staples she bought. She respected his privacy and welcomed his company, cleaned up her own messes and left his the hell alone.

The only thing that bothered him was concern for the private pain of which she still would not tell him, and which she could not altogether hide. She did not tantalize him with it; he acquired only by accident some idea of the depth and extent of her hurt, when he woke quite late one rainy night and heard her weeping in the next room. He nearly went to her then, but something told him that it was the wrong thing to do. He waited, listening. He heard her moan, in a voice softer than her sobs but still plainly audible: "Jacques, who are you? *What* are you?" Then her weeping became wordless again, and after a time it was over and they both slept. In the morning she was so relaxed and jolly that he wondered if he had been dreaming.

He noted certain subtle signs that she was becoming attracted to his good friend Charlie, who lived eight blocks away with three male roommates. Norman gave the chemistry careful thought, and decided that he approved. On the twenty-first day of her residence he saw to it that they were both invited to a party at Charlie's, and that night when it was time to go he announced that a whole day of processing final exams had tired him out, why didn't she go along without him? He was going to turn in at once and sleep the night away, would doubtless be sound asleep whenever she might return, early or late. He smiled to himself at how she tried to keep the pleasantness of her surprise from showing, bundled her out the door, and retired at once to his bed in the den, where he lay with the lights out. In point of fact he was wide awake, but he resolved to lie there in the dark till sleep did come. Charlie, he knew, was not a slow worker, and Madeleine seemed to have a European directness of her own.

Nonetheless, they had not showed up by the time he finally fell genuinely asleep at midnight.

In the morning he tiptoed about, trying to make breakfast as quietly as possible so as not to wake them . . . until he noticed that the bedroom door was open. He found that she had not come home the night before, and went off to work wondering what the hell Charlie had done with his three roommates and the party.

She was not home when he returned, which did not surprise him inordinately, but she had left no message in the phone, which did. He swallowed his prurient curiosity and a solitary dinner and put his attention on the work he had brought home for the weekend. To his credit, it was eleven-thirty before he broke down and phoned Charlie's place.

Charlie answered the phone. The screen showed him in bed with a pleasant-looking Oriental woman whom Norman vaguely recognized. Charlie was quite certain of his facts. Madeleine had arrived at the party, had not been overly depressed at finding Charlie already paired off with Mei-Ling, had stayed and drunk and smoked and laughed and danced with several men without settling on any of them. She had sung them all a devastating impromptu parody of the new Mindfuckers single. She had left the party, unquestionably alone, cheerful and not overly stoned, at about one in the morning.

In his guts, Norman *knew* before he had hung up the phone. But it was a full three days before he could get it through his head as well that Madeleine was never going to come back.

2

1999 I smelled her before I saw her. Even so, the first sight was shocking.

She was sitting in a tan plastic-surfaced armchair, the kind where the front comes up as the back goes down. It was back as far as it would go. It was placed beside the large living room window, which was transparent. A plastic block table next to it held a digital clock, a dozen unopened packages of self-lighting Peter Jackson cigarettes, an empty ashtray, a full vial of cocaine, and a lamp with a bulb of at least a hundred and fifty watts. It illuminated her with brutal clarity.

She was naked. Her skin was the color of vanilla pudding. Her hair was in rats, her nails unpainted and untended, some overlong and some broken. There was dust on her. She sat in a ghastly sludge of feces and urine. Dried vomit was caked on her chin and between her breasts, and down her ribs to the chair.

23

These were only part of what I had smelled. The predominant odor was of fresh-baked bread. It is the smell of a person who is starving to death. The combined effluvia had prepared me to find a senior citizen, paralyzed by a stroke or some such crisis.

I judged her to be about twenty-five years old.

I moved to where she could see me, and she did not see me. That was probably just as well, because I had just seen the two most horrible things. The first was the smile. They say that when the bomb went off at Hiroshima, some people's shadows were baked onto walls by it. I think that smile got baked on the surface of my brain in much the same way. I don't want to talk about that smile.

The second horrible thing was the one that explained all the rest. From where I now stood, I could see a triple socket in the wall beneath the window. Into it were plugged the lamp, the clock, and her.

I knew about wireheading, of course—I had lost a couple of acquaintances and one friend to the juice. But I had never *seen* a wirehead. It is by definition a solitary vice, and all the public usually gets to see is a sheeted figure being carried out to the wagon.

The transformer lay on the floor beside the chair, where it had been dropped. The switch was on, and the timer had been jiggered so that instead of providing one five- or ten- or fifteen-second jolt per hour, it allowed continuous flow. That timer is required by law on all juice rigs sold, and you need special tools to defeat it. Say, a nail file. The input cord was long, and fell in crazy coils from the wall socket. The output cord disappeared beneath the chair, but I knew where it ended. It ended in the tangled snarl of her hair, at the crown of her head, in a miniplug. The plug was snapped into a jack surgically implanted in her skull, and from the jack tiny wires snaked their way through the wet jelly to the hypothalamus, to the specific place in the medial forebrain bundle where the major pleasure center of her brain was located. She had sat there in total transcendent ecstasy for at least five days.

I moved finally. I moved closer, which surprised me. She saw me now, and impossibly the smile became a bit wider. I was marvelous. I was captivating. I was her perfect lover. I could not look at the smile; a small plastic tube ran from one corner of the smile and my eyes followed it gratefully. It was held in place by small bits of surgical tape at her jaw, neck, and shoulder, and from there it ran in a lazy curve to the big fifty-liter water-cooler bottle on the floor. She had plainly meant her suicide to last: she had arranged to die of hunger rather than thirst, which would have been quicker. She could take a drink when she happened to think of it; and if she forgot, well, what the hell.

My intention must have shown on my face, and I think she even understood it—the smile began to fade. That decided me. I moved before she could force her neglected body to react, whipped the plug out of the wall, and stepped back warily.

Her body did not go rigid as if galvanized. It had already been so for many days. What it did was the exact opposite, and the effect was just as striking. She seemed to shrink. Her eyes slammed shut. She slumped. Well, I thought, it'll be a long day and a night before *she* can move a voluntary muscle again, and then she hit me before I knew she had left the chair, breaking my nose with the heel of one fist and bouncing the other off the side of my head. We cannoned off each other and I managed to keep my feet; she whirled and grabbed the lamp. Its cord was stapled to the floor and would not yield, so she set her feet and yanked and it snapped off clean at the base. In near-total darkness she raised the lamp on high and came at me and I lunged inside the arc of her swing and punched her in the solar plexus. She said *guff!* and went down.

I staggered to a couch and sat down and felt my nose and fainted.

I don't think I was out very long. The blood tasted fresh. I woke with a sense of terrible urgency. It took me a while to work out why. When someone has been simultaneously starved and unceasingly stimulated for days on end, it is not the best idea in the world to depress their respiratory center. I lurched to my feet.

It was not completely dark, there was a moon somewhere out there. She lay on her back, arms at her sides, perfectly relaxed. Her ribs rose and fell in great slow swells. A pulse showed strongly at her throat. As I knelt beside her she began to snore, deeply and rhythmically.

I had time for second thoughts now. It seemed incredible that my impulsive action had not killed her. Perhaps that had been my subconscious intent. Five days of wire-heading alone should have killed her, never mind sudden cold turkey.

I probed in the tangle of hair, found the empty jack. The hair around it was dry. If she hadn't torn the skin in yanking herself loose, it was unlikely that she had sustained any more serious damage within. I continued probing, found no soft places on the skull. Her forehead felt cool and sticky to my hand. The fecal smell was overpowering the baking bread now.

There was no pain in my nose yet, but it felt immense and pulsing. I did not want to touch it, or to think about it. My shirt was soaked with blood; I wiped my face with it and tossed it into a corner. It took everything I had to lift her. She was unreasonably heavy, and I say that having carried drunks and corpses. There was a hall off the living room, and all halls lead to a bathroom. I headed that way in a clumsy staggering trot, and just as I reached the deeper darkness, with my pulse at its maximum, my nose woke up and began screaming. I nearly dropped her then and clapped my hands to my face; the temptation was overwhelming. Instead I whimpered like a dog and kept going. Childhood feeling: runny nose you can't wipe. At each door I came to, I teetered on one leg and kicked it open, and the third one gave the right small-room, acoustic-tile echo. The light switch was where they almost always are; I rubbed it on with my shoulder and the room flooded with light.

Large aquamarine tub, styrofoam recliner pillow at the head end, nonslip bottom. Aquamarine sink with ornate handles, cluttered with toiletries and cigarette butts and broken shards of mirror from the medicine cabinet above. Aquamarine commode, lid up and seat down. Brown throw rug, expensive. Scale shoved back into a corner, covered with dust in which two footprints showed. I made a massive effort and managed to set her reasonably gently in the tub. I rinsed my face and hands of blood at the sink, ignoring the broken glass, and stuffed the bleeding nostril with toilet paper. I adjusted her head, fixed the chin strap. I held both feet away from the faucet until I had the water adjusted, and then left with one hand on my nose and the other beating against my hip, in search of her liquor.

There was plenty to choose from. I found some Metaxa in the kitchen. I took great care not to bring it near my nose, sneaking it up on my mouth from below. It tasted like burning lighter fluid, and made sweat spring out on my forehead. I found a roll of paper towels, and on my way back to the bathroom I used a great wad of them to swab most of the sludge off the chair and rug. There was a growing pool of water siphoning from the plastic tube, and I stopped that. When I got back to the bathroom the water was lapping over her bloated belly, and horrible tendrils were weaving up from beneath her. It took three rinses before I was satisfied with the body. I found a hose-and-spray under the sink that mated with the tub's faucet, and that made the hair easy.

I had to dry her there in the tub. There was only one towel left, none too clean. I found a first-aid spray that incorporated a good topical anesthetic, and put it on the sores on her back and butt. I had located her bedroom on the way to the Metaxa. Wet hair slapped my arm as I carried her there. She seemed even heavier, as though she had become waterlogged. I eased the door shut behind me and tried the light-switch trick again, and it wasn't there. I moved forward into a footlocker and lost her and went down amid multiple crashes, putting all my attention into guarding my nose. She made no sound at all, not even a grunt.

The light switch turned out to be a pull-chain over the bed. She was on her side, still breathing slow and deep. I wanted to punt her up onto the bed. My nose was a blossom of pain. I nearly couldn't lift her the third time. I was moaning with frustration by the time I had her on her left side on the king-size mattress. It was a big brass four-poster bed, with satin sheets and pillow cases, all dirty. The blankets were shoved to the bottom. I checked her skull and pulse again, peeled up each eyelid, and found uniform pupils. Her forehead and cheek still felt cool, so I covered her. Then I kicked the footlocker clear into the corner, turned out the light, and left her snoring like a chain saw.

***

Her vital papers and documents were in her study, locked in a strongbox on the closet shelf. It was an expensive box, quite sturdy and proof against anything short of nuclear explosion. It had a combination lock with all of twenty-seven possible combinations. It was stuffed with papers. I laid her life out on her desk like a losing hand of solitaire, and studied it with a growing frustration.

Her name was Karen Scholz, but she used the name Karyn Shaw, which I thought phony. She was twenty-two. Divorced her parents at fourteen, uncontested no-fault. Since then she had been, at various times, waitress, secretary to a lamp salesman, painter, free-lance typist, motorcycle mechanic, and unlicensed masseuse. The most recent paycheck stub was from the Hard Corps, a massage parlor with a cut-rate reputation. It was dated almost a year ago. Her bank balance combined with paraphernalia I had found in the closet to tell me that she was currently self-employed as a tootlegger, a cocaine dealer. The richness of the apartment and furnishings told me that she was a foolish one. Even if the narcs missed her, very shortly the IRS was going to come down on her like a ton of bricks. Perhaps subconsciously she had not expected to be around.

Nothing there; I kept digging. She had attended community college for one semester as an art major, and dropped out failing. She had defaulted on a lease three years ago. She had wrecked a car once, and been shafted by her insurance company. Trivia. Only one major trauma in recent years: a year and a half ago she had contracted out as host-mother to a couple named Lombard/Smyth. It was a pretty good fee—she had good hips and the right rare blood type—but six months into the pregnancy they had caught her using tobacco and canceled the contract. She fought, but they had photographs. And better lawyers, naturally. She had to repay the advance, and pay for the abortion, of course, and she got socked for court costs besides.

It didn't make sense. To show clean lungs at the physical, she had to have been off cigarettes for at least three to six months. Why backslide, with so much at stake? Like the minor traumas, it felt more like an effect than a cause. Self-destructive behavior. I kept looking.

Near the bottom I found something that looked promising. Both her parents had been killed in a car smash when she was eighteen. Their obituary was paperclipped to her father's will. That will was one of the most extraordinary documents I have ever read. I could understand an angry father cutting off his only child without a dime. But what he had done was worse. He had left all his money to the church, and to her "a hundred dollars, the going rate."

Damn it, that didn't work either. So-there suicides don't wait four years. And they don't use such a garish method either; it devalues the tragedy. I decided it had to be either a very big and dangerous coke deal gone bad, or a very reptilian lover. No, not a coke deal. They would never have left her in her own apartment to die the way she wanted to. It could not be murder: even the most unscrupulous wire surgeon needs an awake, consenting subject to place the wire correctly.

A lover, then. I was relieved, pleased with my sagacity, and irritated as hell. I didn't know why. I chalked it up to my nose. It felt as though a large shark with rubber teeth was rhythmically biting it as hard as he could. I shoveled the papers back into the box, locked and replaced it, and went to the bathroom.

Her medicine cabinet would have impressed a pharmacist. She had lots of allergies. It took me five minutes to find aspirin. I took four. I picked the largest shard of mirror out of the sink, propped it on the toilet tank, and sat down backward on the seat. My nose was visibly displaced to the right, and the swelling was just hitting its stride. I removed the toilet-tissue plug from my nostril, and it resumed bleeding. There was a box of Kleenex on the floor. I ripped it apart, took out all the tissues, and stuffed them into my mouth. Then I grabbed my nose with my right hand and tugged out to the left, simultaneously flushing the toilet with my left hand. The flushing coincided with the scream, and my front teeth met through the Kleenex. When I could see again, the nose looked straight and my breathing was unimpaired. When the bleeding stopped again I gingerly washed my face and hands and left. A moment later I returned; something had caught my eye. It was the glass and toothbrush holder. There was only one toothbrush in it. I looked through the medicine chest again, and noticed this time that there was no shaving cream, no razor, no masculine toiletries of any kind. All the prescriptions were in her name.

I went thoughtfully to the kitchen, mixed myself a Preacher's Downfall by moonlight, and took it to her bedroom. The bedside clock said five. I lit a match, moved the footlocker in front of an armchair, sat down, and put my feet up. I sipped my drink and listened to her snore and watched her breathe in the feeble light of the clock. I decided to run through all the possibilities, and as I was formulating the first one, daylight smacked me hard in the nose.

My hands went up reflexively and I poured my drink on my head and hurt my nose more. I wake up hard in the best of times. She was still snoring. I nearly threw the empty glass at her.

It was just past noon, now; light came strongly through the heavy curtains, illuminating so much mess and disorder that I could not decide whether she had trashed her bedroom herself or it had been tossed by a pro. I finally settled on the former: the armchair I'd slept on was intact. Or had the pro found what he wanted before he got that far?

I gave it up and went to make myself breakfast. The milk was bad, of course, but I found a tolerable egg and makings of an omelet. I don't care for black coffee, but Javanese brewed from frozen beans needs no augmentation. I drank three cups.

It took me an hour or two to clean up and air out the living room. The cord and transformer went down the oubliette, along with most of the perished items from the fridge. The dishes took three full cycles for each load, a couple of hours all told. I passed the time vacuuming and dusting and snooping, learning nothing more of significance. The phone rang. She had no answering program in circuit, of course. I energized the screen. It was a young man in a business tunic, wearing the doggedly amiable look of the stranger who wants you to accept the call anyway. After some thought I did accept, audio-only, and let him speak first. He wanted to sell us a marvelous building lot in Forest Acres, South Dakota. I was making up a shopping list about fifteen minutes later when I heard her moan. I reached her bedroom door in seconds, waited in the doorway with both hands in sight, and said slowly and clearly, "My name is Joseph Templeton, Karen. I am a friend. You are all right now."

Her eyes were those of a small, tormented animal.

"Please don't try to get up. Your muscles won't work properly and you may hurt yourself."

No answer.

"Karen, are you hungry?"

"Your voice is ugly," she said despairingly, and her own voice was so hoarse I winced. "*My* voice is ugly," she added, and sobbed gently. "It's *all* ugly." She screwed her eyes shut.

She was clearly incapable of movement. I told her I would be right back, and went to the kitchen. I made up a tray of clear strong broth, unbuttered toast, tea with maltose, and saltine crackers. She was staring at the ceiling when I got back, and apparently it was vile. I put the tray down, lifted her, and made a backrest of pillows.

"I want a drink."

"After you eat," I said agreeably.

"Who're you?"

"Mother Templeton. Eat."

"The soup, maybe. Not the toast." She got about half of it down, did nibble at the toast, accepted some tea. I didn't want to overfill her. "My drink."

"Sure thing." I took the tray back to the kitchen, finished my shopping list, put away the last of the dishes, and put a frozen steak into the oven for my lunch. When I got back she was fast asleep.

Emaciation was near total; except for breasts and bloated belly, she was all bone and taut skin. Her pulse was steady. At her best she would not have been very attractive by conventional standards. Passable. Too much waist, not enough neck, upper legs a bit too thick for the rest of her. It's hard to evaluate a starved and unconscious face, but her jaw was a bit too square, her nose a trifle hooked, her blue eyes just the least little bit too far apart. Animated, the face might have been beautiful—any set of features can support beauty—but even a superb makeup job could not have made her pretty. There was an old bruise on her chin, another on her left hip. Her hair was sandy blonde, long and thin; it had dried in snarls that would take hours to comb out. Her breasts were magnificent, and that saddened me. In this world, a woman whose breasts are her best feature is in for a rough time.

I was putting together a picture of a life that would have depressed anyone with the sensitivity of a rhino. Back when I had first seen her, when her features were alive, she had looked sensitive. Or had that been a trick of the juice? Impossible to say now.

But damn it all to hell, I could find nothing to really explain the socket in her skull. You can hear worse life stories in any bar, on any street corner. Wireheads are usually addictive personalities, who decide at last to skip the small shit. There were no tracks on her anywhere, no nasal damage, no sign that she used any of the coke she sold. Her work history, pitiful and fragmented as it was, was too steady for any kind of serious jones; she had undeniably been hitting the sauce hard lately, but only lately. Tobacco seemed to be her only serious addiction.

That left the hypothetical bastard lover. I worried at that for a while to see if I could make it fit. To have done so much psychic damage, he would almost *have* to have lived with her . . . but where was his spoor?

At that point I went to the bathroom, and that settled it. When I lifted the seat to urinate, I found written on the underside with magic marker: "It's so nice to have a man around the house!" The handwriting was hers. She had lived alone.

I was relieved, because I hadn't relished thinking about my hypothetical monster or the necessity of tracking and killing him. But I was irritated as hell again.

I wanted to *understand*.

For something to do, I took my steak and a mug of coffee to the study and heated up her terminal. I tried all the typical access codes, her birthdate and her name in numbers and such, but none of them would unlock it. Then on a hunch I tried the date of her parents' death, and that did it. I ordered the groceries she needed, instructed the lobby door to accept delivery, and tried everything I could think of to get a diary or a journal out of the damned thing, without success. So I punched up the public library and asked the catalog for *Britannica* on wireheading. It referred me to brain-reward, autostimulus of. I skipped over the history, from discovery by Olds and others in 1956 to emergence as a social problem in the late eighties, when surgery got simple; declined the offered diagrams, graphs, and technical specs; finally found a brief section on motivations.

There was indeed one type of typical user I had overlooked. The terminally ill.

Could that really be it? At her age? I went to the bathroom and checked the prescriptions. Nothing for heavy pain, nothing indicating anything more serious than allergies. Back before telephones had cameras I might have conned something out of her personal physician, but it would have been a chancy thing even then. There was no way to test the hypothesis.

It was possible, even plausible—but it just wasn't *likely* enough to satisfy the thing inside me that demanded an explanation. I dialed a game of four-wall squash, and made sure the computer would let me win. I was almost enjoying myself when she screamed.

It wasn't much of a scream; her throat was shot. But it fetched me at once. I saw the problem as I cleared the door. The topical anesthetic had worn off the large sores on her back and buttocks, and the pain had woken her. Now that I thought about it, it should have happened earlier; that spray was only supposed to be good for a few hours. I decided that her pleasure-pain system was weakened by overload.

The sores were bad; she would have scars. I resprayed them, and her moans stopped nearly at once. I could devise no means of securing her on her belly that would not be nightmare-inducing, and decided it was unnecessary. I thought she was out again, and started to leave. Her voice, muffled by pillows, stopped me in my tracks.

"I don't know you. Maybe you're not even real. I can tell you."

"Save your energy, Karen. You—"

"Shut up. You wanted the kharma, you got it."

I shut up.

Her voice was flat, dead. "All my friends were dating at twelve. *He* made me wait until fourteen. Said I couldn't be trusted.

Tommy came to take me to the dance, and he gave Tommy a hard time. I was so embarrassed. The dance was nice for a couple of hours. Then Tommy started chasing after Jo Tompkins. He just left me and went off with her. I went into the ladies' room and cried for a long time. A couple of girls got the story out of me, and one of them had a bottle of vodka in her purse. I never drank before. When I started tearing up cars in the parking lot, one of the girls got ahold of Tommy. She gave him shit and made him take me home. I don't remember it, I found out later."

Her throat gave out and I got water. She accepted it without meeting my eyes, turned her face away and continued.

"Tommy got me in the door somehow. I was out cold by then. He'd been fooling around with me a little in the car, I think. He must have been too scared to try and get me upstairs. He left me on the couch and my underpants on the rug and went home. The next thing I knew, I was on the floor and my face hurt. *He* was standing over me. Whore he said. I got up and tried to explain and he hit me a couple of times. I ran for the door but he hit me hard in the back. I went into the stairs and banged my head real hard."

Feeling began to come into her voice for the first time. The feeling was fear. I dared not move.

"When I woke up it was day. Mama must have bandaged my head and put me to bed. My head hurt a lot. When I came out of the bathroom I heard him call me. Him and Mama were in bed. He started in on me. Wouldn't let me talk, and he kept getting madder and madder. Finally I hollered back at him. He got up off the bed and started in hitting me again. My robe came off. He kept hitting me in the belly and tits, and his fists were like hammers. Slut, he kept saying. Whore. I thought he was going to kill me so I grabbed one arm and bit. He roared like a dragon and threw me across the room. Onto the bed. Mama jumped up. Then he pulled down his underpants and it was big and purple. I screamed and screamed and tore at his back and Mama just stood there. Her eyes were big and round, just like in cartoons. His breath stank and I screamed and screamed and—"

She broke off short and her shoulders knotted. When she

continued, her voice was stone dead again. "I woke up in my own bed again. I took a real long shower and went downstairs. Mama was making pancakes. I sat down and she gave me one and I ate it, and then I threw it up right there on the table and ran out the door. She never said a word, never called me back. After school that day I found a Sanctuary and started the divorce proceedings. I never saw either of them again. I never told this to anybody before."

The pause was so long I thought she had fallen asleep. "Since that time I've tried it with men and women and boys and girls, in the dark and in the desert sun, with people I cared for and people I didn't give a damn about, and I have never understood the pleasure in it. The best it's ever been for me is not uncomfortable. God, how I've wondered . . . now I know." She was starting to drift. "Only thing my whole life turned out *better*'n cracked up to be." She snorted sleepily. "Even alone."

I sat there for a long time without moving. My legs trembled when I got up, and my hands trembled while I made supper.

That was the last time she was lucid for nearly forty-eight hours. I plied her with successively stronger soups every time she woke up, and once I got a couple of pieces of tea-soggy toast into her. Sometimes she called me by others' names, and sometimes she didn't know I was there, and everything she said was disjointed. I listened to her tapes, watched some of her video, charged some books and games to her computer account. I took a lot of her aspirin. And drank surprisingly little of her booze.

It was frustrating. I still couldn't make it all fit together. There was a large piece missing. The animal who sired and raised her had planted the charge, of course, and I perceived that it was big enough to blow her apart. But why had it taken eight years to go off? If his death four years ago had not triggered it, what had? I could not leave until I knew.

Midway through the second day her plumbing started working again; I had to change the sheets. The next morning a noise woke me and I found her on the bathroom floor on her knees in a pool of urine. I got her clean and back to bed, and just as I thought she was going to drift off she started yelling at me. "Lousy son of a bitch, it could have been over! I'll never have the guts again now! How could you do that, you *bastard*, it was so *nice!*" She turned violently away from me and curled up. I had to make a hard choice then, and I gambled on what I knew of loneliness and sat on the edge of the bed and stroked her hair as gently and impersonally as I knew how. It was a good guess. She began to cry, in great racking heaves first, then the steady wail of total heartbreak. I had been praying for this, and did not begrudge the strength it cost her.

By the time she fell off the edge into sleep, she had cried for so long that every muscle in my body ached from sitting still. She never felt me get up, stiff and clumsy as I was. There was something different about her sleeping face now. It was not slack but relaxed. I limped out, feeling as close to peace as I had since I arrived, and as I was passing the living room on the way to the liquor, I heard the phone.

As I had before, I looked over the caller. The picture was undercontrasted and snowy; it was a pay phone. He looked like an immigrant construction worker, massive and florid and neckless, almost brutish. And, at the moment, under great stress. He was crushing a hat in his hands, mortally embarrassed. I mentally shrugged and accepted.

"Sharon, don't hang up," he was saying. "I *gotta* find out what this is all about."

Nothing could have made me hang up.

"Sharon? Sharon, I know you're there. Jo Ann says you ain't there, she says she called you every day for almost a week and banged on your door a few times. But I know you're there, now anyway. I walked past your place an hour ago and I seen the bathroom light go on and off. Sharon, will you please tell me what the hell is going on? Are you listening to me? I know you're listening to me. Look, you gotta understand, I thought it was all set, see? I mean I thought it was *set*. Arranged. I put it to Jo Ann, cause she's my regular, and she says not *me*, lover, but I know a gal. Look, was she lying to me or what? She told me for another bill you play them kind of games, sometimes."

Regular two-hundred-dollar bank deposits plus a cardboard box full of scales, vials, razor, mirror, and milk powder makes her a coke dealer—right, Travis McGee? Don't be misled by the fact that the box was shoved in a corner, sealed with tape, and covered with dust. After all, the only other illicit profession that pays regular sums at regular intervals is hooker, and *two* bills is too much for square-jawed, hook-nosed, wide-eyed little Karen, breasts or no breasts.

For a garden-variety hooker . . .

"Dammit, she told me she *called* you and set it up, she give me your *apartment* number." He shook his head violently. "I can't make no sense out of this. Dammit, she *couldn't* be lying to me. It don't figure. You let me in, didn't even turn the camera on first, it was all arranged. Then you screamed and . . . I was real careful not to really hurt you, I know I was. Then I put on my pants and I'm putting the envelope on the dresser and you bust that chair on me and come at me with that knife and I hadda bust you one. It just don't make no sense, will you *goddammit say something to me?* I'm twisted up inside going on two weeks now. I can't even eat."

I went to shut off the phone, and my hand was shaking so bad I missed, spinning the volume knob to minimum. "Sharon you gotta believe me," he hollered from far far away, "I'm into rape fantasy, I'm not into rape!" and then I had found the right switch and he was gone.

I got up very slowly and toddled off to the liquor cabinet, and I stood in front of it taking pulls from different bottles at random until I could no longer see his face—his earnest, baffled, half-ashamed face.

Because his hair was thin sandy blond, and his jaw was a bit too square, and his nose was a trifle hooked, and his blue eyes were just the least little bit too far apart. They say everyone has a double somewhere. And Fate is such a witty little motherfucker, isn't he?

I don't remember how I got to bed.

I woke later that night with the feeling that I would have to bang my head on the floor a couple of times to get my heart started again. I was on my makeshift doss of pillows and blankets beside her bed, and when I finally peeled my eyes open she was sitting up in bed staring at me. She had fixed her hair somehow, and her nails were trimmed. We looked at each other for a long time. Her color was returning somewhat, and the edge was off her bones.

She sighed. "What did Jo Ann say when you told her?"

I said nothing.

"Come on, Jo Ann's got the only other key to this place, and she wouldn't give it to you if you weren't a friend. So what did she say?"

I got painfully up out of the tangle and walked to the window. A phallic church steeple rose above the low-rises a couple of blocks away.

"God is an iron," I said. "Did you know that?"

I turned to look at her and she was staring. She laughed experimentally, stopped when I failed to join in. "And I'm a pair of pants with a hole scorched through the ass?"

"If a person who indulges in gluttony is a glutton, and a person who commits a felony is a felon, then God is an iron. Or else He's the dumbest designer that ever lived."

Of a thousand possible snap reactions, she picked the most flattering and hence most irritating. She kept silent, kept looking at me, and thought about what I had said. At last she said, "I agree. What particular design screwup did you have in mind?"

"The one that nearly left you dead in a pile of your own shit," I said harshly. "Everybody talks about the new menace, wireheading, eighth most common cause of death in less than a decade. Wireheading's not new—it's just a technical refinement."

"I don't follow."

"Are you familiar with the old cliché, 'Everything in the world I like is either illegal, immoral, or fattening'?"

"Sure."

"Didn't that ever strike you as damned odd? What's the most nutritionally useless and physiologically dangerous 'food' substance in the world? White sugar. Glucose. And it seems to be beyond the power of the human nervous system to resist it. They put it in virtually all the processed food there is, which is next to all the food there is, because *nobody can resist it.* And so we poison ourselves and whipsaw our dispositions and rot our teeth. Maltose is just as sweet, but it's less popular, precisely because it doesn't kick your blood sugar in the ass and then depress it again. Isn't that odd? There is a primitive programming in our skulls that rewards us, literally overwhelmingly, every time we do something damned silly. Like smoke a poison, or eat or drink or snort or shoot a poison. Or *over*eat *good* foods. Or engage in complicated sexual behavior without procreative intent, which, if it were not for the pleasure, would be pointless and insane. And which, if pursued for the pleasure alone, quickly becomes pointless and insane anyway. A suicidal brain-reward system is built into us."

"But the reward system is for survival."

"So how the hell did ours get wired up so that survival-threatening behavior gets rewarded best of all? Even the pro-survival pleasure stimuli are wired so that a dangerous *overload* produces the maximum pleasure. On a purely biological level, man is programmed to strive hugely for more than he needs, more than he can profitably use. Add in intelligence and everything goes to hell. Man is capable of outgrowing any ecological niche you put him in—he survives at all because he is The Animal That Moves. Given half a chance he kills himself of surfeit."

My knees were trembling so badly I had to sit down. I felt feverish and somehow larger than myself, and I knew I was talking much too fast. She had nothing whatever to say—with voice, face, or body.

"It is illuminating," I went on, fingering my aching nose, "to note that the two ultimate refinements of hedonism are the pleasure of cruelty and the pleasure of the despoliation of innocence. Consider: no sane person in search of sheerly physical sexual pleasure would select an inexperienced partner. Everyone knows that mature, experienced lovers are more competent, confident, and skilled. Yet there is not a skin mag in the world that prints pictures of men or women over twenty if they can possibly help it. Don't tell me about recapturing lost youth: the root is that a fantasy object over twenty cannot plausibly possess innocence, can no longer be corrupted.

"Man has historically devoted *much* more subtle and ingenious thought to inflicting cruelty than to giving others pleasure—which, given his gregarious nature, would seem a much more survival-oriented behavior. Poll any hundred people at random and you'll find *at least* twenty or thirty who know all there is to know about psychological torture and psychic castration—and maybe two who know how to give a terrific backrub. That business of your father leaving all his money to the church and leaving you 'a hundred dollars, the going rate'— that was *artistry*. I can't imagine a way to make you feel as good as that made you feel rotten. But for *him* it must have been pure pleasure."

"Maybe the Puritans were right," she said. "Maybe pleasure is the root of all evil. Oh, God! but life is bleak without it."

"One of my most precious possessions," I went on blindly, "is a button that my friend Slinky John used to hand-paint and sell below cost. He was the only practicing anarchist I ever met. The button reads: 'GO, LEMMINGS, GO!' A lemming surely feels intense pleasure as he gallops to the sea. His self-destruction is programmed by nature, a part of the very same life force that insisted on being conceived and born in the first place. If it feels good, do it." I laughed, and she flinched. "So it seems to me that God is either an iron, or a colossal jackass. I don't know whether to be admiring or contemptuous."

All at once I was out of words, and out of strength. I yanked my gaze away from hers and stared at my knees for a long time. I felt vaguely ashamed, as befits one who has thrown a tantrum in a sickroom.

After a time she said, "You talk good on your feet."

I kept looking at my knees. "I think I used to be an actor once."

"I would have gues—"

Hiatus.

I was standing by the door, facing out into the hall, and she was still speaking. "I said, will you tell me something?"

"If I can."

"What was the pleasure in putting me back together again?"

I flinched.

"Look at me. There. I've got a half-ass idea of what shape I was in when you met me, and I can guess what it's been like since. I don't know if I'd have done as much for Jo Ann, and she's my best friend. You don't look like a guy your favorite kick is sick fems, and you sure as *hell* don't look like you're so rich you got time on your hands. So what's been your pleasure, these last few days?"

"Trying to understand," I snapped. "I'm nosy."

"And do you understand?"

"Yeah. I put it together."

"So you'll be going now?"

"Not yet," I said automatically. "You're not—"

And caught myself.

"There's something else besides pleasure," she said. "Another system of reward, only I don't think it has much to do with the one I got wired up to my scalp here. Not brain-reward. Call it mind-reward. Call it . . . joy. The thing like pleasure that you feel when you've done a good thing or passed up a real tempting chance to do a bad thing. Or when the unfolding of the universe just seems especially apt. It's nowhere near as flashy and intense as pleasure can be. Believe me! But it's got *some*thing going for it. Something that can make you do without pleasure, or even accept a lot of pain, to get it.

"That stuff you're talking about, that's there, that's true. But you said yourself, Man is the animal that outgrows and moves. Evolution works slow, is all." She pushed hair back from her face. "It took a couple of hundred million years to develop a thinking ape, and you want a smart one in a lousy few hundred thou? That lemming drive you're talking about is there—but there's another kind of drive, another kind of force that's working against it. Or else there wouldn't still be any people and there wouldn't be the words to have this conversation and—" She paused, looked down at herself. "And I wouldn't be here to say them."

"That was just random chance."

She snorted. "What isn't?"

"Well, that's *fine*," I shouted. "That's *fine*. Since the world is saved and you've got everything under control I'll just be going along."

I've got a lot of voice when I yell. She ignored it utterly, continued speaking as if nothing had happened. "Now I can say that I have sampled the spectrum of the pleasure system at both ends—none and all there is—and I think the rest of my life I will dedicate myself to the middle of the road and see

how that works out. Starting with the very weak tea and toast
I'm going to ask you to bring me in another ten minutes or so.
With maltose. But as for this other stuff, this joy thing, that I
would like to begin learning about, as much as I can. I don't
really know a God damned thing about it, but I understand it
has something to do with sharing and caring and what did you
say your name was?"

"It doesn't matter," I yelled.

"All right. What can *I* do for *you?*"

"Nothing!"

"What did you come here for?"

I was angry enough to be honest. "To burgle your fucking
apartment!"

Her eyes opened wide, and then she slumped back against
the pillows and laughed until the tears came, and I tried and
could not help myself and laughed too, and we shared laughter
for a long time, as long as we had shared her tears the night
before.

And then, straight-faced, she said, "Wait'll I'm on my feet;
you're gonna need help with those stereo speakers. Butter on
the toast."

3 ≡

1994 The room was ripe with the pungencies of sex and sweat. Darkness was total, and now that their pulse and breathing had slowed, the stillness was complete. Norman tensed his stomach muscles briefly, felt the warm honeyed weight of Phyllis from his left shin to left shoulder, felt the barely perceptible movement with which she nestled a breast more comfortably into his armpit, tasted the sour sweetness of her breath. Idly he moved his left hand up and down the smooth length of her, reflected on how pleasant it was to caress a body whose dimensions were not precisely and thoroughly known, how very pleasant to encounter unfamiliar swellings and taperings, and in the encountering to trigger unpredictable responses and quickenings.

This caused him to wonder why, in all his five years of marriage to Lois, he had never been seriously tempted to be unfaithful. He had been experienced when he met her, aware

43

of the sweetness of novelty, and during the course of their marriage perhaps a dozen women had inspired lust in him at one time or another. But he had allowed only a handful of those temptations to progress even as far as the fantasy stage—and in retrospect those were the only ones where actual fulfillment of the fantasy was out of the question. Ever since their estrangement he had sought no other partner until now. From the vantage point of satiation, he wondered why he had waited so long.

Well, he answered himself, if you consistently pass up a chance at something very pleasant, it must be because you're afraid of risking something else, something that's *better* than very pleasant. There must be something about long-term intimacy, about familiarity, that is sweeter than variety; something more to life than that spiciest of its spices.

He considered the lovemaking just now finished, and he thought, Well, that was definitely more . . . explosive than anything Lois and I have had in years. But he didn't know if he could say it was more satisfying. There had been clumsinesses, false starts, and missed signals. It is a tricky, finicky road to orgasm, different for everyone on Earth. If this woman and he remained lovers for any length of time, they would have to learn each other's ways—such a clumsy, self-conscious process.

And then Norman understood the sweetness of familiarity. Some say it breeds contempt, but he saw now that there was a tremendous security in having someone who knew you inside and out, who had found it worth the time and trouble to learn where your buttons were and when and how to push them, and whose own personal buttons you could find in the dark. It was worth some loss of mystery. In that moment he learned what it had been about his marriage that was so sweet that, over the past half-year, he had bartered away most of his self-respect for occasional morsels of counterfeit.

And with that learning he knew that the thing he still yearned for so badly—having someone so close to you that they become your other leg—was gone for good, and that counterfeit was all he would ever have of it again from Lois—that it was finally and forever over, irretrievably lost, and that he must find someone else and work five more years ever to have anything like it again. The last scrap of hope, nourished for so long, left him at last. His heart turned over inside him, and his eyes stung fiercely.

Phyllis rolled away from him suddenly. It was a single quick movement, but it was made up of many subtle parts, the drag of breast across his chest, the pleasant pulling apart of fleshes cemented by dried sweat, tiny tugs of intertangled hairs separating, moist sounds from her loins. She left a hand palm up on his belly to maintain contact between them, and rummaged in the tangle of clothing beside the bed. She struggled up into a sitting position, replaced the hand with a leg across his leg, and used both hands to shatter the darkness with a struck match.

The effect was rather like that of a star shell going off over a deserted battlefield, for Norman's bedroom was a mess. But he saw only her, the sudden and terrible beauty of her nakedness. She was flat-chested compared to Lois, but he was not comparing her to Lois; Lois was gone from his mind, and his sorrow with her. This was Phyllis, and she was lovely. When her weight had come off him he had automatically taken a deeper breath; now he could not exhale it.

The sight lasted only long enough for her to light two Player's and pass one to him; then she whipped the match flame to death. But he took the opportunity to take several mental photographs, apply fixative, and store for easy access. In the sudden return of darkness, his breath left him whistling. He replaced it with tobacco smoke.

"That," she said softly, "was good enough to be illegal."

"Madam, your son just passed Victorian Poetry."

She chuckled. "You bastard. 'Passed'? That was B-plus at the very least."

"He'll graduate Mama Cum Loudly," he assured her, and she pinched him.

"Seriously, Norman . . ." She drew on her cigarette, and her face and one shoulder reappeared briefly and ectoplasmically. "I don't make a habit of bolstering my lovers' egos, but that was extraordinary."

"Wasn't my doing. Wasn't even our doing. We were both privileged to be present at an extraordinary event."

"Bullshit. It may have taken me till five-thirty in the morning to seduce you, but it was worth waiting for. You're a very good lover, don't you know that?"

A flip answer died on his tongue and left a strange taste. "No," he said finally, "I didn't."

"Well, then, let me tell you: in the last hour or so you fulfilled just about every fantasy I had left, and showed me at least one erogenous zone I didn't know I had. Listen, I'll be honest: I've had better. But I've never had a better first time, and I doubt I ever will."

He could think of nothing to say.

"Hey, look, I don't want to belabor this. I didn't mean to make you self-conscious. I just . . . I guess I just wanted to say thanks. It's . . . well, there's been a long line of guys who couldn't have cared less if I'd been *awake* or not."

It startled him. "Why the hell would anyone want to have fun alone? Given an alternative like you?"

"The ultimate test of cool. Maintain independence even in the ultimate sharing. You, now: you've got more guts than that. You've given me a piece of yourself, and for all you know I might rip you off."

"Phyllis," he said gently, butting out his smoke, "my check-book and credit cards are on the bureau. Clean me out and we'll be about even. You've done me a world of good." He sat up, and she hugged him.

When they separated again, he realized that he could dimly see her outlines now; a warm glow was faintly visible at the edges of the window shade. "Jesus. It's come morning." All at once, and for the first time in many hours, he was immensely tired. He lay back down and closed his eyes.

"Norman?" she began, and from the tone in her voice he knew at least in general where she was going, and started to protest his fatigue, but she kept on talking, saying, "Do *you* have any unfulfilled fantasies?"

Fatigue gone. "Uh . . . sexual fantasies, you mean?"

"Chicken. Come on, be honest. Aren't there any secret wishes *I* can make come true for *you?*" Her hand found him, began working gently.

"Well . . ."

"Come on, you're stalling, trying to think of something else plausible to ask me for, in place of whatever you first thought of."

Even Lois had not pushed *all* his buttons. He made his decision. "How do you feel about being tied up?"

Even in the semidarkness he could tell she was frowning; her hand stopped.

"Further than you wanted to go?" he asked after a while.

"You know," she said slowly, "I'm not sure." She lit another cigarette, cupping it so that all the light was reflected down away from her face. "I had a friend, once. She and her husband were into master-slave stuff, I mean they were incredible. She wore a collar around her neck, had whip scars, and I swear to God she was as proud and happy as hell. I thought it was sick."

"Jesus," he said, "so do I."

"I used to ask her how she could stand to be degraded like that. She said it was like the ultimate proof of her love for him. I asked her if he ever proved *his* love, and she said it didn't work that way, that she gave him what he needed and he gave her what she needed."

"Christ on a skateboard. They still together?"

"Of course not. After a while she had no more proofs to give him, so he dumped her. I haven't seen either of 'em in years."

"Uh . . . that's considerably stronger than what I had in mind. I don't think I'd go for bullwhips and pain and abuse."

It was light enough now to see her grin as her hand squeezed. "But hearing about it got you hard, didn't it?"

He could not deny it.

"I'll tell you something. I think she was off the wall, I mean industrial-strength crazy . . . but once in a long while I think about it and I get wet myself. Isn't that sick?"

"First tell me what 'sick' means when applied to a normal condition. *Nobody* leaves the TV for a snack during the rape scene. That does not necessarily mean that *anybody* wants a rape for Christmas." He took another cigarette himself, and she lit it for him with hers. "Look, my subconscious is as screwed up as anyone's. Just from the little I've told you about Lois and me, you must be able to see that there's probably a lot of hostility toward women buried in me right now, certainly toward one woman. But—well, I don't know if this will make any sense or not, but a fantasy is not necessarily a wish."

"All right, then," she said, and began gently stroking his penis. "Tell me about your *wishes.*" He could make out her features now, and she was looking him square in the eye. He could not look away. Involuntarily his back began to arch, his buttocks to clench.

"I would like to tie you down to this bed," he said thickly, "and tease, tantalize, and otherwise titillate your fair young body until you scream for mercy. The only kind of pain I have in mind—beyond the occasional pinch or scratch we've already tried—is the sweet agony of wanting to come so badly you can't see straight or remember your name."

Her busy hand paused, and she grinned suddenly. "That *does* sound more interesting than scrambled eggs and coffee. I just don't know if I understand the tying-up part."

He disposed of his cigarette and she followed suit. "Well, partly it's the symbolic trust, of course, which is fairly heady stuff. But most of it is a sheerly muscular thing. I mean, sex is a process of allowing tension to build to a peak and then release, right?"

"When you're doing it right."

"All right—but ordinarily there's a certain point beyond which your subconscious will not let you build that tension—because if you did, the sheer intensity of the climax would break your partner's back, or nose, or whatever. But when you're restrained, you can exert total effort safely. Every muscle in your body can turn into steel cable, and it's okay."

She was looking thoughtful. "You sound as if you've had it done to you."

"Once, a long time ago. A woman I lived with."

"You enjoyed it?"

"Very much."

"How come only that once, then?"

"She didn't want to talk about it afterward. I think she was deeply disturbed by how much she enjoyed it. Which was her privilege; I didn't push it."

"But you'd try it again?"

"Well, I have to admit that these days it's not what I'd call one of my premier urges. I guess I just feel like I've had my fill of being helpless, this last year. But if you wanted to, I guess I could get behind it."

"Another time, perhaps," she said softly, and lay down spread-eagled on her back. "Right now I'm yours on toast. Bring on your ropes."

He used neckties, and was careful about circulation.

"Norman," she said as he was securing the last knot, "can you see my handbag?"

"Sure, what do you need?"

"In the inside compartment there's a vibrator."

"Oh." He fetched it, stopped on the way back to the bed. "You know, this is a hell of a first date."

All the tension blew away in their shared laughter.

He opened the shade, and it was well and truly morning now, an impossibly rosy dawn from some Tourist Bureau post-card. He spared it only a glance, then brought his gaze back to her vulnerable nakedness.

"You know," she said, "there *is* something thrilling about being helpless . . . when your subconscious is convinced that there's nothing to be really afraid of."

"Thank you," he said. He tried the vibrator: it sounded like an alarm clock buzzer. He grinned at her. "Never tried one of these."

"The single mother's home companion. It'll be a learning experience for both of us."

"That it will."

After fifteen minutes she begged for a gag. "Honest to God, I've gotta scream so bad, I'll wake up the whole building." He insisted that they work out signals first by which she could communicate the concepts "stop doing that" and "I need a breather." Half an hour later he still had not allowed release to either of them. His penis was iron-hard and uncharacteristically standing completely upright against his belly, and she was in a state somewhere beyond babbling incoherency, when the doorbell rang.

He ignored it, of course. It penetrated his attention only just far enough to cause him to tuck the vibrator under a sheet, muffling it, and continue manually. Phyllis was beyond noticing anything external.

Of course the bell rang again; he was expecting that, and paid it no more mind that he had the first time. From somewhere Phyllis had found the strength to begin whimpering again.

But the third time it rang, long and hard, he began idly wondering who it could be that was *not* going to get access to Norman Kent's attention that morning. Certainly not Lois. From nine at night or two or three in the morning was her visiting range—one reason it had taken Phyllis so long to seduce him. Not Spandrell, he'd have given up after the second ring. Little George could scarcely be imagined ambulatory before noon, and the Bobcat was gone south for the summer. Some stranger? Norman's rhythm faltered slightly.

The fourth time it rang it didn't stop.

Anger welled in him, and his hands ceased work altogether. In ten or twenty seconds Phyllis's eyes had unrolled and she heard it too. By that time he had found his slippers. He was blazing mad, but he did *not* want the first thing she saw to be an angry face, so he made a terrific effort and produced a fair smile. "It's all right, darling," he said, caressing her cheek. "Some impertinent idiot. I'll blow him out into the hall and be back in thirty seconds."

She nodded and he rose and left the room. He stuck his head back in, said, "Now, don't go away," and closed the bedroom door carefully and firmly behind him. As it clicked shut, her leg spasmed; the vibrator dropped to the floor and lay buzzing.

Norman went to the door naked and fully hard, fervently hoping that whoever was on the other side would prove to be shockable. Already composing his opening blast, he slipped the locks and flung the door open, and his breath left him.

Lois took her finger off the bell. "Good morning," she said brightly.

"God damn it," he said, and lost his voice again.

She glanced at his erection and grinned. "Got you up, I see." She gripped it briefly, in a proprietary way, and stepped into the apartment, starched whites rustling. "You always did wake up hard."

Somewhere in his highly educated brain were the words he wanted now, needed now, but all that came to mind was "Get out of here. I don't want to see you now," and he could not say those words to Lois. Moreover, he knew she would not obey them.

"God, this place is a wreck. That's not like you, Norman."

"Lois—" His throat and mouth were too dry to produce speech; hastily he went to the fridge and threw orange juice past his teeth. "Lois, *listen to me*—"

"Jesus Christ, you must have been on some binge last night, you've slept right through your alarm. I hear it buzzing."

"NO!"

Too late, she was already halfway down the hall, he dropped the orange juice and *ran* flat out but she was already opening the bedroom door.

"Lois, God damn it—"

She screamed.

Through the door came the muffled sound of Phyllis screaming too, and with weirdness incredible the screams harmonized. As Norman crashed into his ex-wife he roared himself, a great bellow of unendurable frustration, and when they had landed in a mock-obscene tangle on the hallway floor and the last of his bellow had left him, in that moment of stillness before the world could come crashing down around all of them, the doorbell rang again.

Lois heaved him off her and headed for the door in a stumbling, scrabbling run, nurse's cap askew. For an insane moment he wondered why she should want so badly to answer the doorbell, why anyone would *ever* want to answer a doorbell. Such was not Lois's intention. To her the door was not a gadget for letting people in; it was a gadget for letting them out. Norman heard a loud crash, Lois's war cry ascending the scale, sounds of violent body contact, an astonishing chorus of voices expressing shock and/or indignation, and Lois's footsteps rapidly receding in the direction of the elevator. By then he was on his hands and knees, shaking his head in a perfectly futile attempt to clear it.

"Time out," he said plaintively to the universe in general.

"It's okay," one of his unseen callers told the rest. "He says he'll be right out." Thus reassured, they began entering the apartment—perhaps a dozen of them, by the sound.

Norman had *started* this overtired. He yearned most to race to Phyllis, but he did not want to leave a large number of strangers alone in his apartment until he had at least examined them and learned their business. On the other hand, he was loath to greet them naked. In a few seconds they would have progressed far enough into the apartment to command a view of the hallway. *If only the God damned vibrator would stop buzzing . . .*

All human brains have a component that takes over problem-solving when the conscious mind is stunned. Often it does as well or better. Norman's had gotten him out of the jungle alive six years before, and it did its best now.

"Hang on, Phyllis," he said urgently, and got to the bathroom a split second before the first uninvited guest came even with the hallway. It should have been the work of a moment to deploy a towel, but incredibly he was still erect. Cold water, he thought wildly, and raced for the sink, but halfway there he decided that the noises coming from the living room sounded somehow technological in nature, and he recalled that there was a two-thousand-dollar sound-and-video system in the living room. He whimpered, spun on his heel, and left the bathroom, doing the best he could with the towel.

There is no way to evaluate a dozen people quickly. They looked like a dozen people. The first thing that registered was the source of the technological sounds. Three golf-cart-type video packs with appropriate color cameras, four still cameras, and five audiocassette decks. Every outlet in the room was in use, and two people were setting up high-intensity lights.

Norman stared at the people, and the people stared at him.

An extremely fat lady with a single eyebrow recovered first. "You *were* expecting us?"

"No."

"Oh, dear. I am Alexandra Saint Phillip."

He had never heard of her. It was obvious that he had never heard of her. She could *not* believe he had never heard of her.

"Alexandra Saint *Phillip*," she explained. "And this is René Gérin-LaJoie." She indicated a short dapper man with a monocle. "And Harry Doyle, of course, and Gloria Delemar, and—"

Norman had never heard of any of these people, and every second he left Phyllis alone lowered the already-low probability of his ever seeing her again. "What do you want?"

"The story, of course," Gérin-LaJoie said impatiently. "Today, if possible. There's a fire over on Spring Garden Road we could be covering."

Is that so? Norman thought. "What story? *Hold it,*" he added as a bearded man began to walk down the hall in search of another outlet. The man paused expectantly.

"You *are* the young man whose sister has disappeared?" Saint Phillip asked in astonishment.

In the two and a half weeks since Maddy had failed to come home, there had literally not been a waking hour in which she was absent from his thoughts—until ten o'clock the previous night. Being reminded was like being slapped in the face with a two-by-four.

"Oh," he said weakly. "Oh, my." Pain twisted his face.

"This kitchen's all over orange juice," complained a dwarf with a fake Oxford accent and a Nagra stereo deck.

"He's the one, Alex," Gérin-LaJoie said. "And we couldn't all have gotten the appointment wrong—so MacLeod must have failed to reach him." He turned to Norman. "Obviously our names ring no bell, Monsieur. Perhaps it is more helpful to say that I am ATV News, and Alex is CBC. These other people are the other major Halifax media. We have come at the behest of your department chairman to publicize the disappearance of Madeleine Kent."

"Wait here," Norman said suddenly. "Please, wait right here. I *must go,* I'll be back in a moment. Make coffee if—" The phone rang. The new picturephone in the bedroom. "Oh, slithering Jesus."

"I'll get it," the technician in the hallway said helpfully.

"NO!" Norman screamed, stopping him in his tracks. Alexandra Saint Phillip's single eyebrow became a circumflex, and Gérin-LaJoie's ears seemed to grow points. "Please wait here."

Norman hurried to the bedroom, losing his towel just as he got the door safely shut behind him. Phyllis was bright red;

whether with fury or shame was unclear. He saw at once that it was MacLeod on the phone, in the process of recording a message.

"—concerned after our last conversation," the department chairman was saying, "and then your estranged wife came to see me. She told me a bit more about your situation, and— well, I called in a few favors. I hope you're there, Norman, they'll be arriving any minute now. Lois said she'd drop by and warn you on her way to work, but I wasn't—"

With what was intended as a reassuring smile at Phyllis, Norman spun the phone carefully away from her, adjusted the camera to show him only from the collarbone up, and activated his end. "Yes doctor they're here right now I have to go thank you *very* much," he said, and cut the connection.

He expected MacLeod's image to look startled as it faded out of existence. But: *that* startled? Instinctively, Norman glanced over his shoulder. There was the bureau mirror, perfectly angled to catch Phyllis's reflection.

He literally fell down laughing.

The horror fed the laughter in the vicious feedback loop of hysteria. He made a last massive effort and beat at his head with his fists, barely succeeded in disrupting the loop. Even before he had his breath back he was hunching across the floor toward her like a brokenbacked snake.

He said no word as he untied her bonds, partly from an awareness that it is impossible to apologize to a captive audience, and partly because he could not conceive of anything to say. She stared fixedly at the ceiling until he was done, then rolled convulsively from the bed.

Of course her legs would not support her. No more would her hands break her fall; she landed heavily on her face.

"Are you all right, Mr. Kent?" the technician called from the hallway.

Sure thing, Jimmy, Norman thought for the millionth time in his life, just changing into Superman. *"Yes,"* he roared. "Right out."

"That's what he said the last time," Norman heard the dwarf complain.

He managed to heave Phyllis up onto the bed. She bit him

as he did so, and he let her. When she let go, he began dressing at once. "Phyllis, listen. Stay right there. Get dressed when you can, leave when they're gone. There's no second choice. There's a gun in my desk, I'd appreciate it if you could blow my fucking brains out before you go."

She had the gag down now. "Do it yourself, mother-fucker."

He shook his head. "If I had the guts I'd never have waited this long." He finished sealing his trousers and decided slippers eliminated the need for socks. "Phyllis, I *have* to talk to these people, now. That's CBC and ATV and both papers and most of the FMs out there, they want to know about *Maddy*. I might—it could—she could be—" His jaw worked. "Phyl, for the love of God wait until they're gone. If you go out there now with rope marks on your wrists they're going to think I killed Maddy and ate her. *I've got to get her picture on the air.*"

Without waiting for an answer he left the room, returned at once, shut off the vibrator, left again.

He held up his hands as he entered the living room, partly to head off conversation and partly to save his eyesight—his living room was now hellbright. "Hold it, ladies and gentlemen. I'm still not here yet, it just looks like it. Is coffee made?"

"Let's just get a reading on you, darling," the dwarf said.

"No," he said firmly. "I'm a different color when I've had my coffee."

"See here—"

"No, you see here. Every piece of equipment in this room has its own battery pack, and you're all draining my wall outlets. I'll accept that, because I want the opportunity to shout with your voice. But I will damned well have coffee first."

One of them had figured out the machine; ten cups of coffee were ready. Norman took his cup back into the glare of video lights.

"Now," he said, sitting in his desk chair, "explain something to me. Dr. MacLeod has a good deal of influence in this town—but this big a turnout is ridiculous. I ignore news myself, but you people are obviously the first string. Since when does the first string cover a simple missing-persons story?"

"Since Samantha Ann Bent was found dead in a stand of alders outside of Kentville," Gérin-LaJoie said, coming back with his coffee.

Norman's ears began to buzz. "I don't believe I—" The dwarf thrust a light meter in his face and clipped a mini-mike to his shirt.

"She disappeared from Halifax two days after your sister. She was . . . it was a sex crime. A very ghastly sex crime."

Coffee slopped on his legs. He set the cup down on the desk with exquisite care and lit a cigarette. "Where was she last seen?" he asked mildly.

"Kempt Road," Saint Phillip supplied. "Near the all-night donut place, at about four o'clock in the morning."

"What did she look like?"

"Mr. Kent, I don't know if you want to—"

"Before, dammit!"

"Oh. She was blonde, dyed blonde, and rather short. About seventeen or eighteen, but she looked younger, I should say. Perhaps fifty kilos. A rather bad complexion, and a sort of teenybopper figure, with—"

"They searched the area where her body was found?"

"For others, you mean? Yes, I imagine so. Probably still at it now."

"Any leads on the killer?"

"Nothing yet," from Gérin-LaJoie. "Except that he is very sick."

Norman let out a great slow breath, and worked his shoulders briefly. "All right. I think it's okay. I don't think the same man got Maddy."

Gérin-LaJoie murmured something into his cassette deck. "Why not, Monsieur Kent?"

"Well, I'm not positive—but it doesn't feel right. My understanding is that sex killers pick a type and stick with it. Maddy was—is—thirty-four years old, brown hair exactly the same shade as mine, about three inches taller than I am, and a good sixty-five kilos. Her figure was excellent and her skin superb. When I last saw her she was not dressed remotely like the way seventeen-year-olds dress these days. She dressed sensibly, tastefully. Her clothes were European, with those loose lines, and that air of durability we stopped respecting over here a long time ago." He ran down awkwardly.

"Sex criminals don't always stay with a type," Gérin-LaJoie said. "Some like variety."

"The circumstances don't match. This Bent girl was way over at the North End at 4:00 A.M. Maddy was last seen downtown, on Argyle Street, planning to walk down one block to Barrington and catch a bus, at a little after midnight. The whole MO is different." He puffed on his cigarette and frowned. "Perhaps I shouldn't be telling you all this. If a tie-in gives it more news value—"

"Mr. Kent," Saint Phillip said, "when two women disappear off the streets of Halifax within forty-eight hours, it is news even if one is built like a hippo and the other a giraffe. It is not inconceivable that two killers independently—" She broke off. "I'm sorry, I—"

"No, you're right." Norman's face was stony. "None of this makes things look any brighter for Maddy. But at least I don't think it was your butcher-crazy that got her."

"Monsieur Kent," Gérin-LaJoie said, "forgive me please, I have not had a chance to familiarize myself with your case. Is there no chance that your sister could have . . . taken it into her head to—"

"I don't think so." Norman frowned. "Look, in your business you must hear a lot of people tell you, 'but she had no reason to.' Maddy not only had no reason to, she had reason *not* to. It's too long a story to explain, but—will you just accept it that Sergeant Amesby down at Missing Persons believes she was abducted? He's a rather skeptical man."

"Hell yes," the dwarf agreed. "If *Amesby* says she was snatched—"

"Hadn't she been in Switzerland for ten years?" asked Saint Phillip, who had plainly done her homework. "Couldn't she have—"

"Leaving everything she owned? It's been almost three weeks, and Interpol comes up empty," Norman said.

The bedroom door opened, and Phyllis entered the living room. She wore her own jeans and one of his shirts, with the sleeves buttoned. "Goodbye, Norman," she said icily, and exited. There was a brief pause.

"Look, are you ready to tape?" Norman asked.

"Yes."

He ran his hands through his hair. "Okay." He looked at the largest of the videocameras, told himself it was an old and understanding friend who happened to have one round eye. "My deepest sympathies go to the family of Samantha Ann Bent. I think I know something of what they are feeling now. But I don't believe that the beast who took their girl got my sister Madeleine. Their physical types and the manner of their disappearances are too dissimilar. I'm all the family Maddy has left and I don't know *what* has happened to her." He took a folder from his top desk drawer, selected a large color glossy. He held it up to the cameras, which all trucked in. "This is my sister, Madeleine Kent. She is thirty-four. She was last seen on June twelfth near Barrington and Argyle, wearing a tan calf-length skirt, matching jacket and pale yellow blouse, carrying a yellow purse. She had just returned from ten years in Switzerland, and she tended to speak as though English were a learned language, although she was losing the tendency. If you have any information which could help us locate her, I beg you to contact Sergeant Amesby of the Halifax police, or the RCMP. Complete anonymity can be guaranteed.

"My sister has been gone for eighteen days. I am worried sick. If you know anything at all, if you saw anything unusual near Argyle or Barrington streets on Friday, June twelfth, *please*... call Missing Persons. I—" His voice broke. "I need your help. Thank you." He sucked hard on his cigarette. "Okay?"

"In the can." "Got it." "Good take." At once all the video people and half the others lit cigarettes.

"All right." He drained the coffee, set it on the desk, and took a folio from the same drawer. Most of the journalists came closer, gathered round the desk. "You newspaper people, here is a dossier I've compiled on Madeleine. I gave a copy to Sergeant Amesby, but he won't have let you see it. It contains everything I know or was able to find out about Maddy, everything known about her last evening. Statements from people who were at the party. A copy of the posters I distributed to all the cab companies. Still shots of Maddy, ten years out of date. She had a home videocassette in her belongings that seems fairly recent. I've had some stills made up from that. You can see that she hasn't changed a great deal in ten years."

"More worldly-wise," Saint Phillip said. "A faint flavor of cynical amusement. Of self-assurance. She was a very beautiful woman, Mr. Kent."

Norman clenched his teeth. "And still is, so far as I know."

"Oh, my God, I'm sorry. Of *course* she—"

"As for you print and radio people, perhaps it would save us all a good deal of time if I simply ran off several copies of this dossier for you to take with you. Then if you have any questions you can phone me; I have full-range audio."

"Can we borrow these photos, Mr. Kent?" one of the print journalists asked.

"I'll fax them to you, if you'll all be so kind as to give me your access." He started a notepad circulating. "If there are no more questions, I'll start these through the copier. Please feel free to start a fresh pot of coffee, and there are munchables in the first cabinet on the left."

He collated the dossier and took it down the hall to the library. As paper was stacking in the output hopper, he became aware that he was not alone.

"Mr. Kent?" Alexandra Saint Phillip said.

He did not turn.

"Mr. Kent, it is my business to listen to sad stories all day long. In my darker hours I think of myself as a sob-sucker. I know how to give sincere condolences to people I don't give a damn about. I...I just...I'm sorry, Mr. Kent. I'm sorry for your sister, who looks like she is a hell of a woman. But most of all I'm sorry for you. Whatever happened to her, at least she knows it."

He kept feeding sheets into the copies, perhaps a little more clumsily.

"I've been a journalist a long time, Mr. Kent. You start to get a feeling. I can't be sure, of course, but I don't think you are ever going to know any more than you do now. I don't think she'll ever be found."

Norman stopped feeding the machine. His shoulders knotted. "I don't think so either."

"You are either going to learn how to live with that, or you aren't. I read you as the kind of man who has what it takes to survive something like this. But—forgive me, aren't you in the midst of a divorce right now?"

"That was my ex who greeted you at the door."

"Yes. Look, I have no wish to pry. I'm not trying to get a juicier story, this is off the record. But I think if you own a gun you should throw it away. If you own a straight razor, buy an electric one instead. Perhaps I talk too much. I—if there's anything at all I can do—well, here."

He turned to see her offering a card. Past her he saw the dwarf looking through the open bedroom door. "Get the hell out of there," he barked.

"Certainly, old man. Thought it was the loo."

"Try the one I came out of wearing a towel," Norman suggested bitterly.

"Sorry."

Norman turned back to Saint Phillip. "Madam," he said slowly, *"I* don't know if I'm the kind of man who can take a lifetime of this. But I value your opinion. And your concern. Thank you very much."

She smiled, a very sad smile. "Take the card. It's the one with office *and* home numbers. I don't give it out often. My husband's name is Willoughby. Go on with your copying."

After they all left he noticed that the orange juice had been mopped from the kitchen floor, and knew that she had done it.

That evening he took another walk out onto the MacDonald Bridge. He watched the clouds slide past the moon for several hours, and once he sang a song, and at eleven-thirty he threw his gun over the side into the harbor.

4 ≣

1999 I woke the next morning with less headache than I deserved. The nose hurt worse. I was alone in the bedroom. I heard distant kitchen sounds, smelled something burnt. I found I was irritated. I had not cleared Karen for solo flight yet. That made me laugh sourly at myself, and any kind of laugh will do to get a morning started.

I found her sitting on a pillow in the dining area adjacent to the kitchen. She did not acknowledge my arrival. She was staring expressionlessly at what she had intended to be an omelet. It was the toast that had burned, and these days it's hard to burn toast.

Breakfast with a stranger is always awkward. You come upon each other before you have had time to buckle on your armor. And so the question becomes, how urgent is the need? Even if you made love the night before it doesn't necessarily help: you can get to know someone better than you wanted to over first breakfast. Neither of us was capable of making love, but I knew Karen fairly well, in terms of the pattern of her history. But the Karen I knew had died, had committed suicide. The new Karen I had created by aborting her suicide I did not know at all.

I found that I wanted to know her. As a man who has accidentally caused an avalanche cannot prevent himself from watching to learn the full extent of the damage, I needed to know, now that it was too late, what I had done by my meddling. I wanted to like her. That would make me a hero.

I took the omelet and toast from in front of her. She started indignantly, a good sign. I dumped the stuff down the oubliette and took new ingredients from the fridge. On a hunch I went back and took a sip of her coffee. I pitched that too and got the grounds from the freezer.

I mixed and sliced and grated, assembled and seasoned the resultants, and arrayed them in the cooker. I studied the controls. The combination she had programmed was straight out of the owner's manual, with one plain error. I had figured out the quirks of this particular model—extensive ones—the first day I had been in the apartment. She was a rotten cook. I set it correctly and initiated.

"I think I'm going to move out of this dump," she said.

I nodded. I did not ask where she would go. I prepared cups to receive coffee. Her sugar had been stored in a cabinet, so she didn't take any. Expensive cream was on her shopping list, so she used it.

"Hey, that smells *good*."

I dealt out onion-and-cheddar omelets, bacon, crisped English muffins. I put two straws in a quart of orange juice and poured Antiguan coffee. The shopping-list program had been her own. She was in the habit of ruining some very expensive food. Well, she earned her money. She started to dig in, pulled up short. "You think I'm ready for a meal this size?"

I had reoriented her stomach with tea, soup, and other soft foods. "If it looks good to you, you should certainly have at least a little of everything."

She fell to at once, but ate with some caution. She did not talk while she ate, which suited me. We paid respectful attention to the food. She made occasional small sounds of enjoyment. I found this remarkable. It did not seem that any of the jelly of her hypothalamus had been boiled away. Her pleasure center was functional. Remarkable.

While the food occupied her attention, I studied her. Her hair had been washed, dried, and brushed. She looked squeaky clean. She wore a glossy fluff-collar robe that covered her to the chin. She wore no makeup, no jewelry. Her hands were reasonably steady, her color okay.

After a while she caught me studying her. Without hesitation she began to study me right back. For a few seconds it got like two kids trying to outstare each other, but there is a limit to the amount of time two chewing people can do that and keep a straight face. We shared a small explosion of laughter, then smiled at each other for a few seconds more and went back to our food.

I had given her a portion a third the size of my own. Though she chewed much more slowly, she finished first. At once she reached for a nearby package of Peter Jackson. I did not react, kept eating. She looked down, saw her fingers taking a cigarette from the pack, and put it back. Though I still gave no sign of noticing, I chalked up a point for her.

When I was done, she took the cigarette back out and touched it alight on the side of the pack. "Gasper?" she asked, offering me the pack.

"Don't use it, thanks."

"Grass in the freezer."

"That either."

She was surprised. "You don't get high?"

"'Reality is for those who don't have the strength of character to handle drugs,'" I quoted. "That's me."

She pursed her lips, nodded. "Uh-huh." She took a deep drag. "You're a good cook, Joe. Thanks. Very much."

"Yeah."

She held her cigarettes down between middle and ring fingers. It seems like one of those meaningless affectations, until you notice that with each puff, half of the face is hidden. The inverse is to hold the cigarette like a home-rolled joint between thumb and forefinger tips, minimizing facial coverage. Now that I saw her with her hair brushed, on a head held upright, I saw that the hair too was styled for maximum concealment, in long bangs and forward-sweeping wings. If she'd been a man she'd have worn a full beard.

"Joe what? I forget."

Embarrassing. So did I. "Nixon," I tried at random.

"Temple something. Templar . . . Templeton."

"Well, I knew it was a rat's name," I said. She didn't laugh, of course. She had been a small child when the pack brought Nixon down, and nobody reads *Charlotte's Web* anymore these days. But she could tell that I thought I'd said something witty, so she smiled. She had manners.

"You don't have to tell me the real one," she lied. "It doesn't matter."

Do you ever learn things from your mouth? I have a hundred glib evasions and outright lies on file for the question "What is your name?" To my astonishment I heard myself tell her the truth.

"There is no real one."

"Eh?"

"I don't exist."

She could tell I had stopped kidding, even if she still didn't understand. "You lost me. I'm dumb in the morning."

Nothing to do for it now. "I'm not on file. I'm not on tape. The government and I don't recognize each other. I'm a non-person."

"No shit?" Though she had hidden it well, she had been just a trifle annoyed, thinking I was withholding my real name out of mistrust. Now she was realizing how much I did trust her. So was I. "God, that's fantastic. How did you do it?" She caught herself. "I'm sorry. That's not a proper question."

I was beginning to like her. "It's okay, Karen. I have told two people what I just told you. Both of them asked me how I pulled it off, I told them both the truth, and neither one believed me. Not at first, or ever. So I don't mind telling you."

"Okay. How'd you do it?"

"I haven't the faintest idea."

She thought about it. "Yeah. Yeah, that's kind of hard to get a handle on, all right." She puffed on her cigarette. "I take it there's about a two-hour rap that explains it."

"Yeah. It gets less probable with each sentence."

She nodded. "And you don't especially feel like going into it right now."

Definitely beginning to like her. "Another time. Why'd you stop dealing coke?"

Her eyebrows rose a fraction of an inch. "Tossed the place, eh? I liked it too much. The toot and the loot. Contentment is not in my pattern, if you dig. I'm a Pisces. When the situation's been comfortable too long, I find some way to kick it apart. There are so many. In this case I got involved with my supplier, and when the relationship went sour, so did the career. Of course I couldn't have predicted this without going to the trouble of thinking about it for a second. I believe you, by the way."

"I know."

There went her no-hitter. I hate people who do that, look you in the eye and tell you matter-of-factly how screwed up they are. I have this conviction that screwed-up people are *supposed* to be embarrassed about it. It's as common a vice as smoking these days, and at least as much nuisance to those around you. It lowers the general morale.

On the other hand, I make a habit of bitterly criticizing every aspect of reality *except* myself—which is also bad for general morale.

"After a while I found myself owing considerable money to some very sandy people," she said. "Well, I'd always told myself I could hook if times got bad. I thought it out and made my move, and it didn't work out very well. I mean, I got paid all three times, but I could tell they weren't real happy. They weren't repeat business, they weren't word-of-mouth. A girl could starve that way.

"The fourth one set me straight. We talked afterwards, and he was nice. I told him just a little about me, just that my first time was a rape. 'That's it,' he says. 'You're not a bad little actress, but Señorita, no *way* will you ever convince anyone that you like it.' About a day and a half later it hit me that that wasn't a drawback, it was an advantage, and I changed my PR and tripled my price. I paid off my people in a week. So that's"—she grinned bitterly—"that's what a bimbo like me is doing in a class joint like this." She took a last puff, pinched the filter harder than necessary, and tossed the butt, before it had quite finished going out, in the general direction of the oubliette.

I sat perfectly still. I had scrubbed that floor on my hands and knees—but not by invitation. You don't *own* the place, I reminded myself, you're just robbing it.

But if I had not been irritated (I'm embarrassed to admit), if the effort of not wrinkling up my nose hadn't made it throb, I might have been humane enough to save the obvious next question for another day or two.

"What will you do now?"

She visibly flinched, and dropped her gaze. Of course I felt like a jerk at once. Of course that irritated me more. She rose suddenly from the table. I was between her and one exit, so she took the other. Into the living room.

When she stiffened, I opened my mouth, slapped myself in the forehead, and raced after her. I was days too late. There in the same position between the lamp and the plastic table, from which I had never thought to move it, was the God damned armchair. Framed and lit like a tableau at Madame Tussaud's, lacking only a waxy body . . .

A moist noise in her throat decided not to be a word after all. She looked around, hesitated. She was *not* going to sit those bedsores on the chair that had put them there. But if she sat on the couch she had to *look* at the chair. I stepped past her, turned the chair so that it faced away from the window, and tilted it back as far as it would go, bringing up the footrest. With some throw pillows from the couch, the result was a cushioned flat surface about thirty degrees from horizontal, the high end facing the window.

"Come here," I said in what I hoped was a kindly but firm tone. She did not move. "I'll clear the window. Lie on your belly and watch the sun try to brighten the Hudson Sewer." She still didn't move. "What do you do when you fall off a horse, Karen?"

She nodded, crossed the room, and stretched out without further hesitation. I dialed the window transparent and fetched her cigarettes. She lit one gratefully. "Joe?"

"Yah."

"Would you rub some more of that anesthetic gunk on my ass? And could I have some rum?"

"Just what your system needs. How about some aspirin? If I can find any in that haystack."

She sighed. "Okay."

I fetched cream, aspirin, and water from the bathroom and pulled a footstool near her chair. She lay with her face toward me while I applied the cream, and though she sucked air a few times she didn't cry out. One excellent test of trust is the ability to receive a butt-massage unselfconsciously, and she paid me that compliment. As I worked up to the sores on her back I looked around the room. I had given her story-tapes a B-minus. A boxed set of historical romances had cost her points. On the other hand, she kept a handful of real books, good ones. Maybe the set was a gift. She had a fairly good multipurpose music collection, deficient in classical but otherwise sound; there were items I had already stolen. Her video library was strictly tape-of-the-month club, but with the incongruous addition of some classic early Emsh. An overall rating was hard to decide. A C-plus would have been strictly fair, but a B-minus could have been justified to the . . .

Hiatus.

I was sitting on the couch with half a drink in my hand, and she was looking out the window, smoking a cigarette I didn't remember her lighting. The sun was high over the river now. It looked hot out there. I saw a gull make a dead-stick landing on a distant roof and lay where it hit. What boils up off the Hudson at mid-day would take pages just to catalog. How come pigeons have adapted to pollution and gulls haven't?

After a while she pinched out a cigarette, dropped it on the rug. She got up and put the robe back on. She walked over to the window and stood staring out over lower buildings, watching faraway boats trying to slice the water. "One thing for sure, I've gotta get out of this pit. I always wanted to live in a place like this. My old man's life savings couldn't have bought a month in a place like this. The week before last I found myself sitting in front of the video with the stereo playing and a story on the reader on my lap. I looked around and on the table next to me was a burning cigarette, a burning joint of Supremo, a couple lines of coke, and a drink with the ice all melted. Four kinds of munchies. It came to me that I was bored. I couldn't think of one thing on earth to do that I would enjoy." She turned around, leaned back against the window, and surveyed the room. "It's kind of like that now. I need to change the channel. This just isn't the kind of place where you figure out what to do with the rest of your life."

She was as close as she could come to asking. I was reluctant. "What about, uh, Jo Ann?"

"She lives with two other girls, it's like Times Square."

So think about it. Crazy little hooker with a socket in her scalp, miserable cook, slob, sexual cripple, two kinds of smoker.

Tough as a Harlem rat, in both mind and body. With pretty good manners. She had respected my privacy considerably more than I had respected hers. And she knew what you do when you fall off a horse. In many ways she was the ideal roommate for someone like me, at least for a while. Maybe my own life had gotten a little boring.

"You can crash at my place," I said. "I'll put up with tobacco, but no grass. I do all the cooking, you do all the dishes, I do all the rest of the housework. You can bring five percent of the contents of that medicine cabinet."

Relief was plain on her face. "I'm grateful, Joe. Really grateful. You're sure it's okay," she added, not quite making it a question. I answered it anyway.

"Sure."

"I won't be putting you out any?"

"Karen, why don't you just figure out what questions you want to ask me and ask me? I don't promise to answer any, but we'll save time that way."

She smiled. "Fair enough. You live alone?"

"Yeah."

"Involved with anybody?"

"No."

"Born New Yorker?"

"I don't think so."

She blinked, but let it pass. "Got any family?"

"I don't know."

"You don't *know?*"

"Next question."

"How come you burgle?"

"It's the only job my background has prepared me for. I'm trying to furnish a flat."

"How'd your nose get all broke up like that?"

"I don't know how I got the first break. You broke it the second time, when I unplugged you."

"Jesus wept and died. I'm *sorry,* Joe, I—how can you not know how you broke your nose?"

"I wish to God I knew."

"Jesus."

That ended the Twenty Questions for a while. She paced and thought about what I had said, absently lighting another smoke. I could see her working it out. Most of what I had told her made no sense. Lord, who knows better than I? But I had not been smiling when I had said it, so she believed me implicitly. Therefore there had to be a startling but logical explanation, and I must have reasons of my own for not wanting to go into it.

I wished that were so.

It was a little annoying, how implicitly she trusted me. Perhaps it is vaguely unflattering to be considered harmless. Or a little *too* flattering: more responsibility than I liked.

I was just as annoyed at how implicitly *I* seemed to trust *her.* I depend on my instincts—I have to in my position—but sometime soon I was going to have to sit down with them and ask them exactly why they had had me offer my two most dangerous secrets to her. I must stand to gain something from the ultimate risk—but what?

"Look," she said, still pacing, "maybe there's one thing more we should—" She saw my face and stopped. "No," she said thoughtfully. "No, I guess I don't have to discuss that with you. Okay, look. Can you wait another day or two? I know I promised to help you with these speakers, but honest to God I don't think I could make it to the corner right now. If I don't lay down soon, I'll—"

"Go to bed, Karen. I'll get the dishes. Maybe the day after

tomorrow, maybe the day after that. My time is my own."
Something made that last sentence taste bitter in my mouth.

"Thanks, Joe. Thanks a lot."

"Take two more aspirin."

After she left I got up from the couch and selected one of
her better audiotapes. I intended to steal it, or at least dub it
onto my home system, but my subconscious felt like hearing
it now: Waits's classic *Blue Valentine*. I adjusted the headphones and sat back.

His courageous version of "Somewhere" made me smile
sadly as always. For all us losers and thieves and junkies and
nighthawks there is a place, somewhere. But: *my* place? The
next track also seemed apropos, "Christmas Card from a Hooker
in Minneapolis," but only in that Karen could have written such
a letter. It did not explain why I had answered as I had. I drifted
through the next track, and then my ears woke me up again in
the middle of the hypnotic blues "$29," and I had it. Waits's
whiskey-and-Old-Gold rasp filled my head.

> *When the streets get hungry baby*
> *You can almost hear 'em growl*
> *Someone's settin' a place for you*
> *When the dogs begin to howl*
> *When the streets are dead*
> *They creep up and take whatever's*
> *left on the bone*
> *Suckers always make mistakes*
> *Far away from home*
> *Chicken in the pot*
> *Whoever gets there first*
> *Gonna get himself $29 and an alligator*
> *purse . . .*

I had already taken all her cash myself, and planned to take
other items. Still, there were other thieves on the street who
would consider me shockingly wasteful. If I left her here to
work out her destiny, I was morally certain that she would drift
back to hooking within a week or two. The money is addictive.
But she had been working as an independent for a surprisingly
long time. Such luck could not last; luck had never lasted for

Karen. One day soon she would come to the attention of an entrepreneur. When his training period was over, even a woman as tough and strong as she would be docile, obedient, and tremblingly eager to please. In this largest city in the land of the free, it happens every day.

I could not leave her to the slavers. I hated and feared slavery too much myself.

But it was more than that.

I had meddled. I had forcibly prevented her from ending her life when and as she wished. Stated that way, my action was morally repugnant to me; as a kid I had canvassed and petitioned vigorously for Right to Death, and cheered when it became law of the land. I had no defense now, no excuse: I had acted out of "instinctive" revulsion, which is never an excuse for overriding morality. She had been fleeing from a life that was misery occasionally leavened with horror. If I simply returned her to that life and washed my hands, I was a monster.

I hoped it would not take her too long to find some new kind of direction, some kind of plan or purpose. Because I was stuck with her until she did.

I found myself cursing her for having been so inconsiderate as to pick a slow, pleasant death, and laughed out loud at myself. And went to do the breakfast dishes.

It was actually three days before I clouted a delivery van over on Broadway, and drove us and the plunder I had selected to my place. What I didn't want she left behind. The rent would keep paying itself, the lights would go on and off in random patterns simulating inhabitance, the rugs would clean themselves once a week, from now until her lease ran out in another two years or her credit balance dropped too low. That was the rent she paid to stay at my place: the maintenance of a legal address elsewhere on all the proper punch cards.

I had told her almost nothing about the place. So few people ever see it that it's fun to savor the reactions.

She was neither impressed nor dismayed when we pulled up behind the warehouse. It was a moonless night and there were no lights, but a warehouse does not look impressive even in the daytime. The daytime appearance of mine is, in fact, particularly weatherbeaten and long-abandoned, even for the neighborhood.

It was probably just about what she had expected, and I would guess she had lived in worse circumstances before. "Do we unload now?" was all she said.

"Yeah."

We took the swag in the back way and by candlelight we stacked it, for the moment, where burglar's plunder should be stored, in a corner where casual random search of the warehouse would probably not find it.

An office module formed a block in the center of the warehouse. I led her toward it through the black maze by memory, having left the candles where they would be useful. Most people being led through total darkness are a pain in the ass, but she knew how to move in the dark. As we rounded a stack of packing crates something subliminal warned me. I tightened my grip on her hand and flung her bodily into an aisle between two rows of boxes. That changed the position of my head, so the sap came down on the point of my extended shoulder. My right arm died. There is no good way to get a gun from under your left armpit with your left hand. For me to have tried it would have presented my one remaining elbow to that sap. I back-pedaled, spun, and bugged out.

He followed. Not many could have followed me through my own turf in the dark, but he was one of the few. I tried angling toward the crowbar pile, but he guessed it and moved to cut me off. He pressed me too closely to give me a chance to spill the gun and pick it up. I took us to a cleared space large enough to allow room to work and spun at bay, feeling pessimistic. He pulled up just out of reach and puffed and chuckled. I kicked one shoe up into the air, sent the other in another direction, hoping to misdirect him. He flinched as the first one hit, but by the second he had figured it out. He chuckled some more.

"I couldn't get in your place . . . this time either, Sammy," he puffed. "But you'll take me in . . . won't you? You'll beg for the chance."

His sap arm would be behind him; no matter where or how

I hit him, he'd have a terrific shot at my head. I should have saved one shoe to flip into his face. Dumb.

"Hey, thanks for throwing in the fem, Sam. She'll never find her way outta here in the dark. You saved me another twenty bucks."

I had to make my move soon, he was getting his breath back. Go for the gun? Try to yank my belt free left-handed? Charge and hope for a break? They all sucked.

"Hey, no hard feelings, huh?"

A shinbone was the least risk; I got ready to try a kick, rehearsing what I would do after he broke my leg. "No hard feelings, Wishbone."

If it is possible to grunt above high C, that is what he did then. He came at me in a shambling walk, hissing, and when he cannoned into me he embraced me. I was too startled to react. The hiss ended in the word "Shit," and then he slid slowly down me.

God damn it, was my whole house full of armed hostiles? I stepped out of his arms, bent and searched hastily for the sap without success.

"Twenty bucks, huh?" Karen said. "Mother fucker."

I got slowly to my feet. "What the hell did you do to him?"

"Put a fist through his goddam kidney. Son of a bitch. Help me find his crotch, I want to kick it."

"Take it easy. Your honor is satisfied."

"But—"

"He sapped me. It's *my* turn."

"Oh. Are you okay?"

"I'll be okay for another couple of minutes, until this arm comes back to life. Then I will be very disconsolate for a long time."

"How can I help?"

"Help me drag him over here."

We arranged him on a low flatbed handtruck. He was making mewing sounds. He wanted to scream, but he would give up the idea long before he had the breath. I was glad she had hit me only a glancing blow that first day; full strength and she might have killed me, and wouldn't that have made interesting copy for the *Daily News*?

"Who the hell is he?"

"Wishbone Jones. Small-time mugger and a little of this and that. Skinny as a stork and stronger than I am. Lives down by the wharf. Not bright, but a good fighter. We've tangled." By now I had my gun out. I gave it to her and sat down on the handtruck beside him. My arm and shoulder were just beginning to catch fire, but that was mitigated to some extent by the exhilaration of survival. "Hello, Wishbone."

"H—hi, Sam." He was getting back under control.

"Bad day at the track, Wishbone?"

"Nuh . . . no."

"Then it's got to be basketball or poker."

"Neither one. My ex from Columbus caught up with me."

"Yep. That's kharma for you. Well, I believe we discussed this the last time?"

He grimaced. "Aw, *shit,* Sam. If I go to the hospital they give me the cure."

"We *did* discuss it."

He shook his head. "Ah, shit. Yeah." He gave me his arm.

"No hard feelings, Wish?"

"No hard feelings." He closed his eyes and I broke the arm across the edge of the handtruck as quickly and cleanly as I could. He screamed and fainted.

Karen had not uttered a sound when I had suddenly flung her into the darkness, but she yelped now.

I slumped, exhausted and unutterably depressed. I wanted to vomit, and I wanted to scream from the pain in my shoulder, and I wanted to cry. I stood up. "Let's go inside."

It took one metal key and a five-number combination to get us into the office module. The windows are not boarded, they're plated. The door is too heavy to batter and the roof is reinforced. Still, it is no more secure than the average New York apartment. A cleverer cracksman than Wishbone could have opened it in fifteen minutes with the right tools. There is no such thing as an unbeatable lock, just incompetent craftsmen.

"What about him?" she asked as we stepped in.

"Wishbone will find his way home. To the hospital if he's smart. But Wishbone's not smart. Damn his eyes." I sealed the door and turned on the light.

She was looking at me expressionlessly. She came suddenly close, took my face in her hands, and studied it. Nearly at once she nodded. "You hated it."

"God damn you, did you think I enjoyed it?" I yelled, flinging her hands away.

She shook her head. "No. Not for a second." She backed away one step. "But for just a minute there I was scared to death that you didn't give a damn, one way or the other."

I dropped my eyes. "Fair enough." I turned around and walked a few steps. "Simulating total ruthlessness is, I guess, the hardest thing I've ever had to do in my life. Sometimes it's necessary."

"Yeah. I know."

I whirled, ready to flare up at any sign of pity or sympathy, but there was neither. Only a total understanding of, and agreement with, what I had said.

"Come on," I said. "I'll show you around." My shoulder ached like hell, but as I said, I wanted to see her reaction.

The room we were in had not been substantially altered since the last time it was used as an office, perhaps fifteen or twenty years ago. The alterations I had made had not involved cleaning. There wasn't much to see that was worth looking at, unless she had a thing for busts of President Kennedy the Second. I led her into the back, throwing on lights as we went.

It was obvious that a bachelor burglar of no great fastidiousness lived here. Three inner offices were converted to living space, furnished with things too rickety, threadbare, or ugly to fence. Empties lay here and there, and all the wastebaskets were overflowing. The "kitchen" could produce anything from peanut butter on moldy white bread to a tolerable mulligan, and not much in between, if you didn't count the beer. The office with the toilet had perforce become the master bedroom. A truly astonishing calendar hung on the wall. The mattress lay on the floor, and the sheets had that lived-in look. A rancid glass of orange juice sat beside the bed, next to a sound-only phone and a disorderly pile of recent newspapers all opened to the society page.

She really did have manners. She kept a poker face, made no comment at anything she saw, just looked around at each room and nodded. Perhaps she had lived in worse. Finally my shoulder hurt too much. I decided I had milked it for all it was worth and took her back to the outer office.

She lit a Peter Jackson. "By the way, how many names have you got, Sam?"

"How many are there? Sit over on that desk, 'Sharon.'"

She complied.

"Now lift your feet off the floor, completely, and keep them there."

I waited until she had done so. Initiating dislock sequence while there is additional human-size mass anywhere in the room *except* on the four places where those desk legs meet the floor will cause the room to be blown out of the warehouse. When she was seated correctly I turned to the desk nearest me. I opened the middle drawer. Then I crossed the room and flipped the switch for the ventilation fan that no longer works. On, off, on. I went back to the desk and closed the drawer. What looked just like a battered old Royal manual typewriter sat on a rubber pad on the desk's typing shelf; I typed some words. Karen watched all this without expression, but I could tell that she was wondering if I had sustained any head injuries in the scuffle with Wishbone.

I walked over in front of the bust of Kennedy and smiled at it. Its right eye winked at me. A large section of floor hinged back and up like a snake sitting up, soundlessly. Carpeted stairs led down into a place of soft lights.

"Now I'll show you where I really live."

"You bastard," she said.

I bowed and gestured: after you.

"You bastard," she said again softly. *"This* you *did* enjoy."

I lost control and grinned hugely. "Bet your ass." I gestured again. "Come on. You can get down off there now. Or do you *want* to spend the night up here?"

She came off the desk with a you'll-get-yours grin, tugged her skirt around, and whacked dust from it. "The secret temple of Karnak. Do I have to take my shoes off?"

"Not even your dress." Perhaps an indelicate joke, but I had found that she *liked* being kidded about her occupation.

She grimaced. "That's another buck for ironing, chump."

She came to the stairs and went down. I followed. I didn't crash into her on the bottom step because I was expecting her to stop dead. I waited while she stared, and when she finally stepped into the living room I moved past her.

She was still staring around her, with an astonishment that refused to fade. No matter where she looked, she could find nothing unremarkable. I drank her astonishment thirstily.

Perhaps I am excessively houseproud. But I have some reason to be. The location is a large part of its value, of course—but as a conventional apartment it was worth two and a half of hers, and she had not been living cheaply by any means. I seldom indulge my weakness; Karen was the fifth person to come down those stairs with me. Almost all of the others had lived with me *upstairs* for at least a week before I let them into my real house.

She would not say a word.

"This is the living room," I said, and she jumped. "If you'll step this way...?" Oh, I was disgusting.

She remained resolutely silent during the rest of the tour, but it cost her. It took a good ten minutes; my house has a little more than twice the cubic of the office complex that sits on it.

As we walked I flipped switches and brought the house back up to active status, started the coffee program, and turned up the fans to accommodate her inevitable cigarettes.

The message light on the phone panel was not lit. Maybe one day I will come home and find it lit. When that happens I will drop to the floor and pray that the end is quick.

At last my shoulder made me cut it short. I led us back to the living room and dropped into the nearest Lounger, drawing its attention to my shoulder. "Excuse me," I said. "This won't wait any longer."

She nodded. The chair began doing indescribable things to my shoulder girdle, and I closed my eyes. When I could open them again, she was standing on the same spot in the same stance, looking at me with the same lack of expression. My chair cut back to subliminal purring. I tried the shoulder and winced, but decided against repeating the massage cycle.

"Joe," she said finally, "you are a *good* burglar."

"I'm a very good burglar."

"If that grin gets any bigger, you're gonna split your face clear back to your ears. Just before that happens, would it be all right if I were to ask some of the obvious questions?"

"I'll tell you anything I can."

"All right." She took out cigarettes and lit up. Then she put her fists on her hips. *"What the fuck is this place?"*

"Are you familiar with the expression, 'to go to the mattresses'?"

"Sure. Are you trying to tell me that all *this*"—she swept her hand around the room—"is some kind of gangster's command post?"

"No. But I am telling you that big multinationals sometimes have to go to the mattresses too."

Her eyes widened. "But—that's silly. Multinationals don't have shooting w—well, yes they do, but not in *New York*."

"Not on page one, no. They tend to be much neater, much subtler."

She thought it through. "So it's a corporate command bunker. What corporation?"

"I don't know."

"It looks like it would make a great fortress. How come the original owners aren't here?"

"My guess is undeclared war, a sneak attack. The secret of this place would naturally be known only by a few—presumably 'one grenade got them all.' I estimate that it has been abandoned for almost fifteen years, since about '85. I found it about ten years back, and nobody's come around since, that I know of. Could happen any time, of course."

"So how the hell could you happen to 'stumble across' that song-and-dance routine you did upstairs to open the door?"

"I can't imagine."

She frowned. "Conversation with you certainly has a lot of punctuation. Forget I asked." She looked around again. "Who pays the utilities? Since you don't exist, I mean."

"Nobody."

"What do I look like, an idiot? That's a full-service phone over there, and two powered chairs, and your tape console alone must draw...not to mention that terminal in the bedroom, and lights and climate and—don't tell me. There's an inconspicuous solar collector on top of the abandoned warehouse, no bigger than Washington Square."

I smiled. "I misspoke myself. I should have said 'everybody.' I get my power and phone from the same place you do—I just don't pay for it."

"But they've got hunter programs monitoring for unmetered drain—"

"Programs written and administered by corruptible, fallible human beings. Whoever built this place built it well. I never get a bill."

"I'll be damned." She stared at the phone. "But how can anybody call *you?* You can't have a number, the switching syst—"

"Nobody can call me. It's the perfect phone."

Her grin was sudden. "I'll be go to hell. So it is." She took off her rucksack and checked to make sure she had broken or crushed nothing when she fell. "Where should I stash my stuff?"

"I'll do it. Sit down."

I gestured toward the other Lounger. She put down the sack and went to it, stroked the headrest reverently. "For *years* I've wanted one of these. Never could afford it." She shook her head. "I guess crime pays."

"No, but the perks are terrific. Go on, try it."

She sat, made a small sound as she realized that it did not hurt her sores, then made another as the chair adjusted to her skeletal shape and body temperature. I set it for gentle massage and took her bag to the spare bedroom. When I got back I had her chair mix a Preacher's Downfall for me and a rum-and-rum for her. (I had satisfied myself by then that wireheading had cured her of compulsive overboozing. A marvelous therapeutic tool, save that its side effects included death.)

She did not see me at once; her eyes were rolled back into her head. But after a while her ears told her that ice cubes were clinking nearby, and she came slowly back to the external world. "Joe," she said, smiling happily, "you're a *good* burglar."

It was nice to see her sitting back in a chair, with a smile that I *liked* on her face.

We drank and talked for an hour or so. Then on impulse I put on some Brindle to see if she knew the difference between music you talk over and music you don't. Sure enough, three bars in she shut up and smiled and sat back to listen. When the tape was through she was ready to admire my bathroom, and then I showed her her bedroom. By then she was too tired to admire anything. I started to head for my own room, but she caught my arm.

"Joe . . ." She looked me in the eye. "Would you sleep with me tonight?"

I studied her face until I was sure the question was meant literally. "Sure."

"You're a *good* burglar," she murmured, peeling out of her tunic.

It did feel almighty good to have arms around me in bed. I fell asleep no more than five seconds after we had achieved a comfortable spoon. She beat me by several seconds. From that day on, if we slept at the same time it was together.

I introduced her to the bust of Kennedy, who filed her in his permanents. I showed her the defense systems and emergency exits. I showed her my meditation place down by the river, and how to get there and back safely. She started spending a lot of time alone there, even though she couldn't smoke while filtered and goggled. She did not discuss what she thought about there, and I did not ask. I could search her home, rifle her strongbox, and milk her terminal—but some things are personal. Four days went by this way.

I was sitting in the Lounger having my neck rubbed and planning my next job when I heard the dislock sequence initiate. I glanced up, expecting Karen. But when the door cycled up it was the Fader who came down the stairs, with a tape in his hand.

Fader Takhalous is fiftyish and just as nondescript as a man can be. I have mistaken half a dozen strangers for him, and once failed to recognize him until he spoke to me. He could mug you in broad daylight and rent a room from you the next day. I held much the same relationship to him that Karen held to me, except four years further along. I only saw him two or three times a year, and was surprised to see him now; I hadn't been expecting him for another few months.

But the tape explained it. He nodded hello on his way to the stereo; I nodded back, but he didn't see it. He fed the tape to the heads and turned the treble back to flat. He sat in the other Lounger, leaving it turned off, and stared at the ceiling. I dialed the lights down and shut my own chair off. The music was almost unbearably good, a synthesizer piece that was alternately stark and lush, spare and majestic; that took chances and succeeded. It reminded me of early-period Rubbico & Spangler. The Fader smoked a joint while we listened, and for once I didn't mind the faint buzz that breathing his waste smoke brought; the music made it okay.

And about the time I could tell that the unknown composer was building to the finish, Karen did come home, the music masking the noise of her arrival. I had not thought this through. As she came down the stairs she took in the scene, threw me a hello smile, and headed for the kitchen, carrying groceries.

When she returned she sat on the couch without a word and listened, staring at the ceiling. The Fader raised an approving eyebrow, then returned his own attention to the music.

When it had ended we awarded it ten seconds of silence. Then the Fader rose from his chair. He bowed to Karen. "You listen well, Miss—".

"Karyn Shaw. That was worth listening to."

"They call me the Fader. Which is what I'm about to do. A pleasure to meet you." She offered her hand and he kissed it. Then he turned to me. "Pop me that tape, son. I'll bring it back for duping another time. I just remembered I left the kettle on."

I got the tape and gave it to him. "What's your hurry?"

"A small matter of business." His eyes slid briefly to Karen.

"She's okay, Fader. She's a friend. She's *here*, right?"

He relaxed slightly. "I've got a mark up to Phase Two, and I just now thought of a way I could take him straight to Phase Four in one jump. If it works it cuts down the seed-money investment substantially—but it has to happen *now*. I'll let you know how it turns out."

I grinned. "Ah, the delicious urgency of the creative impulse. Good luck." He smiled and nodded at Karen again, and was gone.

"Nice old duck," she said when the door had closed behind him. "I get the funny feeling maybe I . . . frightened him away somehow. I'm sorry if I did, that music was *nice.*"

"You're the sorriest thing I've seen all day," I said. "What did you buy us for dinner, and why aren't you pouring it?"

"Whups." She left and came back with whiskey and cashews and raisins. "I'm cooking stew."

"The hell you say."

"God damn it, Joe. *I* know I'm no good with a microwave. My folks were too poor to have micro. But you've got that old-fashioned stove that still works in there, and a perfectly good pressure cooker, and that's what I learned at my mother's knee. So shut up and wait till you taste it before you—"

"All right, all right, I'll take a chance."

She found the Fader's joint on the rug, which thank heaven is burnproof, and looked up inquiringly. I nodded, and she toked it back to life. After two or three deep puffs, she set it down on what we still call an "ashtray" even though it's been years since cigarettes or joints produced ashes, probably because "buttrest" seems indelicate. "Hey, Joe. Guess what? I think I figured out what I want to do when I grow up."

I sat up straighter and felt myself smiling. "Tell me about it." It was the best news I'd had in a long while. I hadn't been sure whether her meditation was helping or hurting her.

"You remember that conversation we had back at my place, back on Day One? About joy? As distinguished from pleasure?"

"Sure."

"So there's two kinds: the kind from doing a good thing, and the kind from passing up a real tempting chance to do a bad one. The second kind's easy. It is really tempting to go back to the life, the money's fabulous—and it's giving me great joy not to, because the life is a bad thing."

"You don't rationalize that it's therapeutic for the customers?"

"If acting out aggression drained it, there'd be fistfights *before* football games instead of after. I did my customers no favor, and I charged 'em plenty for it.

"But dumping that is only a kind of negative joy. I've been looking for a *good* thing to *do*. Something really worthwhile, something to benefit the world in a significant way, and commensurate with my talents and background."

"Uh-huh."

"Well, that's the hard part. I've never learned how to do anything really useful except fuck and fix motorcycles, and I can't go back to bikes because I can't stand working on the junk they make nowadays. Besides, the existence of motorcycles in good running order isn't all *that* great a boon to mankind. I figure I can do better than that."

"I'm sure of it," I agreed. "What have you selected?"

"Well, I got to thinking about this socket in my skull. I got to thinking about people who have 'em put there, and why. Self-destruction's too quick an answer. I've been over it in my head a lot, and I can't be certain, but I think if that option hadn't been there—if there hadn't been a friendly neighborhood wireshop all of six blocks away—if wireheading hadn't come along and presented itself, I do *not* think I would have just found some other way to suicide. Other than tobacco and a risky lifestyle, I mean.

"I mean, I don't think dying is what I wanted at all. I don't think hardly any of the people the juice has killed wanted to die, as such, exactly. I think we just . . . just wanted to *have it all,* just for once, just for a little while to have it all and not be hungry anymore. And if dying was the ticket price, well, okay."

I wasn't certain I agreed, but then I'd never asked a wirehead's opinion. Very few people ever get to. I remembered the great lengths she had gone to with the water bottle to prolong her own last ride as far as possible.

"So it seems to me, now, that the existence of that option is an evil thing. An attractive nuisance, like the swimming pools and old refrigerators little kids get into. It makes it so that people past a certain point of instability are unbearably tempted. Maybe I'm rationalizing, trying to shift some blame for what I did from myself."

She finished her drink and lit a Peter Jackson, masking the last fragrances of the Fader's joint. "So what I'd like to do is everything I can to remove that option."

I sat there trying not to frown. "How, exactly?"

"I haven't exactly got detailed plans yet—"

"Phone your congresscritter? Write a letter to *The Village Voice?* Shoot every wire-surgeon in town?"

"The shock docs don't matter one way or another. They'd just as soon be botching abortions and faking draft deferments. It's the corporations that make and market the hardware that are the real villains."

"Anybody can put together a juice rig."

"The wire and transformer, sure—but the droud itself, the microfilaments and the technology to place them properly, that's not workbench stuff. Without the corporations, wireheading just wouldn't happen."

"Do you have any *idea* how many corporations are involved?" I asked sarcastically. I had no firm idea myself.

"Three."

"Nonsense. There have to be at least—"

"Three. The shock doc I picked took it out in trade, and he felt talkative afterward. I didn't think I was listening at the time, but I was. There are over a dozen juice-rig models on the market, but they all get their basic modules from one of three corporations. There used to be five, but two of them went under. And the doc said he had his eyes and ears open, and he had a hunch that two of the three were really different arms of a single outfit that nobody knows."

"How could a juice-head company go broke?"

"How should I know? Sampling the merchandise, maybe. Anyway, all the basic patents are held by a Swiss outfit, so that makes a total of three targets and four avenues of approach."

"Infiltrate and destroy, huh?"

"Something like that. Free-lance industrial espionage."

"I repeat, what's your plan? See how many executives you can poison before they get you?"

"I thought of it," she admitted.

"Pointless and stupid. Honey, you start killing sharks, they just start showing up faster than you can kill them."

"Yeah, but that's not why I gave up the idea. I don't think I've got it in me to kill."

That impressed me. Most of the children of television are convinced that they have in them what it takes to murder in cold blood. The overwhelming majority of them are wrong. Surprisingly few have what it takes to murder in *hot* blood, or even self-defense. "Congratulations."

"But there are other ways. There's no such thing as an honest corporation. A hooker often learns things, without even trying, that the IRS would love to know. Or the Securities and Exchange Commission. Or the Justice Department, or—"

"Or *Newsday,* right. They pay the best, you might as well get a terrific coffin out of the deal. I'm certainly glad to hear that you have no death-wish."

"I'm not especially afraid of death. Not anymore. Someday, no matter what I do, random chance is going to strike me dead. I might as well be doing something worthwhile at the time. It should be a shame that I died."

"It sure will be. Karen, the kind of people you're talking about have all the access they could ever want, and more leverage than you can believe. There is no way you can sell that kind of information and not be traced. Hell, they'll be able to follow the path of the check."

"I won't sell the information, then. I'll give it away."

"Don't be silly. Who'd trust free information?"

"But I could—"

"Damn it to hell, listen to me. I was professionally trained to infiltrate and destroy once, by experts. I've been on the con for a long time now, and I have a unique advantage you don't share. I can't be traced. If my *life* depended on it, *I* wouldn't get within a hundred miles of a scam like this. With a crack team of about a dozen, and an unlimited bankroll, you could maybe put a big bruise on people like that and live to admire it. No way is *any*body going to bring them *down.* Let alone a single commando, let alone a crusading hooker with a hole in her head. Get serious, will you—"

"Shut the fuck up!"

I am not used to being outshouted. I hadn't even known I was shouting.

"Don't talk down to me! I don't care how old you are, don't talk down to me. I'm sick of that shit. I don't have to listen to that. I have been around, chump. I've been in on enough scams to know what I can do. I'm pretty smart and I'm pretty tough, and I don't scare worth a damn. God damn it, I've been hooking for almost a year in this town and *nobody owns me.* I'm a fucking independent, do you know that? Do you know what that means?"

Of course I did—but I had never thought it through, never considered the cleverness and strength it implied. She saw me working it out and grinned. "There's a sucker out on the street now with three new creases on his face. One that I put there, and two from worrying about where I might put the next one. Joe, *I know the way things are.* I know this job is too big for me, and I expect to enjoy it right up to the end, and I don't need any lectures. Oh, *Jesus,* the stew!"

She leaped up and galloped to the kitchen. I sat there with my empty glass, listened to the squeal and hiss and clatter of the silly obsolete pressure cooker, listened to oh-shit noises turn to dubious *mmms* and finally to mollified *nnns* and a last triumphant *ha.*

Once I blew a radiator hose on the highway. A Good Samaritan stopped to help me. He acted very knowledgeable about cars. While I was getting the spare hose out of the trunk, he helpfully topped off my transmission fluid for me. With the brake fluid I kept behind the right headlight. "Oh, it's all the same stuff," he assured me. "They just put in different dyes and charge you more money." It took me three days to get a tranny shop to flush and refill the system, and for those three days the transmission slipped so badly that I nearly went crazy. The engine would roar smoothly in response to the accelerator, while the car crept along in fits and starts as it slipped in and out of gear. It was a helpless, frustrated feeling. I had all the horsepower in the world, and it took me two city blocks to coax her up to thirty.

At the moment that was the inside of my head. High revs, but it wouldn't *go* anywhere. I attributed it to the pot smoke I had breathed. The thought train went like so:

(I'm much too agitated.) (Well, sure I am, my new friend is planning something dangerous and stupid.) (No, there's more to it than that.) (Something else?) (Yes.) (What else?) (. . . my new friend is planning something dangerous and stupid.) (No,

there's more to it than that.) (What else?) (... my new friend
is planning...)

Pull back on the accelerator and try again.

(Why must there be something else?) (Because I'm much
too agitated.) (Why?) (Because my new...)

Same loop. Try again.

(Why do I feel my agitation is "too much"?) (Because if I
were only concerned about my friend, I'd be trying to persuade
her to drop her plans.) (And...?) (And getting agitated is the
wrong way to persuade her.) (Sure?) (Yes; it will only strengthen
her resolve.) (Conclusion?) (I'm not really trying to talk her
out of it.) (What *am* I doing, then?) (Getting very agitated.)
(Why?) (My new friend is planning something...)

Christ.

The aroma of stew struck like a symphony, disrupting the
inner loop. I heard silverware being assembled, bowls being
ladled full. I saw the cigarette she had left burning give one
last puff of smoke and expire. Stop the brain, put it away,
maybe after dinner...

(What *should* I be doing?) (Talking her out of it.) (How?)
(By going along with the gag.) (By—?) (Wait for her own
doubts to emerge, wait for her to falter—and she will—and
then nudge.) (Con my friend?) (That, or stubborn her up and
send her out there alone. There's no third choice.) (I can't do
that.) *(Why not?)* (It's dangerous.) (What do you mean, dangerous?) (It makes me very agitated.) (Why?) (My new friend
is planning to...)

(I'm trying to talk *myself* out of it!)

She brought two bowls into the room, and the symphony
of smells crescendoed. She put them on the coffee table, left,
and reentered with a jug and two glasses. She poured for us.
She left again for garlic-and-butter-toasted French bread, and
then she sat opposite me. I started to dig in.

"Joe? It should cool a little first."

"Right."

"Look... I just did some thinking. I had no call to blow up
at you that way, no right. It's just that you came on kind
of... paternal, and you're about forty." That made me wince.
In my head I'm twenty-eight. "About the same age as *he* was

when . . . I'm sorry I yelled at you."

"I'm sorry I yelled too. I don't know why I did."

We ate the stew. It was superb, and I told her so.

"Joe?"

"Yeah."

"Look, you've done an awful lot for me. You saved my life, you put me—"

"Please."

"—back together again, let me say it, you gave me this place to come to and a warm bed every night, you never ask when I'm gonna get it together and *do* something, you give me all this and I give you bupkiss."

"My ass. I got all your cash and a terrific pair of speakers."

"You're a good man, Joe, and only a selfish bitch would ask you for anything more."

"The way you're about to?"

"The way I'm about to."

I tried to sigh, but a belch spoiled it. "Ask away, honey. Your stew has softened my heart."

"Your terminal has just about all the access there is. I want you to get me readings on all my targets."

The fear was back, a muffled yammering in a distant compartment of my skull.

"Just give me a deep reading of each one. That's all. I'm not asking you to come in on the scam. It's not personal with you, it's not your crusade. But you could save me weeks of legwork—maybe months."

"I'm sorry, Karen. I can't."

"Why not?"

(Why not?) "The kind of information you're talking about is ringed around with alarms, tricky ones. If I trip one, a tracer program could start hunting me back."

"So what? You don't exist, not on tape."

"Exactly. How come you're still an independent? Forget about how tough and smart you are—what's the main reason?"

She frowned. "Well . . . my johns don't talk much. Not even to their best friends."

"Bullseye. How long do you think you'd last in this town if The Man heard about you and decided he could use you? A couple of gentlemen would call on you, and when they were done you'd be terribly, terribly anxious to do any little thing that might please them. Now suppose that you're a big-time corporate shark. The kind whose attention The Man himself tries not to attract. Somebody tries to crack your shields, and when you investigate you discover that the interloper has no legal existence. Could you not find uses for such a person? Important uses? Would it not be worth a *lot* of time and trouble to track him down and enslave him? Honey, I continue to exist as an independent for the same reason you do, or anybody else with something special to offer. The bastards haven't noticed me yet. Should I stick my nose in their window and start sniffing?"

We both listened to the argument as it came out of my mouth. It convinced her, and it should have convinced me. My subconscious had done a good job on it. It was a pretty good argument, with only a couple of holes in it, and it was indeed something to be afraid of. But it wasn't what I feared. I could tell.

But she bought it. She didn't even bother poking at the holes in the logic to see what I had them stuffed with. If a good friend doesn't want to do you a favor, there's no point in arguing.

"I guess you're right. I hadn't thought it through." She sat crestfallen for a moment, then squared her shoulders. "Well, there are other keyboard men in town."

"Sure. Professionals with equipment almost as good as mine. Better connected, better protected. But Karen . . . listen, no matter how you go about this, it's suicide city, I'm telling you. Give it up."

"Two weeks ago I was willing to die just to find out what pleasure was like."

"If all you want is a socially useful kamikaze mission, just stop paying off your draft board. You'll be on the New York police force the next day, and stiff in the South Bronx before the year is out."

"And chase guys like you? And chippies like me? Don't be silly. Look, I've got to piss—you stay here till I get back. Surprise dessert in the kitchen." She leaped up and was gone.

I sat there trying to figure out what I was really afraid of.

It was astonishingly, frustratingly difficult. I knew that the answer was in my possession, that some part of my mind held the knowledge. I could even tell in what "direction" that part lay. But every time I steered that way and gave her the gas, the transmission slipped. It could run away faster than I could pursue. Stubbornly, hopelessly, I stalked it, knowing only that it tasted like nightmares.

Something yanked me out of my brown study; the outside world was demanding my attention. But why? Everything looked okay. I smelled nothing burning, all I heard was the distant sound of Karen urinating . . .

I played back tape, and discovered that I had been hearing that sound for an impossibly long time.

I didn't even bother to run. She had found a small length of hose under the sink, and used adhesive tape to run a siphon from the toilet tank, to simulate the sound of urination. Then she had left, by the second of my two emergency exits. The one I had not told her about. On the face of the lid she had left a lipstick message: "Enjoy the speakers, Joe. I'm glad that fucker landlord didn't get them. Thanks for everything."

I nodded my head. "You're welcome," I said out loud. I went to the kitchen, made a pitcher of five-to-one martinis, frowned, dumped it in the sink, made a pitcher of six-to-one martinis, nodded and smiled, brought it into the living room, and hurled it carefully through the television screen. Then I rummaged in the ashtray for the Fader's roach, and got three good deep tokes out of it before I burned my lip. I had not smoked in many years; it smacked me hard.

"Lady," I said to her empty stew bowl, "if you can con me that well, maybe—just maybe—you've got a snowball's chance."

5 ≡

1994   Norman halted just outside the front door of his apartment building, let it close behind him, and sighed. Fall had always seemed to him a silly time to begin the new school year. Like hibernating bears, scholars sealed themselves away from the world just when it was at its most beautiful. A farmer would have been his most involved with the outdoors now, trying to outguess the frosts and prepare his home for winter. Norman could not even yield to the temptation to kick apart heaps of rainbow leaves in his path, for an assistant professor in public can no more take off his dignity than his trousers.

It was only a block to the campus, but Norman was running late. He sneered at his briefcase, turned right, and began the walk to work. As he passed the underground garage ramp it blatted at him and emitted a Toyota. Norman watched the car as he got out of its way, wondering for the thousandth time why anyone living in this city would want to own a car. Walking was much cheaper, much less trouble—and healthier too.

If you're such a health nut, he asked himself, why have you let yourself get so badly out of shape? In the six years since he had left the army, Norman's only sustained regular exercise had been this daily two blocks' walk to and from the university. He had long since given up even pretending that he was trying to control his tobacco habit, and he knew he weighed more than he should. He could remember what it had felt like in the army, to be in shape, and wondered why he had let such a good feeling go out of his life upon his discharge, without a backward glance. He had known an echo of that easy confidence, that readiness for anything, the night when Maddy arrived and he had thought her a prowler. But the absurd failure of his charge that night proved that it was only an echo, an adrenalin memory, that he no longer deserved that confidence. Norman resolved to begin a rigorous program of calisthenics that very night, and to sign up for swimming privileges at the university pool that very afternoon, whereupon he lit a cigarette.

This whole thought-train had occupied only the space of time necessary to glance at the puffing Toyota and then down into his jacket pocket for his cigarettes. His cupped hands came away from his face, and the one holding the match began to shake it out, and instead held the match upside down long enough to burn him. Lois stood before him on the pavement— tall, slim and beautiful—frosting at the mouth and shivering. She wore no coat. Her hair and makeup were impeccable, and her expression was somewhere between afraid and exhilarated.

"I'm late," he said at once, and then, "Ouch." He disposed of the match, making his hundredth mental note to switch to the new self-lighting cigarettes.

"I know. I nearly froze my face off waiting in my lobby for you to come by." She could not meet his eyes, though not for lack of trying.

"Lois, for God's sake, it's the first *day*. I've got—"

"I planned it this way. First I thought I'd have you over for coffee and spend about three hours leading you around to it, and then I decided that would be dishonest and you'd resent being manipulated, so I thought I'd just say it bang and let you have time to think about it before you say anything. That way you sort of don't just say something, like, spontaneously, and then feel like you have to live up to it or something."

This was a more or less familiar ritual with them. When she had, say, lent five hundred (Old) dollars they couldn't spare to a friend who couldn't possibly be imagined repaying them, she would begin the news like this. And he would think, What is the most horrible thing she could possibly say next? and then he would be relieved when it wasn't that. So he thought now of the most horrible thing she could possibly say next, and she said it.

"I want to come back to you."

He stared at her, waited for a punchline, for the alarm clock to go off, for a freak meteorite to come and drill him through the heart.

"I'm off today at three, I'll be home all night, call me when you're ready."

She was gone.

Since his path was no longer blocked, he resumed walking. At this particular time her proposition—no, damn it, her proposal—was simply and literally unthinkable. He placed it firmly out of his mind and walked on, thinking of pushups versus situps and wondering if the bookstore had gotten his texts in yet. When he had gone about twenty steps he paused, spun on his heels, and roared at absolute maximum volume, *"What about the plumber, then?"*

Across the street a second-floor landing window slid open on Lois's building. "He moved out a week ago," she called back, and closed the window.

A handful of students on either side of the street were motionless, staring at Norman with some apprehension. He glared back, and all but one resumed their own migrations. That one continued to stare, quite expressionlessly, past glasses that doubled the apparent size of his eyes.

"Moved out of his own apartment, by God," Norman muttered to himself. He puffed furiously on his cigarette. There had to be *some* way to make that insolent bookstore manager show a little respect. Norman couldn't complain to Mac-Leod . . . but perhaps he could mention it to someone who *would* tell MacLeod. Yes, that idea had promise...

He walked on.

His first sight of the campus delighted his sense of irony. The original layout designer had placed concrete walkways where he thought they would look nice. Generations of students had taken more convenient paths, destroying grass and creating muddy ruts. Generations of administrators had taken this as a personal affront, and had struck back with strict, unenforceable prohibitions. The current administration had faced reality: all the previous summer they had torn up and reseeded the walkways, poured new ones where the students' ruts were. Now Norman saw at once that the majority of the upper-class students were ignoring the new walkways and following the old paths they had always scorned, through the new grass. In one place a small circular flower plot stood precisely on a no longer-extant path; Norman watched a student walk directly to it, circle its perimeter carefully, and continue on the imaginary walkway.

Having just made himself a public spectacle before students who might well be his own, Norman walked where he was meant to walk. But he resented having to do so.

He picked up memos and schedule revisions at the department office, stored his hat and coat in his office, and went to deal with the bookstore. By a stroke of luck the assistant departmental chairman was present when Norman said in a slightly raised voice, "Another *month?* But these were ordered in March. Of last year." The assistant chairman glanced up, and Norman had the satisfaction of hearing the store manager hastily give an excuse that was not only patently false, but checkably false: a memo from the Chancellor would reach the manager within twenty-four hours, and Norman's students would have their textbooks before the close of the add-drop period. He reached his first class, Introduction to Joyce, in a cocky, go-to-hell state of mind, and when he looked about the room and saw at least a dozen versions of the same mask—eager interest mixed with respectful politeness—something clicked in his head and he made an impulsive decision. Norman had always been rather conservative for an English teacher, had never needed to be given MacLeod's Number Three Lecture on The Irresponsibility of the Maverick, had always respected even the forms and traditions which he personally found silly. Ever since the army he had been willing to pay lip service to any ritual-system that promised stability—or even only familiarity. But all at once he heard himself say to his students the very same words that had nearly ended his father's career twenty-five years before.

"Is there anyone here who does not want an A?"

Total silence.

"I say, is there anyone here who objects to being given an A in this course, for the semester, here and now?"

One hand rose near the back, a skeptical woman sensing some kind of trap. (Norman's father had drawn three of them.)

Norman nodded. "Okay. Come see me in my office sometime, we'll discuss it. The rest of you, you've all got an A in this course. You can go home now."

Pandemonium. Hands shot up all over, and no one moved from their seats. (Twenty-five years before, several students had whooped with glee and left the room by this point.) When the general outcry reached its first lull, Norman spoke up and overrode it.

"I am perfectly serious. Those of you who signed up for this course because you needed another three credits in English may now leave, satisfied. You have what you paid for, and are spared six months of diligent hypocrisy."

"And then when we take you up on it and leave, you fail us, right?" said the woman who had first raised her hand.

Norman frowned. "You have nearly managed to insult me, Ms. . . ."

"Porter."

"Ms. Porter. Let me assure you: I say what I mean, and vice versa. Those who choose to leave have my blessing, and my thanks. I will not even make a list of your names, since everyone except Ms. Porter is getting the same grade. I will not so much as look with private disapproval on those of you who choose to go. I fully understand that the existing system pressures you to matriculate at the expense of learning about anything you're interested in, and acquiring a necessary job credential seems to me as valid a reason as any for attending a university. God help us. If that is your purpose, accept it and be proud of it and do it efficiently. And don't clutter up my classroom. Because you see, I happen to be enormously interested in—and greatly confused by—the writing of James Joyce. Some of the things he wrote stir up my brains and haunt my off-hours, and other things he wrote mystify or bore me to tears. And I propose to spend a couple of hours a week for the next several months in the *exclusive* company of people who are also enormously interested in the writing of James Joyce. I believe this will increase my own knowledge and appreciation of Joyce, and I'm confident that it will increase yours."

A young man who wore the only necktie in the room besides Norman's spoke up in a nasal voice. "Will there be any tests?"

"Well, I should hope there will be at least one or two in every classroom period, but not the way you mean, no."

"Papers?" asked a short rat-faced woman.

"Anytime you feel you have the makings of a paper, cogent or otherwise, write it up and leave it in my office. The very best I will help you to have published, if you're interested. Those and the second best will be photocopied, distributed, and discussed. The bad ones will be discussed privately. They'll all get A's."

The necktied young man supplied Norman with the straight line he'd been hoping for. "But Dr. Kent, if we've all got A's... what's supposed to motivate us to work?"

Happily, Norman again quoted his late father. "Why, bless you, the intrinsic interest of the material itself."

Blank faces stared at him. He waited, and after a few moments a third of the class left the room. Ms. Porter was among them. Most of the remaining two-thirds looked mightily interested.

Be damned, Norman thought, history does repeat itself.

He repeated the procedure at Victorian Poetry, his only other class that day, with similar results.

At nine o'clock that night he stubbed out an expensive marijuana cigarette, set his phone for *record*, shook his head at it, and said, "Not a chance." He played it back, nodded, and punched Lois's number. When his board told him that she had answered, he fed the recording on a loop. His own screen stayed dark, and after a while she hung up. He put Lambert,

Hendricks, and Ross on the stereo, lit another of the cigarettes, and after some while cried himself to sleep.

The next morning history continued to repeat itself. The summons was waiting on his desk, and the reaming was thorough. It did not help at all that MacLeod knew the story about Norman's father. MacLeod had made all the allowances he was going to make for Norman's personal misfortunes; for the rest of the semester, and perhaps the year, Norman was on sudden-death overtime. The next mistake would be his last. He was obliged to contact all the students who had left and advise them that he had been overruled. No part of that was fun.

Thoroughly sobered at last, lusting again for any kind of security, Norman became over the next three or four months a model teacher—that is, a tireless and blindingly efficient robot. He shouldered a tremendous course load including two freshman World Lit courses and a two-night-a-week seminar, and performed brilliantly in all of them. He completed and published an exemplary paper on Dwyer's 1978 "Ariana Olisvos" hoax, which was anthologized nearly at once. He took over the campus literary magazine when old Coxwell died, restructured the staff to tremendous effect, and figured out a way to get the printing done at half cost. He kept his promise to himself: he spent every hour not used for work or sleep in hard exercise at either the gym or the pool. He gave up tobacco and cannabis and cut down on alcohol. Good physical condition came back hard at his age, after nearly seven years of neglect, but he pursued it hard. His students either loved or hated him; none was indifferent. MacLeod allowed himself to become friendly again.

To those around him Norman came to seem almost unnaturally alert and rational. In fact, he was in a kind of trance, the peace of the dervish.

At Christmastime came Minnie and the Bear.

Both sets of parents had guessed wrong. A man christened Chesley Withbert should not be very tall, very broad, immensely strong, and covered all over with curly black hair; it is unfair to those tempted to laugh. His inevitable nickname was first given to him at age eight. Similarly, a woman born Minnie Rodenta should not be five feet high and mouse-faced, but no nickname had been found for her yet that was not worse. To Norman they were beloved friends, not seen in three years and frequently missed. He was greatly cheered by their arrival in that loneliest of all seasons, which of course was why they had come.

Norman and the Bear had served together in Africa; each had saved the other's life once. Norman had been wounded and discharged first, but by the time he was out of the hospital the Bear too was out of the army, and had moved to Nova Scotia. While Norman was sitting in New York, pondering what the hell to do with his life, he got a letter from the Bear, inviting him up to Halifax for a couple of weeks. Halifax is one of the few remaining North American cities from which one can reach raw nature in ten minutes' drive; by the middle of the second week Norman knew that he could never go back to New York. There was a regional shortage of trained English teachers, the only job for which his prewar degree had prepared him; he overcame his lack of experience with a brilliant interview and was hired. Presently the Bear and his new lover, Minnie, introduced him to a girl Minnie worked with at Victoria General Hospital. Named Lois. Both couples spent a great deal of time together, swapped twice experimentally, and gave it up when it seemed to interfere with their friendship. They were married within three months of each other.

Then three years ago Minnie's work had taken her to Toronto. Bear had by then established himself as a copy-hack, and was earning a fair living knocking out tecs, sits and scifis for several software networks; he had no strong objection to moving. Since that time the two couples had communicated largely by birthday phone call, and in the last year even that had been interrupted by the collapse of Norman's and Lois's marriage. The reunion now was explosively enthusiastic on both sides.

"Jesus," the Bear rumbled as he released Norman from one of his classic hugs. "You're in great shape, man."

Norman's grin flickered momentarily. "Some ways, brother, some ways," he said, and then Minnie was taking her hug. Her first words were, "Sorry it took us so long, Norm. It's been crazy out."

"Nonsense. I'd've been too busy to be a proper host if you'd come sooner. God, it's good to see you two. I've been on eleventerhooks ever since you called." He took their suitcases, showed them where to put their coats and boots and where to find the liquor cabinet. As soon as they were all seated in the living room he raised his glass high. "To great friendship," he said, drained the glass, and flung it across the room. It smashed on the baseboard heater.

Minnie and the Bear broke up. They faced each other, said in unison, "We've missed him," and followed his example.

"Missed me again," he said exultantly, and then, "Oh, God, I've been hanging out with ordinary people for so long. Thank you two."

"There are crazies in Hogtown," Minnie said, "but few with your elegance." Norman rose from his chair, bowed, and produced more glasses, threading his way carefully through the scatter of glass on the carpet.

"This is fantastic," he said wonderingly. "You two have been here less than a minute, and it's as though you'd never left. All the time between has just disappeared." He giggled. "How thoughtful of it." Suddenly he looked away.

The Bear lay in magnificent repose in one of Norman's huge beanbag chairs, looking rather like a beached whale covered with colorful tarpaulins and black seaweed. He made a joint appear, tapped it alight, and sucked hugely. "So? Which side brings the other up to date first?" He passed the joint.

Norman hesitated, decided training was shot to hell anyway, and took a toke. "Is yours cheerful?" he croaked, passing the joint to Minnie. With her nose wrinkled up she looked even more mouselike.

The Bear looked thoughtful. "Yeah, on the whole. A couple of real bright spots, and one genuine tall tale."

"Then we'll save it for catharsis, okay?"

The two nodded at once. "Lois?" Minnie asked economically.

"Yes and no," Norman said. "Not really; I think I've got that under control now. It's more Madeleine. And, I suppose, mostly it's me. It's been a hard-luck voyage, mates. I—you didn't get here any too soon."

"Damn straight," the Bear agreed. "I still see double yellow lines and headlights coming at me. So talk."

Norman brought them up to date, beginning with Lois's first request for a separation and including his botched suicide, Maddy's arrival and disappearance, and subsequent events. The Bear interrupted frequently with questions, Minnie more seldom.

"Argyle, Barrington area, huh? Pedestrians around there all night long on a Saturday."

"And a little bit of residential. Enough so that a scream could *not* go unheard."

The Bear nodded. "Two blocks over nobody'd pay any attention. But right there it'd cause phone calls. And you're sure she didn't know anyone in Halifax well enough to get into a car with them at 1:00 A.M.?"

"No one in North America. Except Charlie, who was occupied."

"And alibied by many witnesses," Bear clarified. "So, that leaves two possibilities."

"Psycho cabbie or rogue cop."

"Right. Nowhere except in the crap I write do you take an armed and able-bodied citizen off a public street with no fuss at all. Only a fool would try it. And from what you say, she could take care of herself. You checked out both angles?"

Norman produced a file folder from his desk, took two sheets of paper out, and gave one to each. "This is the poster I put up everywhere a cabbie might conceivably see one. It's got a good recent picture, her description and the circumstances of her disappearance, and my phone number. While I was putting them up I questioned all the dispatchers and half the drivers in town. I pieced together people's memories and accounted for every driver seen in that area during that time, with some computer assistance."

"That leaves a cop." The Bear frowned. "Hard to track."

"Sergeant Amesby at Missing Persons brought up that theory before I could think of a graceful way to phrase it. He's been running his own check with a lot better data, and he comes up empty too."

"Yeah, but is he really looking?"

"I've been living in Amesby's pocket for months. I know him. He looked."

"A cop with no partner can fake his whereabouts."

"Not so Amesby couldn't catch it. Believe me, Bear, he's good."

"Most fortunate. We'll dismiss the notion of a citizen in a cop suit."

"That he sewed himself, right." He passed them the rest of the folder's contents, mostly press clippings and blowup facials of Madeleine taken over a period of fifteen years. "The firm she worked for in Zurich supplied some company videotapes with footage of Maddy in them, and I had stills made."

"You got terrific coverage," Minnie observed.

"Saturation. A woman named Saint Phillip has been very helpful. No woman in the Maritimes has died mysteriously without a paragraph mentioning that police do *not* believe this case is connected with the disappearance of Madeleine Kent, followed by a three-paragraph synopsis. I've been on all three local stations and the CBC twice each. Lots of results, none worth talking about."

The Bear finished off the joint and lay back thoughtfully into the chair. "Well," he said, gazing at the ceiling, "when you have eliminated the impossible, whatever remains, however improbable, et cetera. So a total nut pulls up to the curb, shoots a total stranger in the head with a silenced gat—"

"In the *back* of the head. She went armed, and she was fast."

"Right. Yanks her into his car before anybody comes around the corner, and departs at a moderate speed, takes her out up into the maples. He's local, woods-wise enough to find a spot where no one will walk—which is *much* harder than a city killer could imagine—and he's immensely strong, because he can haul the corpse of a pretty big woman *to* that spot without aid. In the dark. Oh, goat berries, I don't believe it for a second." He grimaced ferociously.

"Wait a minute," Minnie objected. "Why does it have to be woods, just because there's so much of 'em around here? How about that business from your last, darling? The newly poured concrete?"

The Bear nodded. "And the psycho who happens to have unrestricted access. You will recall that I didn't put my own name on that one."

"But I mean what about some urban or suburban disposal site?"

The Bear looked pained. "Darling, this was *summer*."

"Oh. That's right. Well, what about the harbor?"

"Darling, remember how many summer Friday nights we tried to find a spot along the water uncrowded enough to make love? Imagine trying to dump a corpse. You *might* pull it off— but would you bet on it?"

Norman suddenly smiled. "You know, except for Amesby, you two are the first people I've spoken to since Maddy left that don't use euphemisms. I can't tell you how grateful I am."

The Bear grinned back at him. "Damn straight. Not many people are understanding enough not to be understanding. You, for instance, are not one of those offensively oversolicitous hosts, who fusses about making sure one's glass is full and offering one coffee and such."

Norman shook his head sadly. "How can you live with such a snide bastard, Min?" He got up and headed for the coffee-maker.

"I beat him regularly."

"Damn straight," the Bear agreed. "I keep thinking: *this* time I'm gonna fill that straight."

"You fill practically anything, dear." They grinned lewdly at each other.

"I'm about ready to fill a strait*jacket* myself," Norman called from the kitchen. "You two still take cinnamon?"

"Yeah."

He came back with three coffees and cake on a tray. "So what all this comes d—what are you doing?"

The Bear was lighting another joint. "Dr. Withbert's famous bluesectomy procedure. First get nuked with good friends, then . . . haven't we done this before?"

Norman hesitated. It was a Friday night, but . . . "I've been keeping myself on a short leash the last few months. The accumulated stash—"

"Is what we came a thousand miles to drain," Minnie said

firmly. "Listen to the doctor."

"Remember the Ukrainian proverb," the Bear boomed. "'The church is near—but the roads are icy. The tavern is far—but I will walk carefully.' How long has it been since your last confession, my son?"

Norman remembered, and set down the coffee. "Gimme that joint."

"So what this all left me with," he went on a few puffs later, "was the natural logarithm of one."

"I still like the rogue-cop idea," Bear said, gulping coffee. "Who else could be confident of getting away with it?"

"Maybe," Minnie said, "but the trouble with any psycho theory, cop or civilian, is that psychos usually aren't one-shots. They keep on performing until they get caught. But you say there's been nothing with a similar MO—"

"Psychos make their own patterns, my love," the Bear said drily. "Maybe he takes six months to wind up to each one. Maybe he's wealthy and does this in a different city each week for sport."

"I don't buy either one," Minnie persisted.

"So what's left?"

"Well, if it's not a flat-out killcrazy, it's got to be someone she'd lower her guard for. Norm, how would she react if, say, a carful of *women* offered her a lift?"

"She's like me, she loves to walk. It was a beautiful night. She'd spent the last ten years in *Europe*, Minnie. I don't think she'd accept a ride from any stranger."

"Hey," the Bear said, sitting erect with some difficulty. "How about that? Somebody from Switzerland?" He frowned again. "He locates her at 1:00 A.M. on a Friday night without asking memorable questions of anyone she knew here. Bear, you *are* a jackass. Forgive me."

Norman squinted at the Bear. "That last joint get you high?"

His old friend recognized the beginning of a litany that had been written in the jungle years before, grinned, and gave the antiphon. "Nah. You?"

Norman frowned and stuck out his lower lip. "Nah."

The Bear shook his head sadly. "Cheap weed."

"Blackskin man give me bad deal."

"Burned again."

"Yeah, Sarge."

"Only one thing to do."

"Check."

The Bear produced the pack, and they chorused, *"Smoke some more!"*

Minnie had endured all this with patience and, since she had not heard it in three years, some amusement. "Count me out, thanks. I'm not about to try and keep up with you two."

But by the time the third joint was half consumed, the smiles had faded and the topic remained. "I kind of liked the Switzerland angle myself. She was hanging around with some *very* comfortably fixed people, and she dropped a few teasers about an unhappy affair. But Amesby's got some friends at Interpol that he respects, and anybody Amesby respects I respect, and they come up empty. As near as we can learn, no one she dealt with in business had any motive to have her kidnapped or hit. It wasn't that kind of business. Electrical supply, micro-electronics widgetry and software, related items. They have an excellent reputation, as a stodgily honest old firm, just big enough to be unambitious. Harbin-Schellmann is the name, I think. They were sorry to see her go, but not that kind of sorry. Anyway, as you say, a Swiss hit squad passing through town would be bound to leave spoor. So that's out too." He took the last toke, held it awhile with his eyes closed. "So I consulted a couple of psychics."

The Bear opened his mouth and then closed it firmly. Minnie only nodded. "What'd you get?" she asked.

"The first one was recommended by the RCMP, they'd worked with him several times with pretty good results. He was about sixty and looked like a grocery store clerk, dressed like one, everything. He was very irritable, very disinclined to try and like you. That made me suspect he might be into something."

Minnie nodded. "Nurses have to learn that one. Patients are clients, problems you try hard to solve. You become their friend only if they've *got* to have one, and then you get chewed up some."

"I saw it happen with Lois. I think she got a shade *too* good at disassociating."

"We'll carve that one next," Minnie said firmly. "Let's close up this one first. What did the psychic say?"

"How much did he ask?" the Bear wanted to know.

"He got every known salient fact out of me—he said straight out that as far as he was concerned his only talent was for having very reliable hunches, which required *all* available data at a minimum. He got things out of me about Maddy that I hadn't known I remembered. Then he . . . well, it sounds anti-climactic, but he just seemed to sit there and think about it awhile."

"While you were watching?" Bear asked.

"I saw him forget me. Except as part of the puzzle, I mean. After about ten extremely boring minutes he told me that Maddy was in a house, a private home, on the order of a hundred and fifty klicks from here. Direction uncertain. Two men were with her. He said he didn't feel any hostility or violence or aggression in them, but their relationship to Maddy was not clear. He said she came through as so passive that she might have been drugged or simply ill. She had not been physically harmed or mistreated, and she wasn't being interrogated. He said there was a large body of water right out in front of the house, but he couldn't tell whether it was the Bay of Fundy or the Atlantic or what. One other house in sight nearby, uninhabited. He told me that it was a very beautiful spot, woods all around the house and a brook nearby that was unsafe to drink. He said he had not felt any fear from Madeleine. He apologized for the fact that all this information was perfectly useless, and he charged me fifteen dollars for an hour of his time."

"Do you think he was into something?" the Bear asked, leaning forward intently.

Norman shook his head. "I don't know. I don't know, Bear. I was straining not to be skeptical, and I found I didn't have to strain so hard. I'll stipulate that he's sincere. But I just don't know. The damned evidence always turns out to be unobtainable, doesn't it? But I keep getting this funny feeling. Like the story makes so little sense that it makes sense." He giggled. "Does that make sense?"

"It butters no parsnips," the Bear said, sitting back. "What'd the second one say?"

"The second one was recommended by some friends of

Lois's, which made it harder to be open-minded. But I was desperate. He religioned it up a good deal more. He said 'cosmic' and 'universal' a bit too often to suit me, but—"

"So did Gandhi," Minnie interjected.

"Right. He shaved his head and wore fake Tibetan clothes from Eaton's and one gold earring and he had no last name, but I have no really valid reason to sneer at any of those things either. And even if I did, nothing says a jerk can't be psychic." Norman rubbed the bridge of his nose. "He was strange. Kind of . . . well, I started to say 'wild-eyed,' but that's not accurate. He looked . . . subtly *wrong* somehow, off-register in some indefinable way. You had the feeling that at any moment you would put your finger on it. It kept you just a little bit off balance, but he didn't seem to realize that or exploit it in any way.

"Anyway. His rap . . ." Norman consulted some notes from the folder. "He said she was in a motel, no idea where or how far away but definitely not in Halifax Metro. Two men were with her, and she loved them both very much. He thought they might be her brothers until I told him she had none but me. Anyway, she was not being held against her will, she very much wanted to be there and was having a wonderful time. She had not been in the motel for very long, she had been brought there recently from the country."

The Bear's eyes flashed and he shifted his weight in the beanbag chair.

"Right. Let's see, right at that point he reversed himself a little on location, said the motel was definitely somewhere in the Annapolis Valley. I asked him how he knew and he said he 'recognized the spiritual flavor of the region.' He said she had just come from somewhere up over the mountain, very close to the Bay. He repeated that she loved and trusted the two men very much."

"Did he mention if they were Swiss?"

"He said he couldn't feel them at all directly, only Maddy's perceptions of them. I told him a little about her background and asked if he could get their nationality, but all he could say was that she thought about them in English. *All* the rest of this, by the way, he gave me with no information whatsoever, using only a picture of her and a rosary of hers he had me fetch along."

"All he had to do was read a paper or watch the news," the Bear noted.

"I know, I know. He said he hadn't, but who knows? But honestly, it was hard to picture him reading the crime news. Anyway, he—"

"What's this about a rosary?" Minnie interrupted.

"He'd asked me over the phone if I had access to any small 'religious objects' belonging to the missing person. She had a rosary our mother gave her when she was a little girl, I'd run across it in her things. He said that would be fine, bring it along."

"Point for him," she muttered. "Go on."

Norman consulted his notes. "That's about it. Oh, wait, he said one man seemed to be the dominant one, smarter or stronger than the other. The other deferred to him. That was all he got, and for his fee he made me donate two hundred New dollars to the UN Disaster Fund. He wouldn't take a cent himself."

"A motel in the valley..." Minnie said thoughtfully.

"A week later," Norman continued, "the first man called me back. He said he'd seen the same house again, in a dream this time. He said it was empty now, but it was a very clear night and so now he could make out New Brunswick on the horizon, pick out the lights of a large city against the sky."

"Fundy shore," the Bear breathed. "Up over the mountain from the Annapolis Valley. It fits." He interlocked his big fingers and played tug-of-war with himself; his triceps bulged, then relaxed. "No help. Blue sky pieces."

"Eh?"

"You know him and puzzles," Minnie said. "The two stories don't contradict; they interlock pretty good, like jigsaw pieces. But they're blue sky pieces: no useful informational content."

"Except in context," the Bear agreed. "Which we don't have yet. I assume your Lieutenant Amesby checked with Valley RCMP?"

"Sergeant. Of course he did—I tell you, the man is good at what he does. Good enough that I can't understand what he's doing in the Halifax Police Department. In addition to that, I had copies of the poster put in every bank, credit union, post office, and Liquor Commission outlet from Digby to Wolf-ville. Result: the cube root of fuck-all."

"Plus the number of sentient beings in Parliament," the Bear agreed. He placed his knuckles together; this time it was his biceps that swelled alarmingly. "Well, my son, this is some hard bananas you bring me, but fortunately you've come to the right man. A trivial problem, really, although I can see that some of its subtler aspects might well have eluded a mere trained professional such as Amesby—or a workaday genius like yourself, Norman—for several months. 'Watson, you know my methods?'"

Minnie nodded. "Certainly, Holmes." She turned to Norman. "He comes up with the cube root of fuck-all."

The Bear beamed. "Excellent, Watson. A very concise summary."

Norman felt all his breath leave him with a rush. "Bear, you don't know how much I hoped you'd come up with a decent hunch," he said bleakly. "I've gone over it and over it until my head spins, I wake up in the morning trying to *make* it make sense, and nothing. You two have got maverick and supple brains, and I was hoping you'd see something Amesby and I missed. Damn it, there *is* no probable answer. Least improbable would I guess be some variant of the random-psycho theory—and at this point I'm afraid I'd be grateful if I could just believe it and get started with the mourning. But it's so bloody *unlikely*." A brandy decanter stood nearby; he uncapped it and drank, passed the bottle.

The Bear looked greatly distressed now. "*Compadre,* I'm sorry to say I don't even have suggestions, and the day I can't give bad advice . . ." He smote both thighs with his fists, hard enough to make the beanbag chair start violently.

"I've got suggestions," Minnie said.

Both men looked at her.

"Two of them. First, can we all stop lying to each other?"

Norman and the Bear flinched guiltily.

"All three of us know better. When there is no logic, you go on feelings, and I think we all have the same hunch, am I right?"

The two men exchanged glances. "All right," they said together.

"Allow me," Norman said to his friend. "Okay, the only reasonable hunch is Switzerland. Someone from there, call him . . . well, for the sake of argument let's call him Jacques. Maddy mentioned that name once. If the psychics are even close to accurate, it *has* to be Jacques. Nobody else could have the resources. Even if the psychics are both frauds, it has more logic than the lone-psycho theory. Okay so far?" His friends nodded. "So the logical next step—"

"—is to go to Switzerland and nose around," Minnie finished. "And you're hesitating."

"I'm right on the fence," Norman agreed. "Have been for a couple of weeks. I was hoping you two would help me decide one way or the other—"

"—and instead, he who defecates in arboreal regions here tried to play dumb. And you let him," Minnie said. "And now he and I are being as neutral as we can manage. All right, you're doing great, keep going: Why are we being neutral?"

"Because I've got a job and responsibilities, and if you agree with me that Switzerland is the key, I'd dump the job in a minute and blow my career on a hunch. And you're friends, so you don't want—"

"Think again," the Bear said grimly.

Norman looked puzzled.

"Brother," the Bear went on, "if that's the only reason you can think of, I just got you down off that fence. On this side."

"I don't follow."

"Exactly. Look, postulate Jacques. For reasons unknown he reaches across an ocean, locates a particular person without the slightest difficulty, leaving no trail, and puts on her a snatch so perfect that a pro like Amesby doesn't smell him. Jacques tap-dances around everybody from Interpol on down and vanishes without a trace. Now tell me, and this will sting a little but hang on, it's the killer: *What has a guy like that got to fear from an English teacher?*"

Norman opened his mouth, closed it, and seemed to deflate. He looked down. "I can take care of myself."

"Norman, look at me. Listen to me. We were in cocky

khaki together, and I'll certify that you were sudden death with both hands, okay? Just looking at you I can see that you're in real good shape, maybe *almost* as good as you were when you were a kid, even. Norman, our whole platoon couldn't have made Jacques uneasy. Not with full combat ordnance and the air support we never used to get. The *best* you can accomplish is quick suicide."

Norman's face was in his hands. "But Bear," he said hoarsely, *"she could still be alive."*

"Certainly. That's why suicide is the best you could accomplish. Look, if he's got her, best guess is she's involved in something he wants kept secret with a capital S. If she's still alive, it's because he doesn't absolutely need her to be dead. But if *you* come poking around..."

"But maybe I could—"

"FORGET IT, NORMAN!" the Bear thundered, and furniture danced.

"Your subconscious made the right decision," Minnie went on in what seemed a murmur by comparison, "even if it didn't keep you informed. There is nothing you can do that will help. We could all be wrong—it might be a nut that got your sister—and if so there's no point in blowing your job. If we're right you might endanger Maddy. If you ever get *proof* that she's dead, and that a Swiss did it, *then* maybe I'd say it's time to go lose your life in something too big for you. But not now—you don't dare."

Norman was silent.

The Bear shifted his weight uneasily. "My dear, a while back you said you had two suggestions. I've only heard one."

Minnie's face lost all expression. "There's only one thing you can do, Norman."

"Go on," he said.

"Kill her."

Norman jumped.

Her voice was mercilessly hard. "Sit back in a comfortable chair. Get thoroughly stoned. Pick a psycho killer from Central Casting and replay Madeleine's murder in your mind. In complete and vivid detail, 3-D stereo, a couple of instant replays. Feel the pain and the fear and the *unfairness* of it. Pick a

possible method of corpse disposal and walk him through it—
say, he walks her out onto the MacDonald Bridge to where he
has wire and weights waiting. Picture her drifting in the currents
under the harbor, bloating and being chewed, and when the
horror is more than you can bear, cut it off. Sharp. Get drunk.
Have her declared dead, and have a symbolic funeral. Picture
her *in* that empty coffin, throw flowers on it, and begin formal
mourning. Say goodbye to her in your heart, Norman, and get
on with your own life. Pray that they catch the poor crazy
before he does it again, but *say goodbye to Maddy*.

"Otherwise you'll—" She caught herself. "You could crack."

Norman sat perfectly still, features expressionless. But his
skin was pale and his palms were sweaty. There was a moment
of silence.

"God, this is depressing," the Bear boomed finally. "What
a party. Let's talk about something cheerful for a change.
How'd your marriage come apart?"

Norman broke up, and his friends joined him. The laugh
went on for some time, faltered, steadied, became one of the
great laughs, one of those where every time it starts to pause
for breath, someone gasps out another punchline and it's off
again. A great laugh with the Bear participating took on epic
proportions.

Whereafter in due course Norman documented the decline
and fall of his marriage, Minnie described life in the Neuro
Ward of a big-city hospital, and the Bear narrated an intricate
and hilarious story of revenge on a critic, which had generated
income as a side effect. Having compared the water lately gone
under their respective bridges, they let their conversation become more general, and by the time the brandy was annihilated
and they had switched to Irish coffee they had remembered
and retold all the jokes, puns, and anecdotes they had been
saving for each other, and were waxing philosophical. The
Bear propounded his Leech Theory of Economic Dislocation;
arguing that no organism can survive without some control of
the size of its parasites, he called for the establishment of a
legal Maximum Wage. Then Minnie tried to explain in lay-
man's terms why the researchers attempting to crack the information-storage code of the human brain, who had been so

confident fifteen years before, were now frankly stymied.

That triggered Norman to bring up the newest and most alarming campus problem: a few students were having a plug surgically inserted in the skull, which allowed direct stimulus of the hypothalamus. Wireheading baffled Norman to the soles of his feet, and he said so. Minnie spoke at length about medical and psychological aspects of the new phenomenon, and the Bear described it as the natural bastard child of the two cultural imperatives *be happy* and *be efficient,* with a postscript on why wireheading would *not* be made illegal as lysergic acid had been thirty years before. That led them into recounting old drug experiences, which they gradually came to realize everyone present had already heard anyway, and by then the coffeepot was empty and the hour was late. Norman showed them the guest room, bathroom, and location of breakfast makings, hugs were again exchanged, and all three went to bed.

Norman hovered on the edge of sleep for what seemed a long time before he heard his door click open. He rolled over slowly, and found his arms full of Minnie.

"Where's Bear?" he asked sleepily.

"Too tired," she whispered. "Heavy driving plus heavy drinking zonks him out. Just as well, this bed's too small anyway."

"Heavy drinking zonks me out too."

Her lips touched him delicately at a place where neck joined shoulders, and simultaneously two of her fingernails found a certain precise spot with a facility that, all things considered, implied either terrific tactile memory or a high compliment. She pulled back and examined the results. "Wrong."

"Uh, I take a long time when I'm drunk."

"No, love. You *give* a long time when you're drunk. I remember. Now stop being so fucking polite and shut up."

"Make me," he punned, and she did.

6 ≡

1999 I sat there for an indeterminate time after Karen had left, paralyzed by internal confusion: the slipping-transmission phenomenon mentioned earlier, except that now there were *several* thought loops cycling simultaneously. Intuitively I felt that something urgent needed doing, but I could not for the life of me imagine what it might be.

No matter how many times I ran it through, I got the same answer: I had discharged all my moral obligations to Karen Scholz. She and I were square, all debts paid. I had meddled in her suicide, an immoral act. In reparation I had done all I could to ease her transition back into living. I had made her a present of my most essential secrets, given her the power to tamper with my own obituary date if she so chose. I had supported and maintained her at the absolute peak of creature comfort while she took stock and decided what to do next. When what she came up with was a more elaborate form of suicide, I had done my best to talk her out of it. Perhaps I had been small in refusing to get her the computer readings she wanted, but the procedure really was uniquely dangerous for me, and any of a dozen other professionals in New York could oblige her with less risk.

She would have her crusade, and perhaps she would manage to die with joy, and perhaps it *would* be better than dying with pleasure.

In any case, it was her choice and my responsibility was ended. It saddened me that she intended to kamikaze, but I had no rights in the matter. She had made it plain that she did not want my advice or assistance. Case closed. Exit Karen, urinating.

Exit Karen.

Yes, that was the way of it; she would surely fall. As a fighter she was all heart and no style at all; they would crush her like a bug. More likely sooner than later. Doña Quixote on a spavined horse, armored in rust, fielding a balsa lance against a twenty-megawatt, high-torque Wind Energy Module, in defense of righteousness. In defense of the right of people not to be tempted to their deaths. She wanted to slay the Sirens, she who had heard their Song and lived.

She was welcome to try. If she saw herself as Doña Quixote, that was her business. I saw no percentage in playing Pancho Sanza. I am not capable of that kind of love. I think I was once, but something happened to me in a jungle. Enough brushes with death will permanently inhibit your urge to place your life on the line for *any* cause. When that final day came, when I heard the click-snap-*spung!* and saw the mine pop up to head height and ducked to try and take it on the helmet, I had a very clear idea of the sacrifice I had made for my country. When, much later, I discovered that I had survived the event, and the war, it left a lasting impression. As Monsieur Rick said, I stick my neck out for nobody. (And I *never* burgle veterans.)

Furthermore, I was not at all certain that I approved of her crusade. If I had been wrong to meddle in her suicide, what right had she to tamper with the suicides of the hundreds, perhaps thousands, who would plug themselves in over the next few years? People *wanted* juice rigs. It seemed to me a self-correcting problem: in a few generations all the people who could be tempted by pushbutton ecstasy would be bred out of the race.

People like Karen...

Who, let's face it, was a loser. The term *loser* does not necessarily denote incompetence, stupidity, or major personality defect. It says that you lose a lot. She had been, through no fault of hers that I could discern, consistently unlucky all her life long. That can break even the toughest fighting spirit.

Perhaps wireheading bred the race not just for competence and survival drive...but for luck?

If so, was I *that* strict a Malthusian? Misfortune was no stranger to me, and might remember me at any moment. Out there in the jungle I had smoked opium admixed with heroin, though I had known it was insane. What would I have done if someone had offered me a juice rig then? What would any of us in my unit have done?

This was stupid. Stipulating that the existence of the wire-head trade was undesirable, Karen's silly secret-agent stunt was the wrong way to go about abolishing it. Lone operators do not bring down big multinationals. At best she would bring about a restructuring of personnel, a redivision of the pie. I did not see *any* effective way to put the egg back into the shell. Certainly, prohibiting wireheading could accomplish nothing useful, and I couldn't design an effective way to regulate it.

Regardless of whether or not I could see any right answer, I knew Karen's way was a wrong answer. So I certainly did not want to chase after her to join her. There was no point in chasing after her to try and dissuade her; I'd had one fair try at that and failed. And there was no way in hell I was going to chase after her and forcibly restrain her. I had, in short, no visible motive to chase after her.

And I wanted to get up from my chair and track her. It scared me to death.

If we had even once made love, or even fucked, I could have attributed it to my glands. I had never so much as had an erection over her.

What in *Hell's* name was wrong with me?

After a time I got tired of running it through, and decided to snap out of it. Find something useful to do.

It was not hard. As soon as I let my eyes see what they were looking at, my search was ended. My television was a total loss. Its gaping glassfanged face had long since ceased to drool good gin on the carpet beneath. The air conditioning had left only a memory of a very bad smell.

I got up and dried the carpet, cleaned up the glass, and disconnected the tube from the system, not bothering to reset all the tripped circuit breakers. The way I had it wired, not only had I lost phone, commercial and cable TV programming, computer display and storyscreen, but I would not have stereo until I could scare up some more patchcords. The most efficient system design is not necessarily the best. All I had left was books and booze.

So the first thing to do . . . no, the first was to dispose of the dead telly. That took me fifteen minutes. The *second* was to steal another.

It was a good plan. It steadied my mind, for while I am working I do not chew over my problems. I give it my full attention, by long habit.

First I had my computer ask the power company computer for a list of customers whose power-consumption profile had been identical for more than five consecutive days, just as usual save that I had to work with printouts instead of display. When the list was filed down to a twenty-block radius from my home turf, it contained eighteen possibles. I had the computer dial all eighteen phone numbers and strike from the list those that had a record-a-message program active. Those absentee tenants probably planned to be home soon. The no-answers numbered seven. I asked the NYPD computer for information on defensive structures of those seven buildings, and selected the one that was hardest to crack. That tenant would have the most expensive TV. Standard procedure would then have been to tell that building's security cameras to recognize me as a bona fide tenant, and take it from there. But this particular building also employed live guards in the lobby. Still no problem: the pigeon had recorded a message-program in his own voice, it just wasn't in service. I hooked in the voder and had my computer use his phone and a fair imitation of his voice to call downstairs. It told the door guard to expect a TV repairman from TH Electronics. The guard welcomed it home, and it thanked him. It hung up and printed out a work order for me.

My computer has so many interesting capabilities that to use it for something as trivial as grand larceny is almost a crime. But to exploit anything like its full potential I would have to compromise an even greater asset: invisibility. I am the man no one is looking for, and I like that a lot.

I am deeply curious to know more about the extraordinary person who had that machine built and programmed. Almost I yearn to meet him or her. My recurring fear is that I shall: intuitively I know I would not survive the encounter.

But surely he or she must be long dead. That's what I tell myself when I wake up sweaty.

I wiped all records of my transactions at both ends, stood up, and got disguise number four from the closet. Faded green coveralls, a GI jungle cap, grimy work boots laced with speaker cable, a tool belt that would have made Batman laugh out loud, and a stained shoulder satchel bulging with assorted electronic testing gear. I checked the picture ID in the wallet that went with the outfit, and corrected my facial appearance to match. It is a part of my job I really enjoy: trying on new faces. None of them, even the one I start and end with, ever looks familiar. I can't imagine what would.

I spilled coffee on the work order, blotted it with a dirty cloth, wadded it up and stuffed it in my breast pocket, and left. I was back within two hours with the tube and a couple of interesting audiocassettes from the van I'd clouted. I wired the new glass teat into the system, ran a few tests, and made a few adjustments. I punched for news display and sat down in front of it. I had the chair make me a bourbon and distilled water. After two sips I killed the news readout and concentrated on the drink. I had nearly finished it before I allowed myself to ask me:

What is the *next* thing to do?

(Follow Karen, of course. Do what you said earlier: play along and wait for her own momentum to falter, then give her something to distract her attention. Once she gets the readings she wants from someone else, the immediate danger to you is past.)

Yeah, but getting those readings from *anybody* could make *her* hot. I could catch something meant for her.

(Yeah, you're really hooked on a safe, sedentary lifestyle. I can see that.)

All right, I find a moderate amount of risk stimulating . . .

(And you won't do something stimulating to save a friend's neck?)

But how do I know she'd let me—

(She's used to you meddling in her life. For some reason she doesn't mind.)

Yeah. Father figure.

(Okay, jerk. You adopted her. Be a responsible father. You're *in loco parentis,* just like—)

Hiatus.

I was sitting at the terminal keyboard, fingers at rest on my lap. I didn't recall resolving the internal debate, but evidently my subconscious thought it was settled. I even had some idea what I intended to program. Instead I swore, spun the chair around, hugged myself, and folded over until I hit the floor. My mouth was wide open, my teeth clenched tight, my forehead knotted, and I snarled softly in the back of my throat. When I could, I pounded the rug with my fist and wept.

I *hate* them. Those sudden gaps in my life, those sudden jump-cuts like slipshod editing, like little bits of tape snipped out of my recording. It must be much like this to have epilepsy, except that I never seem to convulse, or hurt myself while I'm blacked out. Some sort of automatic pilot cuts in; other people rarely even notice. But I resent those missing bits of tape. One of them is six years long.

It all comes of being careless in jungles, I guess.

I was pretty used to it by now. I rarely threw that kind of frustration tantrum anymore, *never* when I was not alone. But I was about to involve myself in something that I could sense was much more dangerous than my average heist, and it was maddening to be reminded that I did not have guaranteed access to my own brains.

But eventually I had cursed and cried out all the fury and

frustration. I got up off the rug and sat back down at the terminal. I had wasted enough time.

Karen's credit account showed no activity, either savings or charge, since she had left her apartment to move in with me. She had left my place with enough cash to rent a flop, but she had not yet paid a deposit to a keyboard man. I set up a monitor on her credit, so that when she did pay I would know who she hired. I knew, or knew of, perhaps half the boys in town, and I could locate the rest and pick up her trail. If she paid in advance, as she almost certainly would have to, there was an excellent chance I could "tap the line" and listen in on whatever her operator found out. That would be less dangerous than initiating the probe myself—although more dangerous than simply trying to trail her physically from the site. If her operator *did* trip a guard program, it might be sophisticated enough to notice me "listening on the extension." I wondered if it was worth the risk. If I knew what she knew, I could figure the first place she'd go and get there first, be waiting for her. It would be a good argument for taking me on as a partner.

I realized something and cursed. Karen didn't have to touch her credit. If no friend was willing to lend her a couple hundred, she would surely know how to locate at least a few of her regular customers. They would be happy to make any requested donation, and they would *prefer* to use cash. I wasn't thinking clearly.

Damn it, that left me flat. There was nothing she had to do that had to appear on tape somewhere in the network. She could get her sightings, pick a target, and skip town without leaving a trace in the system. She couldn't get through a dragnet, but I am not a dragnet. I could not find Karen if she did not wish to be found, not quickly anyway.

Perhaps I would after all have to run the inquiry program she had asked me for.

That decision could be postponed. "If she did not wish to be found . . ." That was the key. I suddenly recalled the wording of the goodbye message she had scrawled on my toilet seat; she had *not* written, "Don't bother to try and come after me." Could I assume that she was trying to prevent me from trailing her?

I decided to see how the hand played out. I left my watchdog program monitoring her credit account, wired to light and sound alarms. Any withdrawal or deposit would bring me out of a sound sleep. If she wanted to be found, or didn't care one way or the other, she'd trip that alarm. If she was actively trying to shake me off, if she hadn't touched her credit or reentered her apartment within, say, twenty-four hours . . . well, then I could sit down and decide whether I wanted to catch up with her badly enough to stick my neck out. I told her apartment terminal to notify me if it was used.

I nodded and got up from my terminal, rotating my head to pop my neck. What's the *next* thing to do?

It was a tight contest between go *to sleep* and *get piefaced drunk*. I didn't feel remotely sleepy, and I didn't want to answer that alarm drunk or hung over. But finally I was forced to admit that I was so wound up I would probably be more effective hung over. And I might not have to answer any alarm . . .

Nor did I. The hangover was somewhere between average and classic. I could find no music that would soothe it. Finally I gave up and took aspirin. It muted the headache and increased the queasiness. I let the Lounger rub my neck for almost an hour, and as my strength came trickling back I used it to get agitated again. After a while I became aware that I had for the past ten minutes been composing variations on the expression "hair of the dog." Puppy fuzz. Cur fur. Pug rug. *Toupé du chien*. I said a powerful word out loud and went out for a walk. I knew I would not drink among strangers—and I wanted to go see some people, in the same way that other people infrequently feel like going to the zoo.

And on the streets I found signs and wonders, things strange and different. I saw a man with one leg walking a dog with three. I saw two women dancing together on the roof of a station wagon; oddly, neither one seemed to be enjoying it. I passed three young toughs in leather and mylar, cheeks tattooed and noses pierced, the oldest of them perhaps fourteen. (This is the first generation of "juvenile delinquents" whose resignation from society is irrevocable. They cannot change their minds when they get older. It will be interesting to see how that works out.) I saw a pimp feeding cocaine to his golden retriever. On a sloping street I saw a short squat ancient woman in a black print dress and babushka stop on the opposite sidewalk, sigh, squat a little more, and begin urinating copiously. A vast puddle gathered at her feet and rushed down the hill. I stood frozen, as though at some personal religious revelation, vouchsafed to me alone. It was not that everyone else on that street ignored the woman. They literally did not see her. People sidestepped the rushing river without noticing it. The hair stood up on the back of my neck and my head throbbed. The old woman urinated for a full minute; then the flood ceased, she straightened, sighed again, and resumed walking uphill, leaving damp footprints of orthopedic shoes. A few minutes later I shook off my trance and resumed my own walk.

I passed a sidewalk cockfight; noticed that they were betting Old dollars. I passed an alley in which a young whore was on her knees before a cop, paying her weekly insurance premium. He was looking at his watch. I passed six pawnshops in a row, then a political party's precinct headquarters, then four pornshops in a row. I rounded a corner and nearly tripped over a wirehead sitting on the sidewalk in front of a hole-in-the-wall hardware store.

He was new to it: the air had not yet grown in around his droud, and he had obviously just learned the one about wiring in a third battery to produce a threshold overdose. He grinned at me and I saw Karen in his face. I hurried past; almost immediately my stomach knotted and I had to sit down on a stoop with my face in my hands. Out of the corner of my eye I saw the hardware shop proprietor stick his head out of his shop, look around furtively. He bent over the wirehead and extracted his wallet. The boy blinked up at him, grinning, then suddenly understood and roared with laughter. "Right, man," he said, "square deal," and he laughed and laughed.

I found myself walking toward the proprietor with no idea why. He flinched when he saw me, flinched again when he saw my face, then became aggressive. "This man owes me money—you just heard him say so. Mind your own—" He shifted gears, held out the wallet, and said "please," and then I jacked one up under his ribs, his gut should feel like mine.

As he went down and backwards the wallet flew into my hands. I took all the money that was in it and tore it into tiny shreds, tossed the shreds down a sewer. The wirehead laughed and laughed. I threw the wallet in his face and walked away. Behind me I could hear him, ripping up all his identification and photos and giggling.

I bought a Coke at a dog-stand. It tasted like burned sugar. I used it to wash down four drugstore aspirins and decided to go home and check my alarms. Automatically I took a different route toward home, and so passed something genuinely unique:

A wirehead shop with a large sign taped in its window saying "FREE SAMPLES."

I stopped in my tracks and stared at that sign.

Free samples? How in God's name could you give free samples of radical neurosurgery? *And what if it were true?*

I entered the shop.

The shock doc was old and thin and red-nosed. His clothes were baggy everywhere they weren't shiny. His hands shook at rest. They were almost the only sign of life; his face and eyes looked newly dead. A potential customer was gibbering and gesticulating at him like a speed freak, babbling something about installment plans, and he was not reacting in any way at all, not laughing or anything. Eventually the customer realized he was wasting his time and went for his gun. It was a sure sign that he was stone crazy—was he going to hold a gun on the doc through surgery?—and I started to backflip out the door. But the doc stood his ground; one of those shaking hands shot up and slapped the man, *crack, crack,* forehand and backhand. They stared at each other over the gun. The excited man was no longer excited, he was quite calm. He put his piece away, spun, and brushed past me on his way out. His expression made me think of Moses traveling away from the Promised Land. When I turned back to the doc he was giving me precisely the same dead stare he had given my predecessor.

Now I noticed that his other hand was in his pocket. It was not alone in there. He looked me over very carefully before he took it out, empty.

I was doing my best to look like a man at the very end of

his rope; con man's chameleon reflex. The room helped. Surely to God his operating theater was bright and well lit, but this office-anteroom was dingy and dark and depressing as hell. Unnaturally depressing; I suspected subsonics at high gain. The predominant color was black, and it's not true that a black wall can't look dirty. Even the storefront window was blacked over; the only illumination came from a forty-watt bulb on the ceiling. There was no decor. Behind the doc an L-shaped affair that might have been either a counter or a desk grew out of the wall, a chair on either side. One had to pass the thing to get to the door that must lead to the operating theater. On the opposite side of the doorway from the desk was a tall steel cabinet with a good lock. A black box sat on top of the desk, and connected to it by telephone cord was what looked like an oversized black army helmet.

I shuffled my feet. "I, uh . . . good, uh . . ."

"You saw the new sign and you want to ask me some questions," he said. His voice was flat, sepulchral. "That sign is going to make me rich."

I have known cripples and cops and killers, people who *must* learn how to get numb and stay that way, and I have never met anyone remotely so inhuman as that man. It was impossible to picture him as a child.

"I, uh, always understood there was no way to . . ."

"Until this year that was correct," he agreed. "It still can't be done anywhere but here. Yet. The device that makes it possible is my own invention." He displayed no visible sign of pride. Or, for that matter, shame.

"How does it, uh . . . ?"

"It is based on inductance principles. I do not intend to discuss it further. My patent application went in this week; that sign has only been up for an hour."

"Well, but I mean, how would I . . ." I trailed off.

He stared at me for a long time, hands shaking. "Step over there against that wall. Behind the sonoscope."

Hesitantly, heavily, I obeyed. The sonoscope looked just like the one in every emergency room, rather like an old fluoroscope, except that the face of the display had a fine-mesh grid inscribed on it. I stood in the proper spot while he candled my head with ultrasonics. He grunted at his first look. "Trauma there. And there."

I nodded. "War wound."

"Hold your head still. I will have to offset the droud a bit—"

"Hey, listen," I interrupted, "I'm not sure I'm going to do this. I just—"

His shoulders slumped a little more. "Of course. The sample first. This way."

He led me to the desk counter, sat me down, and went around behind it. He made three adjustments to the black box, one to the inside of the "army helmet." He passed it to me. "Put this on. That way front."

I eyed it dubiously.

He did not sigh. "When I activate this unit, it will set up a localized inductance field in the area where I calculate your medial forebrain bundle to be. For a period of five seconds you will experience intense pleasure. The effect will be almost precisely half as strong as that produced by a conventional droud from standard house current."

"What if my medial thing isn't where everybody else's is?"

"That is unlikely. If so, the most probable result would be that you would feel nothing, and I would recalibrate and try again."

"What about *least* probable? Are there any potentially dangerous near-misses?"

"Not lethal ones, no. There is a chance, which I compute as less than five percent, that you might experience a feeling of either intense heat or intense cold. If so, tell me and I'll disconnect."

"This thing has been tested a lot?" I temporized. "I mean, you said your patent thing just went in this week."

"Exhaustively tested, by me, for a year at Bellevue."

I raised an eyebrow. "Volunteers?"

"Mental patients." No, in other words.

I kept on looking at the damned helmet.

What was I doing here? Research? Investigating the subject of Karen's crusade, so that I could understand it better, understand her better? What was to be gained here that was worth sticking my head into a giant homemade light socket?

Was it really that tempting? To know pure pleasure for once, for just this once, to let go all the way and find out what happens when you let go? If I did let go, could I find my way back?

"Doctor, do you consider conventional wireheading addictive?"

He didn't flinch. "Yes."

"Is *this* addictive?"

"No."

"Is it habituating?"

"It can't be. One free sample per customer. I am not a candy store."

I had a thought. "Can you cut it back to one-*quarter* droud strength?"

"Yes. That would still be your only sample."

Still I waited and debated. He was making no slightest effort to influence my decision either way, or to hurry it along. He was dead. I thought of Karen in the harsh light of her living room lamp, and of the young wirehead I had left shredding his identification. I thought of what Karen wanted to do. She wanted to commit financial and/or physical violence on the people who ran this industry. She wanted to abolish this practice. I intended to try and con her out of it. *I had to know what it was like*.

I put my hands on the helmet, and I closed my eyes and tried to imagine what ecstasy would feel like, and—

Hiatus.

I was halfway out of my chair, rising, spinning toward the door, all in slow motion. The helmet was in mid-bounce. Just before the shock doc's face slid out of my peripheral vision, I thought I saw the mildest, most feeble trace of relief flicker across it. I was conscious of every muscle-action of running toward the exit. Someone was screaming; I didn't know his name. My time sense was so stretched out that I was able to open the door at a dead run, leaning out to pull it towards me, yanking my torso back away from it as it opened, pivoting on the handle so that I flung myself into the street. I hit the pavement feet first, perfectly banked for my turn; after three skidding steps I had my stride back and within ten I was settled into it. Shortly I had to brake for a busy intersection. As I did, my time sense suddenly snapped back to normal. I sat down on the curb, rushing traffic a meter from my shoes, and bent over and puked and puked into the gutter. The nausea lasted, off and on, through four or five light-changes. When it passed I sat there for another couple, and then I heard cat feet approaching and looked up to see who was desperate enough to roll a drunk in broad daylight. So I happened to be looking in the direction of the wireshop, a full block behind me, when its front wall danced across the street, hotly pursued by brightness intolerable, and struck the vacant storefront opposite like some monstrous charge of Brobdingnagian buckshot.

I flung myself back and sideways, away from traffic and into blast shadow, and the sound reached me as my face hit the pavement. I stayed down until it seemed like everything that was in the air had landed, then rolled to my feet fast.

My would-be mugger was glancing back and forth from me to the smoking wreckage, clearly of two minds. I put my hand on my gun butt. "Not today," I said, and he licked his lips and sprinted for the shop. He had delayed too long; five or ten people were already gingerly entering the store, wrapping various things around their hands so they wouldn't burn their fingers. They were a gang; two of them stood guard.

I joined the rest of the crowd. We stayed a half-block away on either side and stared and cursed the looters for getting there first and swapped completely bogus eyewitness reports. I decided it probably had not been an accidental explosion. It had taken artistry and skill to place a charge that would utterly wreck the wireshop without bringing down the floors above or seriously damaging the adjoining buildings. God is an iron, but He is seldom that finicky in his irony. That left me in three simultaneous states of mind. I was impressed. I was scared. And, strongest of all—

I was enormously intrigued.

I made my way home quickly, and when I smiled at President Kennedy he winked his *left* eye. I had a guest. One that Kennedy had recognized and admitted, or he would have winked both eyes several times. I am allergic to surprises, and never more so than that afternoon. My first thought was that anyone smart enough to crack my house was smart enough to tell the

President which eye to wink. I wondered why I had never thought of that. I pulled my gun and made sure the collar wasn't in the way of the knife and told myself that it was purest paranoia to think the wireshop bombing could have anything to do with me. The hypothesis yielded a bomber of infinite resources, great ingenuity, and complete incompetence. More likely my guest was the Fader, who was about due. Or Old Jake, come with his guitar to play me a new song...

And when the door raised itself, music did indeed come drifting up the stairs. But it wasn't Old Jake. It was the Yardbird, these forty-four years dead.

Whoever was down there was a friend.

It was Karen who sat in my living room, crosslegged on her usual chair. Even if the music had masked the sounds of my arrival she could not have helped seeing me peripherally, but she gave no sign, kept staring at the place where the far wall met the ceiling. I sat down quietly in the other Lounger, dialing for tea.

She was listening to one of the last Dial sessions at WOR, in '47, when Bird finally got the band he wanted in New York. Miles and Max Roach and Duke Jordan. And all the smack he wanted. There's a Mingus piece, usually called "Gunslingin' Bird," whose full title is "If Charlie Parker Was a Gunslinger, There'd Be a Lot of Dead Copycats." As my tea arrived, the thought jumped into my head: if Charlie Parker had been a wirehead, all those copycats would have had to work for a living.

When the last note of "Bird of Paradise" cut off, and not a moment before, Karen turned the stereo not down, but off. I remembered that the Fader had liked her.

"Hi, Joe."

"Hello, Karen."

"Anticlimax. The runaway child comes back home."

"Why?"

She took her time answering. "I don't know if I can put it into words. You...you've done...a lot for me, and, and that means that you must...care about me some and I'm gonna go do something that's gonna get sticky and you wanted to talk me out of it and I didn't give you a *chance*, I got defensive and took it personal and cut you right off." She paused for air. "I mean, I'm gonna do this anyway but I just thought you'd feel better if you did your best to talk me out of it first, you know, like you'd be easier in your mind. It was wrong of me to leave like that, it was . . . it was like . . ." She was slowing down again. ". . . like not caring about *you*."

I was looking at my hands. "And you're not afraid I'll try to prevent you?"

"No. You're not my father."

"Have you hired a reader yet?"

"Not yet. I've been thinking."

I looked up and met her gaze. I had decided on the way home. "Good. You don't need one anymore."

She twitched her shoulders violently. "I—you—but—" She stopped herself and closed her eyes. She drew in a big lungful of air, pursed her lips, and blew it sl-o-owly through her teeth, *ssshhhoooooo*, did it again slower. Then she opened her eyes and said, "Thank you, Joe."

My hangover was gone.

"When do we start?" she asked after a moment.

"Have you eaten?"

"I brought cornbread, and some pretty good preserves, and some Java coffee."

"We start after brunch."

As we were setting the table she took me by the shoulders and looked at me for a long moment. Her expression was faintly quizzical. Suddenly she closed in and came up on tiptoe and was kissing me thoroughly, her fingers digging into the back of my head. I had salad bowls in either hand and could neither resist nor cooperate. She did not kiss me the way a whore kisses her biggest spender. She kissed me the way a wife kisses a husband who remembered their fifth anni—

Hiatus.

She was two meters away, leaning back against the wall with her hands outspread. Her eyes were round. Salad dressing stained her blouse and dripped from her cheek, and there was lettuce all to hell and gone between us. I looked up at the ceiling. "Dammit," I cried bitterly, *"that* one wasn't fair!"

"Joe, I'm sorry, I'm sorry, I didn't—"

"I wasn't talking to you!" I stopped myself. I tried her exhaling trick and it helped a lot. "Karen, *I'm* sorry. That had nothing to do with you, nothing at all. It was—"

"I know. Somebody in your past."

I shrugged. "It could be. I honestly don't know." I told her about my blackout condition. I had never told anyone before— but she and I were going to go to war together, and she had a right to know.

When I was done explaining, all she said was, "Let me see if there's a safe dosage," and then she came into my arms and hugged me and kissed me, the way a friend kisses a friend, and that was just fine.

And we ate, and that was just fine too, and then we adjourned to the living room. Where I pulled the terminal out of the wall recess and heated it up. And the next two hours were interesting indeed.

There are many better keyboard men than me. I came quite late to programming, and will never have the genius level of aptitude that some are born with. On my good days I consider myself a talented amateur. There are enormous holes in my knowledge of computers, and probably always will be. But blind chance gifted me with a computer the equal of any in North America, with programmed-in owner's manual, at a point in my life during which I had nothing better to do than study it. It is so supple and flexible a machine that I have never been tempted to anthropomorphize it. It can interface with almost any network while remaining effectively invisible. Its own capacity is four terabytes, four times ten to the twelfth bytes.

Karen watched for the first half hour, but after the first ten minutes she was just being polite. Finally I told her to go dig Bird on the headphones, and she did. At that point I was only puzzled. Subsequently I did some things with that most versatile of computers that would have shocked the IRS, a few that would have fascinated the CIA, and even one or two that might have surprised the computer's original owner if he or she were still alive. I went from puzzled through intrigued to mystified, stayed there for about an hour, then moved on to baffled, proceeding almost at once to frustrated. Karen heard me swearing and came over to sit wordlessly beside me with her hand at the base of my neck. Within another fifteen minutes, frustrated modulated into vaguely alarmed, and stayed there.

Finally I ordered hard copy printout and cleared. "'You got it, buddy,'" I growled in my best Tom Waits imitation. "'The large print giveth, and the small print taketh away.'"

"What is it, Joe?"

"I'm damned if I know, and I'm sure I can't explain it very well. You haven't studied economics, let alone business economics. It's—" I broke off, groping for an analogy within her experience. "Like a motorcycle. You can break down what a motorcycle does, chart the path and interaction of different forces and materials, follow the power flow. If you can visualize the motorcycle as a series of power relationships, you can locate its weak points—where it can be most disabled with least effort. That's what I've been trying to do with the wirehead industry. But I can't get a computer-model that *works*. If you built a motorcycle like this it would whistle 'Night In Tunisia,' make a pot of coffee, and explode. I can't make sense of the power flow . . . and it seems to have only the most peripheral relationship to the money flow . . . damn it, there's nothing the IRS could object to. Stupidity isn't illegal. But it just . . . *feels* wrong, feels like something is being juggled. But I can't understand how or why or by whom. That makes me highly nervous."

"So, since you can't diagram out this motorcycle, you can't find the weak points?"

"I can't be sure. We've got to get inside and nose around, learn things that aren't in *any* computer. Field work."

She nodded. "Fine. *Where?*"

"That's another problem. There are three major corporations, as your source told you—and by the way, if two of them *are* really the same outfit, I can't prove it. We might get useful information at any of three places."

"Where?"

"Germany, Switzerland, Nova Scotia."

"Which is better?"

"The biggest outfit is the West German one, in Hamburg. That'd be the hardest to crack. I don't speak German—"

"I do."

"Point. The smallest of the three, and that ain't small, is in Geneva. We can get by with English in Switzerland but I think there's the least information to be had there. The middle-size bear is in Halifax—"

"...and the Canadian border is a joke. That settles that. My stuff's still where I left it? I'll pack."

"Yes, do that," I said, and set immediately to making my own preparations for departure. I wasn't sure why she was impatient to be going, but I knew why I was. I could not shake the nagging fear that I had tripped some subtle watchdog program without knowing it. There are ways to avoid being back-tracked, and I believed I knew the best ones.

But I wasn't positive.

We took four days getting to Halifax. We had to keep changing vehicles, and one does not want to enter a strange city exhausted from travel. Especially not if one wishes to vanish as quickly as possible into the shadows of that strange city. We found a cheap apartment house that still accepted cash in the old part of town, on a sorry, broken-down sin-strip called Gottingen Street. If you went up on the roof you could see the harbor and the bridge to Dartmouth. You could also leave the building in any of three directions without special equipment, which was what closed the deal. We took a year's lease on a two-bedroom as Mr. and Mrs. Something-or-Other, and by the time I hitchhiked back from where I'd dumped our final car, Karen had us unpacked and food in the fridge, coffee made.

"Oh, Joe, this is exciting. This town is so strange; I think I'm going to like it. Let's go for a walk and plan our first move."

"Wait," I said. "I don't think we should do either one just yet. I haven't needed to bring this up until now, but... let me tell you what happened to me on my last walk in New York." I did not do that, but I did give a brief outline of the wireshop incident. Her eyes were wide when I was done. "Do you see what I mean? It has the same *wrong* feel as I got when I took the readouts. That zombie was no genius inventor. When I saw that homemade helmet of his, I couldn't believe someone else hadn't thought of it five years ago. Hell, they could have built one of those in the eighties. But he had the only one I ever heard of. And he got blown away, along with the Mark I, the week his patent application went in—" I broke off and frowned. "You *can't* burgle the Patent Office's computer files. But maybe I can find out whether anyone has made official inquiries through channels about that particular patent. That's public record."

Before I had left my home I'd had my computer select three different acceptable but unused phone numbers in Halifax, diddle the Atlantic Tel computer into believing they were high-credit subscribers in good standing, initiate conference calls from all three, and leave those circuits open, on standby. Why not? I wasn't paying for it. I dialed one of those numbers now, and when I was put through I got out the portable terminal I travel with and clipped its squeaker to the phone. I was interfaced with my home computer.

I asked it my questions, frowned, and rephrased my questions. This time I got an answer, and it couldn't have been on screen for more than three seconds before I was ordering the computer to break circuit, wasting that means of access. I was scared enough to wet my pants.

"There is no such application on file," I said in a shaky voice. "No patent remotely related to wireheading or inductance or anything to do with the goddam brain has been sought by anybody in the last year. Current to three o'clock this afternoon."

"So either that shock doc was stone crazy—"

"Or someone can subvert the U.S. Patent Office. And we know about it. God's teeth. The only people with interest enough and leverage enough are the big wirehead outfits—and why the hell would they take risks like that to suppress something that would probably triple their income or better?"

"Jesus."

"It's wrong, it feels wrong, it's all just...*off*. And I'm getting very nervous. Let's *not* go for that walk."

We watched TV instead, curled up in the master bedroom, until we fell asleep. I slept poorly. Bad dreams.

When a week had gone by without incident or alarm, I began to relax. Until that time we made believe that we had never heard of wireheading, and kept to ourselves. We talked a lot. The entertainment facilities of our room were a joke, and I was not going to call home again until and unless I had to. Part of our talk involved practical matters of planning, a good many hours inasmuch as we had almost nothing to go on. We were able to kill much time inventing new contingencies. But there was a limit to how far we could stretch that, and finally there was nothing left for us to talk about except the stories of our lives.

Karen started it. She talked about her childhood, starting with the happy parts because they came first chronologically. They didn't last long. Her father had been a monster in almost a biological sense. She told me a great deal about him over the course of perhaps a week, first in a two-hour monologue she ended by vomiting to exhaustion, and then in a series of long conversations that wandered everywhere but always led back sooner or later to that extraordinary man. I use that last word reluctantly, but I can find no legitimate excuse to disown him. I wish I could. His death should have been celebrated. Well, it had been—by Karen surely, and likely many others— but I mean nationally. Planetarily.

But although he had never been especially intelligent, Wolf- gang Scholz had always had the animal cunning never to hurt anyone who could effectively complain about it.

About her mother, Ilse, Karen told me little, and most of that simply involved incidents at which the woman had been present. Apparently she was one of those cipherlike people that true sadists keep around. Having no personality to destroy, they cannot be used up.

The telling of her life was good for Karen. She had told most of these anecdotes to others over the years—but she had never told anyone *all* of them. In telling them all together, perhaps she was able to perceive some kind of gestalt pattern she had previously missed. Perhaps by replaying every minute of her life with her father she was better able to exorcise him, one step closer to being able to accept and forget him. Every time you play the record, the signal-to-noise ratio gets worse. Her consumption of alcohol dropped steadily to zero. She cut way back on tobacco. She actually began to display signs of neatness, become more careful in personal grooming.

And finally it was my turn.

And of course there was nowhere to start but at the beginning.

I remember, as an infant remembers womb dreams, the click and the sight of the mine coming up like a featureless jack-in-the-box and very bright light and then very dark dark. And then I was born.

When I realized that I was alive, my first thought was that VA hospitals were better than I'd heard. I was in a powered bed in what looked like the bedroom of a captain of industry, with no medical equipment in sight. My head did not hurt nearly as badly as I thought it should, and nothing else hurt at all. Well, I said to myself, you've managed to come up smelling like a rose again, Corporal—

And paused.

Because what I intended to end that sentence with was my name. And I did not know it anymore.

It was not really *that* much of a shock, then. In all the books and movies, amnesia is always temporary. But I yelled. A man came in the door with an icebag. A man so completely nondescript that I could not tell whether I knew him or not. I thought that was symptomatic too at the time, but of course it was the Fader. He sat down and put the ice on my head and told me that he had gotten the son of a bitch.

I'm not sure which questions I asked first, but within a couple of days I had as much information as the Fader could give me. By the end of a month I knew almost all I was ever going to know.

When the mine went off in the jungle I was, as best I can reconstruct it, twenty-four or thereabouts. When I woke up in that bed under the offices of that deserted warehouse, for what I believed was the first time, I was—again, best guess—about thirty.

Of what I did, where I was, during the intervening six years, I have no slightest recollection.

Of my life before the mine went off I have only random shards of memory, disordered, fragmentary, incomplete. I do not for instance know my name, nor have I been able to discover it.

It's like a million file cards scattered across a great field, more than half of them facedown. Random bits of information are clear and sharp, but there is no context. I remember a family, remember childhood incidents involving three vividly recalled people, but I do not know their names or what has become of them. I remember growing up in a small town; if I ever see it I'll know it, but I doubt I'll ever find it. I remember that we moved to New York in my early adolescence, but in the four years since the Fader put that icebag on my head I have walked through most of the five boroughs without finding that street. Ten years is a long time in New York. It may not exist anymore.

I remember enlisting and bits of Basic and there's a lot of chaotic, badly edited video footage of the horrors of war—in fact, the army days are probably the period I retain most of. But to my sour amusement I cannot recall my serial number.

What the Fader had to say was mighty interesting. We had met a couple of months before in a bar. I had busted a stein over the head of someone who was attempting to knife him. We had become friends, and a couple of weeks ago I had invited him home, and a week ago I had showed him my *real* home. The Fader stated that he was a composer—who, the times being what they were, dabbled in the small-time con (mostly variations on the classic Man in the Street) and an occasional mugging. He told me that I was a burglar, apparently for the sheer love of it since I obviously had, as he put it, adequate resources.

How had I found my home? How would he know? He had been too polite to ask, and I had not volunteered the information. Or, unfortunately, much else.

One guess suggests itself. One of the two emergency exits from the underground apartment is a long tunnel, which at its far end is camouflaged, quite realistically, as an abandoned sewage outfall, malodorous and unattractive to inspection. Could I have been so afraid of someone or something that I tried to hide in there, and found myself in Wonderland?

The Fader said that we had been coming back from a large

"mutual adventure" when a hijacker tried to take its proceeds from us. The hijacker had laid a sock full of potting soil against my skull, and the Fader had killed him with his hands. Then he had dragged me the rest of the way home, and since he knew the dislock sequence but had not been filed in the perms yet, he had a hell of a time propping me up in front of Kennedy to get the door open. (I added the weight-activated explosives later.) He had been nursing me for the past few days, through delirium and nausea, had run several medical texts through the reader before he decided he could safely refrain from taking me to a hospital.

This last because I had told him my secret: that I did not exist, that I was an invisible man.

At some point during my missing six years, and after I had stumbled upon my home, I must have seen the possibilities of its computer, and decided to resign from the human race. I had done a hellishly efficient job. God is an iron.

In between talking with the Fader, I watched and read a lot of news—and I heard nothing that made that decision seem like a bad idea.

I could, to my only mild surprise, think of no better place for me in the world than the one I seemed to have made and lucked into. Every goal or dream I ever had that I can recall was destroyed in the jungle. I looked around me and found it good, or at least tolerable. And I could imagine no other occupation or lifestyle that was.

The Fader showed me what ropes he knew, helped me relearn what life was like in the underworld, steeled me to the rogue. He helped me comb through the ragbag of my mind for scattered bits of memory; helped me try, with the aid of the computer, to find out who I was; helped me get drunk enough on the night that I finally accepted, emotionally, that I might never know. He had done for me what I later did for Karen, and when he had finished it he politely made his excuses and left me alone, visiting frequently for a while and then tapering off. He even found me women, until it became clear that it was a waste of everyone's time. According to my memory shards I had nothing against sex—but now I found myself as asexual as Karen herself.

"Jesus," Karen said at this point in my narrative, speaking for the first time in hours. "How could I read it so wrong? You never wake up hard in the morning, you never get hard at all, and so I figure you must be gay. What a jerk."

I looked away. "To be totally accurate," I said tightly, "I'm a little bit more than asexual. Maybe antisexual is closer."

"How do you mean?"

"Arousal frightens me. Angers me. I can remember enjoying sex in the past, but now on the rare occasions that I become aroused, I—I usually have one of those blackouts."

Karen shook her head. "Different with me. I just don't get anything at all. Not since I was a kid."

Suddenly I was crying, explosively, convulsively, and she was holding me, holding my head against her breast and rocking me in her lap, and I was hanging on to her for dear life. "I thought *I* had it tough," I heard her whisper, and I wept and wept. It was the first time in a long while that I had wept for anything but rage, and it drained away an enormous amount of pain and fear and left me spent. Karen half-carried me to bed, and it was like leaning on a rock with a soft surface.

There was a new bond between us the next day, and so it was late that afternoon that Karen had her own blowout, that her own psychic kettle came to a boil. I think it was that night that she finally forgave God for creating her father, and I ended up holding her until she fell asleep. A deep and profound sleep, complete exhaustion plus successful catharsis. She never felt me undress her, never noticed me leave the bed, never heard the TV I watched as I mixed myself a drink and finished it. I took another one to the corner chair with the directional reading light, and I sipped while rereading computer printouts for the thirtieth time, trying to make a sensible pattern out of them.

The drink was long gone when I heard the first sensual moan.

I looked up and dropped the printout. She had worked the sheet off in her sleep and lay writhing on the bed. She was obviously having a deeply erotic dream. I had never known this to happen to her before, had never expected it to. I felt a trace of the faint distaste that sexual arousal usually elicits in me and wanted to look away.

But Karen—scarred, frigid little Karen, my true friend Karen—was whimpering with lust. Perhaps for the first time in years.

Something had finally unlocked, some door in her mind was opening. If it could happen in sleep it could happen in waking life. My patient was at a crisis. But *was* it happening? She thrashed on the bed, clenching and unclenching her thighs, making small sounds as she searched for release. Her hands flexed and grasped at her sides; she had never learned to masturbate, could not work it into whatever fantasy was stimulating her.

Surely a lifetime of deprivation should provide enough back pressure to allow release without any physical stimulus. But what if it didn't? If this attempt at sexuality ended in frustration, would it be repeated? When would conditions ever be better? Or as good?

I got up and approached her. She did not seem to feel my weight come on the bed. I looked her over from head to toe, dispassionately, as an intellectual problem. I thought it out. The more input I gave her, the more she had to work into the script of her dream; eventually the effort might bring at least partial awareness and failure. Her arousal was coming in slow waves that built to a peak, ebbed, then caught again. When I sensed a peak coming I reached out carefully. With infinite gentleness I put the tip of an index finger just above the top of her vulva, so slowly that for her there was probably no defined border between not feeling it and feeling it. As the peak arrived I moved my finger delicately down the shaft of her clitoris toward the glans. She was breathing in gasps, whistling on the exhale. As I approached the nub I began using a little fingernail, and when I had reached it my thumb was beneath it, trapping it, and she groaned and went over the edge.

It was not the spectacular, backbreaking orgasm I had rather expected. It was a mild thing, a gentle upwelling. But it was definite and unmistakable, and it left her soft and buttery and totally unconscious, all angles rounded, all edges softened. It left me with tears on my face and awe in my heart and a hollow feeling that hurt as bad as anything I've ever known. My sleep that night was an endless round of nightmares, and when I woke the sheet was pasted to me.

Two nights later the sequence essentially repeated. Except that she woke up after orgasm, and figured out what had just happened. We hugged and cried then. I had no nightmares that night. The next day she taught herself to masturbate while I was out shopping. She reported her success proudly, and I smiled and congratulated her, and was jovial as hell all that day, but I believe she caught on because she never again mentioned it or did it in my presence.

But she started spending a lot of time in the bathroom.

I was confused about my own feelings. For her I felt genuinely happy and gratified. And relieved: I never again remembered that there was still a droud in her skull, which she could still use.

For me I felt nothing.

Then came the day when our impatience overcame our paranoia and it was time to begin our campaign. Karen had more than one motive to return to her profession now. Oh, she had cautioned herself not to expect too much. Sex with a random stranger whose only known attribute is that he or she has to pay for it is not liable to be great. But whatever happened, she could definitely abandon her former specialty and switch to straight whoring. She now knew, at least, how to pretend enjoyment. And as it turned out she was third-time-lucky, came several times, and refunded his money. From then on she went about one for three, as near as I could tell.

My own cover identity was pimp, part-time second-story man, and occasional dope runner. If I was home when she brought a client home, I remained discreetly out of sight in the other bedroom, with my eyes on the TV and my ears cocked for trouble. I wasn't always there; I had fish of my own to fry and she could handle herself. A good part of what I was doing was running down exactly how, after we had established our personae, we would begin expanding her client list to include the people we wanted to get to know better, without its being too obvious that we were moving in that direction. I had to tail a couple of them to the homes of the whores they did patronize, learn what kind of women they liked and what they liked to do with them. I was able to get some information from three women by pretending to be looking for recruits for my own stable. With one of them it was necessary to express horror and shame at my unprecedented attack of impotence, and be laughed scornfully out of her room. I tried a fourth woman, and her man put a notch in my ear and a trivial slice on the back of my arm before I could apologize sincerely enough to suit him.

It was going well. We were both acquiring authentic reputations in the Halifax underworld, and I was learning just what class of johns our targets represented, so that we could specialize in that type and acquire them in the natural course of events.

I had decided to actually move a little coke for the sake of my cover, and I returned from a negotiating session in a pool hall with a tentative commitment and a good deal of optimism. When I got home, two coats were on the living room couch and the door to the working bedroom was closed, so I took coffee into the other room and watched a TV special about a zero-gravity dancer, in orbit. Very interesting stuff, very beautiful. I wondered why no one had ever thought of it before. After a while I heard the phone start to ring, but Karen must have picked up the extension at once because it cut off before I could move. Shortly I heard her door open, then the apartment door, then a male voice in brief conversation with Karen's, then the door closing. I put my coffee down; Karen's customer had gone and I wanted to ask her some things.

Only the customer wasn't gone. She and Karen sat at the kitchen table, both dressed, portioning out the pizza I had just heard being delivered. I stopped and waited diplomatically for my cue.

Karen looked up and brightened. I could tell that this had been one of the good ones. "Hi, baby. I didn't know you were home. Want some pizza? This is my old man," she said, turning to the client, and then her smile vanished.

The woman was not a regular. She was about my age, blond and tall and slim, quite beautiful by conventional standards. In my first glimpse of her, bending over the pizza, I had noted in her face and carriage small trace indicators of self-indulgence and bitterness, but I had also sensed strength and courage and will. She wore a starched white uniform, quite unwrinkled and spotless except for where it had been stained when the pizza leaped from her fingers.

She was staring at me, mouth open, eye bulging with shock, hands gripping her elbows so tightly that the knuckles were turning white. She was looking at me as if I were death, as if I were all horror and all evil, and I could not for the life of me imagine why.

"Lois," Karen cried, "what's *wrong?*"

Her mouth worked. She swallowed. "Norman," she rasped and swallowed again. "Oh, my sweet Jesus fucking Christ you *are* alive." She tilted her head as if she had heard something, and fainted dead away.

7 ≣

1995 The last two factors in the complex causal-event-
tree that killed Norman Kent were Semester Break and an old
address book.

Each factor by itself was necessary but not sufficient cause.
Norman might have gotten through Semester Break if it had
not been for the address book; the book would probably not
have killed him at any other time of the year. But the two
factors coincided, and Norman's death ceased to be a matter
of statistical probability and became virtually inevitable.

He even knew this when it happened.

He had followed the advice given him by Minnie and the Bear,
had done his level best to declare Maddy dead in his mind. He
had gone so far as to initiate the lengthy process of having her
declared legally dead, which he had been putting off. The
horrible impersonality of the procedure helped make the idea

of her death more real to him. In his academic world the tendency was to smother the unpleasant realities of life in empty form—in dozens of empty forms, to be filled out in quintuplicate. It seemed fitting and correct that the bureaucratic world should deal with that most unpleasant reality of life—death—in the same way: by chanting the dry cold facts over and over again, on paper. It made it official, made it real.

The lesson was clear: pain could be buried, with enough shoveling. Norman had allowed himself to relax for the duration of his friends' visit, because this let him appreciate them. But when they left he plunged gratefully into the work that had backed up in a week of relaxation, and was soon producing like five driven men again.

His students began to transcend themselves, reaching new plateaus of insight and understanding almost against their will. He published a new paper, in which he coined a new critical term of fourteen syllables that meant nothing whatsoever and was to remain in serious critical usage for half a century after his death. Under his direction the campus literary magazine not only doubled its circulation and quintupled its readership, but brought several of its contributors reprint fees, and one a book contract. Norman practiced, and even came to enjoy, the art of Lunching for Advancement, which he had formerly considered an unpleasant obligation. Three jealous colleagues tried but failed to knife Norman; one was ruined by boomerang effect. Eighteen students, singly and in groups, in series and in parallel, failed to seduce him. Three carefully selected faculty wives succeeded. MacLeod, who was married to one of them, began to publicly praise his own sagacity in giving Norman one more chance to Find Himself, and dropped hints about early Total Tenure. Even the Chancellor deigned to nod to Norman when they passed one day on the quadrangle, both scrupulously following the unnaturally natural pathways.

Respect of a similar yet different kind was given to Norman by other teachers and students who were in no way connected with the university. Monday night was Fitness Canada Night at the YMCA, the basic RCAF program with assorted frills: Norman was first made a class demonstrator and then offered a part-time job, which he declined. Tuesday night was Jazz

Beginner class at DancExchange: he was by now in the first row. Wednesday night was T'ai Chi, that splendid blend of dance and unarmed combat. Thursdays had given Norman a problem for a while: no course for which he was eligible involving physical exertion was offered anywhere in the city on that night. He settled for a pistol marksmanship class given by the police department. Friday night was unarmed-combat class at the Forces post on South Street, where again he was made a demonstrator. He jogged to and from all these activities—he jogged everywhere he went off campus—and did some serious running on weekends down at Point Pleasant Park. Every night he slept like a dead man, a kind of rehearsal.

He gave up forever tobacco and alcohol and marijuana and reading for pleasure and sex for pleasure. They were all ways to relax, and he had no wish to relax. He canceled the cable-feed service that brought entertainment and news to his video console. He abandoned all social life save that which would enhance his professional position, and pursued that with energy and something that was frequently mistaken for gusto.

He attained, in short, as has been said, a drastic kind of dynamic stability, the peace of the dervish, and maintained it for some time. As the work pressure on campus swelled, growing inevitably into the tidal wave of Exam Week, he rode it like a master surfer, until at last, when he was humming along at absolute peak velocity and efficiency, the wave suddenly broke and deposited him, shipwrecked, on the shores of Semester Break.

All the work, all the students, most of the faculty, all *went away*. Norman was far too organized to need to plan his next semester, and there was no First Semester work left undone. There was nothing to fill his days.

His evening prospects were not much better. Three of his five evening classes were also suspended while the students were away; marksmanship and hand-to-hand would continue, but it was easy to see that he would come home from them insufficiently exhausted. As for what might be called his curricular extracurricular activities, only one of his three faculty wives had failed to leave town for the vacation—and by Murphy's Law she was the least tiring, most tiresome, and least available of the three. There was not much to fill Norman's nights.

For the first few nights he bounced around his apartment like a Ping-Pong ball in a blender, a workaholic evading savage withdrawal. He added final touches to already exemplary housekeeping, got his apartment looking like an advertisement, then frowned and rearranged virtually every piece of furniture in it, three times. He cooked himself elaborate meals that required hours of preparation and extensive cleanup—then hours later he would realize that he had forgotten to enjoy them. He designed a way to increase the efficiency of his apartment's layout by tearing out a single wall, and gave it up only when the building super proved to him that the wall was load-bearing—that every wall in the massive tower was load-bearing. In desperation he dug out his novel, but put it aside after an hour. Writing was hard work, but it was not the kind of work that kept him from being alone with his thoughts.

He cast his mind back to the days when he had had both time and inclination for a hobby. He had once been something of a low-key computer enthusiast, had in fact built his own Other Head (a machine so versatile that its brand name was fast becoming a generic term) from a kit. He spent two days familiarizing himself with the state of the art, then redesigned and rebuilt and overhauled his system, hardware and software. After a day of playing with it he was again restless and irritable. He found himself hurling a glass against a wall because the grapefruit juice in it had become lukewarm.

Inanimate objects and total strangers began to conspire to drive him mad. An essential component of his typewriter snapped under no provocation at all—the dingus that held the paper against the platen-roller (it irked him immensely that he could not recall the name of that dingus). Norman did most of his typing on his processor, but the few uses he still had for the old IBM—official documents, fill in the blank forms, and the like—were *just* important enough to make it a necessity. Typewriter repairmen overcharged mercilessly. Norman decided an epoxy repair might just hold up and reached for his epoxy. Used up in rebuilding his Other Head. He went out into the bitter cold and bought more. When he opened it at home, the resin was solid throughout its tube; he had been sold epoxy several years old. Swearing, he went out again—it was snowing fiercely now—to a different store and purchased a cyanoacrylate adhesive, the kind that bonds skin instantly. He found that the tiny tube was too frail to withstand the force required to break the seal inside its tip, even with a very sharp pin and much care; two of his fingers bonded together before he could react and instinctively he yanked them apart, tearing the skin. Adhesive dripped down the length of his hand, dropped on his expensive slacks. He wanted to clench his fist in rage and did not dare. He bellowed and ran to the bathroom, flushed his hand as clean as possible, and dressed the bleeding finger; when he returned to his office the tube was bonded to the desk. He pierced the side of it to get some fresh adhesive, and made his repair job. The stuff claimed to bond in "seconds," so he gave it an hour. The join failed instantly on the first test. With trembling hands, Norman removed the tube of adhesive from the desk, scarring the desk irreparably and getting adhesive on his shoes. He found himself in the living room, holding the massive IBM over his head, the power cord tangled on one arm, and realized that he was looking for the most satisfying object through which to hurl the thing. He set it down with great gentleness on the rug, then stood erect and filled his lungs. People who live in apartment towers do not generally visualize God as their upstairs neighbor, but Norman looked upward now and screamed, *"What is it, then?"*

Silence came for answer.

"You've got my attention, damn your flabby heart! *Now what the fuck are you trying to tell me? I'm listening!"* He swayed on the balls of his feet, shoulders hunched, breathing heavily. His head ached, his fingers throbbed, his throat was torn by the violence and volume of his challenge. *"Well?"* he shrieked, damaging it further.

At this third provocation the woman living above Norman called out to her husband. That man's name was Howard, but there was a floor and a ceiling and a perfunctory attempt at insulation between the woman and Norman, so that the word he heard filtering down to him from on high was:

"—coward?"

His eyes bulged. The blood drained from his head.

"—coward, what's he doing?"

He bent and grabbed the IBM, heaved it up to chest height. But the cord had his ankle now, so he yanked his right foot out from under him; he lost the IBM and went down howling. He saw the great gray bulk coming down at his face, rolled convulsively out of the way, and smacked his skull solidly into a leg of the coffee table. It was excuse enough to lose consciousness.

His awakening was strange, only partial. He had no recollection of the incident, did not ask himself how he came to be lying on his living room floor with a sore head and assorted aches. He simply got up, moved the typewriter to where he kept the trash, and made coffee. Thoughts of any kind came slowly and far apart. One fragment of the metaprogramming part of his mind recognized that he was in shock, but did not care. Decisions were handled by something like a random-number generator somewhere in the murky cavern of his brain; Norman went along for the ride, his consciousness on hold, or perhaps "on standby" would be more accurate.

He found himself seated at his desk, rubbing a finger uselessly over the new scar as though it could be erased. His coffee was cold. He recalled that there was an immersion coil in one of the desk drawers and looked for it. He got sidetracked: the desk badly needed straightening out. Been meaning to get this organized, he thought, and began weeding out superfluous items.

One of the first was the address book.

It was quite out of date. Norman had built his Other Head on his honeymoon, with wedding money; both he and Lois had fed their address and phone files into it and dumped the original books and lists. This was an old one that had been overlooked. Norman was about to trash it—it was surely obsolete—and then he hesitated. Some part of his somnolent mind decided that he might just run across the name of some forgotten old friend or lover he could call or look up, as a means of harmlessly killing some time. There might be one or two other items worth adding to his computer files. He opened the book and began browsing.

The first twenty pages were just what he could have expected: a mildly bemusing, mildly depressing trip down memory lane. I wonder if she ever forgave me. Say, I remember that jerk. And Ed, so promising, yeah, dead in the Second Riot in Philly. Old Ginny, wow, what are the odds she's still single? On and on for twenty pages—right up through the J's. There was nothing worth salvaging.

Then he turned the page and saw Madeleine's old address and phone code in Switzerland.

The violence was all internal this time, too titanic to escape his skull in any form whatever. The full recollection of the evening past came crashing out of its cage, the surface of his soul fissured and split to reveal something disgusting, the last seven years of his life snapped suddenly into meaningful pattern, agonizing pattern, he understood at once that he *must* now undo every single day of that seven years and that their undoing would almost certainly bring his death to him within a period measured in days—and an unobservant person seated across the room would probably have failed to notice a thing. Norman did not so much as flinch. He sat quite still for perhaps ten seconds, forgetting to breathe. Then, very gently, he sighed.

"All right," he said, looking straight ahead at nothing. "I hear you."

Then, sitting bolt upright, the address book still perched on his lap, he fell asleep in the chair.

Some hours later his eyes opened. It was just morning. He rotated his head on its socket three slow times, cracked his spine, put his hands on the desk, and stood carefully. The book fell unnoticed from his lap; he would never notice it again. He knew what he needed to do and what he needed to learn and much of how to do it. Most of all he knew how much it would cost him—and was only glad he had the price.

It was quite simple. Somewhere in the African bush he had decided to hell with self-worth, given it up as a lost cause, settled for mere pride. A villain or a coward may have pride. Academic life had gradually eroded most of that pride—not because he failed at it but because he succeeded at it, turning out generations of students whose imaginations had been stimulated precisely where the department chairman wanted them stimulated and nowhere else. He had sold everything for security, gelded himself for security. Small wonder his wife had left him for someone more dangerous. When he had failed to learn from that lesson, life had, with the infinite patience of the great teacher, spent more than a year kicking him repeatedly in the heart, brain, and balls. You didn't need to catch Norman Kent between the eyes with the million-pound shit-hammer more than forty or fifty times before he got the message:

Pride is not enough to get you through this world. You have to have self-worth too, or you won't be able to take the gaff.

Sam Spade had hit the nail squarely, more than half a century before. When a man's partner is killed, he's supposed to do something about it. Madeleine Kent had been, for a brief time but in full measure, Norman's partner, and someone had come and taken her away, and Norman was supposed to do something about it. Self-worth required it.

To die in pursuit of self-worth is much better than to live without it. So said all his life since the jungle days, now that he had the wit to read it. The supersaturated solution had at last crystallized, all at once. Norman caught himself humming as he headed for the door, and realized on some preconscious level that he was happy for the first time in a long while.

He walked south to Point Pleasant Park while he planned his campaign. The horrid cold sharpened his thought.

Known for certain: Madeleine was gone. Period.

High probabilities, in order: Maddy was dead. She had been killed by a man known to her and perhaps named Jacques, or by agents of that man. Jacques was very puissant and very clever, possessed of enormous resources.

Slightly lower probability: Jacques had been a colleague or business associate of Madeleine in Switzerland. Perhaps not— he could be a tennis pro she had met in a bar, or the man who came to fix the microwave. But would she then have felt it necessary to leave her job, leave the career she had built so painstakingly, leave her ten-year home in Switzerland, and come to Canada to avoid Jacques?

She had not left Switzerland because she *feared* Jacques,

of that Norman was certain. She had not been even half expecting to be kidnapped or harmed. During her stay with Norman, Maddy had sometimes slipped and showed hurt; she had
never shown fear.

Assuming all this, she must without realizing it have possessed information that Jacques considered damaging to him.
No other motive made sense; a lover spurned does not take on
Interpol and the RCMP. Norman yearned mightily to possess
information that Jacques would consider damaging.

How do you approach an enemy ten times your size?

In disguise, smiling.

First step: locate Jacques. Without being caught at it. Norman did not intend to underestimate Jacques; he assumed that
his Other Head and his credit account were bugged and monitored. He could not afford to access information about Maddy's
firm from any terminal in Halifax Metro, for that matter, if he
wanted to be *certain* of coming up on Jacques's blind side.
There must be no evidential record even hinting at Norman's
interest in Jacques. One day soon Jacques might have reason
to wonder if someone was taking a bead on him, and if he
could learn that someone in Metro had been asking questions
about him at or shortly after the time that Norman Kent had
dropped out of sight, he would add two and two. Norman
needed information that had already been accessed, which left
only one way to go, and so he gave ten dollars to the first wino
he met at Point Pleasant Park.

He stood outside the phone booth, watching a filthy super-
freighter belly up to the containerport across from the park,
while the wino phoned up the city police and asked for Sergeant
Amesby. Norman kept better track of missing-persons stories
than most citizens, had discussed most of them at length with
Amesby. Thus briefed, the wino was able to convince Amesby
that he was in possession of important information regarding
a recent case quite unconnected with Maddy's, and demanded
a face-to-face meeting at a remote spot near St. Margaret's
Bay, many kilometers to the west. He had corroborative data
not known to the general public. Amesby went for it. The
drunk hung up grinning, and Norman gave him the additional
twenty he had promised for a successful job. With three of

Norman's ten-dollar bills in his hand, the unshaven and tattered man asked Norman for a quarter. He used it to call a cab, to take him to the Liquor Commission store.

Norman walked to police headquarters. Amesby was gone when he arrived. Norman was known there, and had long ago made it a point to be liked there; they brought him to Amesby's office and let him wait.

Thank goodness for the cheapness of the voters! Amesby's files were actual files of paper, in big bulky drawers, rather than electrical patterns on tape or disc. Norman used gloves, and within half an hour he knew everything that Amesby knew about Maddy's situation in Switzerland, her acquaintances, and the firm she had worked for. He used Amesby's battered IBM to note down a few addresses, phone numbers, and bits of information.

Amesby was efficient, and had paid attention when Norman told him about Maddy's single cryptic mention of the name Jacques. In the web of acquaintances that Amesby had had Interpol draw up for Madeleine, there were two men named Jacques, with dossiers for each.

The first and seemingly most obvious candidate was her immediate superior at Harbin-Schellman, Jacques DuBois. But Norman rejected him at once when he saw the photograph. Maddy could not have become emotionally involved with that face. The second was a man named Jacques LeBlanc. Norman could read nothing at all from his face; the man was nondescript. He was executive vice-president of Psytronics International, the much larger consortium that had absorbed Harbin-Schellman in the last year. He apparently had had extensive contact with Maddy in the course of the takeover, would have been an ideal candidate for a lover, save that Interpol could not turn up even a rumor of a romance between the two. What made that lack of evidence significant was that LeBlanc was not married. If he and Maddy had become involved, there would have been no reason to conceal it. Unless . . . could he have been using Maddy for secret leverage in the takeover? No, she would not have played along; Maddy had old-fashioned ideas about loyalty.

All right. Jacques's last name was LeBlanc, until events proved otherwise.

Amesby's copier was down the hall, useless to Norman. He typed an abbreviated version of LeBlanc's dossier, removed all traces of his work, and left. On his way out he told the desk man it was nothing important, not to bother telling Amesby to phone him.

He stepped from the police station into the incredible wall of wind that howls past Citadel Hill in winter, and leaned into it. With the wind-chill factor, the sudden temperature differential was on the order of a hundred and ten Fahrenheit degrees; Norman ignored it and plodded on, making plans.

On his way home he got twenty dollars worth of change from a bank. He fed some into a sound-only pay phone in the quiet basement of a moribund restaurant and called Zurich, where it was now three o'clock in the afternoon.

It was necessary to locate Jacques; according to Interpol, he traveled a lot. It would be difficult enough for Norman to get to Switzerland untraceably—but it would be stupid to manage it and find that his quarry was in Tokyo or Brasilia. The dossier mentioned an interest that Jacques shared with Norman, and it gave Norman an idea. They both collected classic jazz. He summoned up the New York accent that he had by now almost succeeded in obliterating, and located in his wallet the number of the illegal New York tie-line that one of his faculty wives had told him about.

"DiscFinders, N'Yawk, callin' long distance for Mr. Jock Le Blank."

"One moment, please."

So Jacques was in Switzerland. That was all Norman wanted to know—but he was curious to hear his enemy's voice. He decided to try and sell Jacques a rare Betty Carter side.

But the next voice was female. "Monsieur LeBlanc's office, may I 'elp you?"

"Hullo, this is DiscFinders in N'Yawk, lemme speak to Masseur Le Blank, please."

"I yam sorree, Monsieur LeBlanc is out of the city at present." Norman was glad he had waited. "When's he comin' back?" Slight hesitation. "Not for some time. May I 'elp you?"

"Well, where is he?"

"I yam sorree, I cannot give out that—"

"Listen here, sister, what I got here is a mint copy of Betty

Carter's birthday album, on her own label, there can't be another one mint inna world. Five thousand bucks expenses Mr. Le Blank fronted us to find it, another fifteen on delivery. I think he wants to hear this record, what do you think?"

"If you will send it 'ere, we—"

"Bullshit, lady, didn't you hear me? Fifteen grand, New dollars, the day Mr. Le Blank gets this record in his hand. You think I'm gonna ship it over there and let some clown in your mailroom leave it on the rad for a week before he forwards it fourth class? I send it direct to Le Blank by courier, *personally*, or I peddle it elsewhere."

"Monsieur, I yam afraid I must—"

"I am the best record finder in the world," Norman roared, desperate. "I don't need this bullshit. I know three other people, old customers, 'ud buy this fuckin' thing in a minute, I'll send Le Blank a registered letter tellin' him where his expense money went, how did you say you spell your last name?"

"Monsieur LeBlanc is vacationing in Nova Scotia, in a place called Phinney's Cove. The postmaster in the town of 'Ampton can direct your courier. 'Ave him say that Madame Girardaux approved it. You understand this information is to be absolutely confidential?"

"That's more like it. Pleasure doin' business wit' ya, Miss Jeerado." Dueling Accents. He hung up.

His first reaction was elation at his lucky break. Jacques was right here in the province, a scant hundred and fifty kilometers away. Norman owned a small cottage and a couple of acres not twenty klicks from Phinney's Cove—which community comprised perhaps fifteen homes along the Fundy Shore—and knew the area fairly well.

He had not been looking forward to stalking Jacques on the latter's home ground, in an unfamiliar country, and he was immensely cheered to find Jacques on something like his own turf.

Then he had second thoughts. The hair prickled on the back of his neck. Jacques had been standing unseen just behind his back for an indeterminate time; perhaps this was not wonderful news after all. Could Jacques be wondering if Maddy had passed on something incriminating to her brother before she'd been killed? If so, he must by now have concluded that Norman did not *know* he had anything incriminating . . . mustn't he? Or was he even now deciding to play it safe and have Norman killed too? Norman went from joy to fear like a speeding car thrown suddenly into reverse.

Then he had third thoughts. He remembered what the two psychics had told him about Maddy's surroundings after her disappearance. The descriptions given would fit Phinney's Cove—the city lights on the horizon would be St. John, New Brunswick, across the Bay of Fundy. *Perhaps Maddy was not dead!*

He forced himself to leave the restaurant at a slow walk. A block away, after satisfying himself that he was not being tailed, he did run the remaining three blocks to his home.

He had to take a small risk, then. He needed information he could only obtain from his own Other Head. But it was not the sort of information that Jacques would be likely to find significant, even if he learned of the accessing. From long years of living with Lois, Norman still had a line to the data banks of the hospital just up the street. To play it safe, he charged the tap to Lois's code; someone reviewing the record might reasonably suppose that she had made a routine retrieval while visiting her ex-husband.

The readout he got in response to his query elated him. A male Caucasian of Norman's approximate age and size had died within the confines of the hospital during the previous forty-eight hours. More important, the late Aloysius Butt had been a pauper with no known relatives, was awaiting burial by the province. Since the demographics of Halifax bulged markedly in Norman's age bracket, this could not be considered an incredible stroke of fortune, but Norman definitely took it for a good omen. Aloysius Butt was the one lucky break Norman required for the plan he was forming. Had Aloysius not had the grace to die so timely, Norman would have had to postpone his campaign until a suitable candidate presented himself, and Norman could not bear the thought of enforced inactivity at this point. He did not want too much time for reflection, for doubt and worry. Fortunately fate had given him the one factor that his wits could not provide, just when he needed it. It was railroading time!

Now for traveling cash. Back out to another pay phone.

"This is me, no need for names."

"Not if you say so," the other said agreeably. "To what do I—"

"I am prepared to sell you, under certain conditions, my entire collection. You know what they're worth, can you get that much cash by tonight?"

"What conditions?"

"You tell nobody where they came from. I don't mean just Revenue Canada Taxation or your mistress, I mean *nobody*. You get them in different jackets—same goods, in Angel sleeves, but the jackets'll be from junk, I keep the original jackets. And it has to go down tonight, at 3:00 A.M."

"Without the jackets, the resale value depreciates. There would have to be a small dis—"

"No it doesn't and no there won't. You have no intention of selling them. Book value, take it or leave it."

"I don't know if I can get that much cash by tonight. Can I give you a check for the last five thousand or so? You know I am good for it."

"My friend, this is a one-time-only offer, and nothing in it is negotiable. The Swede wouldn't treat these as well as you would, he wouldn't *appreciate* them—but I know he'll have the cash at home."

The barest hesitation. "Come up the back way and knock two paradiddles. Thank you for thinking of me."

Details filled the rest of the afternoon. Norman picked out two complete sets of clothing, put on the first and folded the second into a compact package. He carefully filled a backpack, his two prime considerations being that the backpack should sustain him for an indeterminate time on the road, and that no one subsequently searching his apartment should be able to deduce that such a backpack had been filled. He did not, for instance, pack his salt shaker, but poured half its contents into an old perfume vial of Lois's. Any essential of which he could not leave behind a convincing amount in its original container he abandoned, to be replaced out of his operating capital on the road. When he was done with his preparations he examined his entire apartment in detail—and shook his head. I am, he thought, an unreasonably neat man. The apartment was, as always, so neat and organized as to give the impression that its owner was away on vacation—which was exactly wrong. He un-neated it a little, gave it a spurious kind of lived-in look. He went so far as to cook himself a dinner—an undistinguished one, when what he wanted was a grand Last Feast, a farewell to his gourmet's kitchen—and leave the dishes in the sink.

He spent the next six hours in his armchair with headphones on, saying goodbye to his music. At midnight he shut off the system and transferred a carton full of extremely rare jazz records, many of them deathgifts from his mother, into the jackets of cheap ordinary records, and vice versa. He put the disguised rare records into another carton, then selected eight more mundane records from his shelves and put them, in their original jackets, into the carton full of rare records. In three unobserved trips, he brought both cartons, his backpack, and his spare set of clothing down to the lobby, stashing them in the dark community room.

One A.M. Lois should have just returned home from work by now.

He flinched at the cold as he left his building. He hurried across the street, noting that the window he wanted was lighted. He used a key he had possessed for some time, but never before used, to let himself into the ancient three-story apartment building. The hall heaters were not working, and more than half the lightbulbs were dead. There were no security cameras to record comings and goings. Norman climbed to the top floor, located a door. He had a key for this door too, but did not wish to use it; he knocked.

Lois answered the door. She started with surprise when she recognized him. "Why, Norman!" she said in a voice that seemed a bit too loud. "What brings you here?" She made no move to step aside and let him in.

"I've got to talk to you, Lois. Business, very urgent."

"Can't it wait until tomorrow? I just got in from work and—"

"Sorry. It can't wait."

She hesitated.

"Come on, it's cold out here. It won't take a second."

Still she hesitated.

"I always let *you* in."

She let him in. A woman, also in nurse's uniform, was seated in Lois's living room; as he saw her, her hands were just coming down from the top button of her smock. Pillows were spread on the floor before her, and he noted that the stockings below her uniform were distinctly non-regulation. He turned back to Lois and, now that the light was better, observed a lipstick smear on the side of her throat. So Lois was trying to change her luck, and was embarrassed about it. Wonderful! She would be flustered, anxious to get rid of him, and the presence of her lover would allow him to be as vague as possible.

"Leslie, this is Norman, my ex. Norman, this is Leslie; she and I have to prepare a report together by tomorrow. What can I do for you?"

"Those records you borrowed. King Pleasure, Ray Charles Trio, Lord Buckley, the Lennon outtakes. I need them all back, right away."

Lois bit her lip. "Uh . . . I haven't had a chance to tape them yet."

"It's been over a year."

"Well . . . can I borrow them back and tape them later?"

Lie. "Sure."

If she had been alone she would have argued. "Well . . . wait here, I'll get them."

She left the room. Norman smiled sweetly at the other nurse, and sat down across from her. "Hello, Leslie. Or should I call you Lez?" He was ashamed at once of the cheap shot, but it could not be recalled.

Leslie started to speak, then changed her mind and stood up. "Excuse me," she said coldly, the only words she had spoken since he arrived. She left, following Lois, and shortly he heard the buzz of low conversation in the adjoining room. Lois came back alone with eight records, each jacket sprayed with preservative plastic.

"Here. Take them and go."

Now for the dirtiest trick. Well, it couldn't be helped. "Lois—let me borrow your car for tonight."

"I need it tomorrow."

"No problem. I'll leave it under the building, keys in the usual spot. But I've got to do a lot of traveling tonight, and a taxi just won't make it."

She frowned.

"Lois, this cancels us, okay? I'll never ask you for another favor. *Please.*"

Again she hesitated. Then: "Norman . . . promise that it won't be the last favor you ever ask me, and you've got a deal."

That one hurt; it was an effort not to wince. "Okay," he lied at last.

She handed over her key ring, and unexpectedly she kissed him—a long, smoldering kiss that was painfully evocative. For the thousandth time in his life, Norman wished there were some truly effective way of erasing memories. The worst of it was having to cooperate in the kiss, to put a false promise into it. "I'll be here alone tomorrow night," Lois murmured as the kiss ended. "Come tell me about your night's travels." Norman was silent, regretting. She searched for words that would bind him to her, and what she came up with was, "I miss your prick." The regret faded; he promised and made for the door.

Still he paused on the threshold. "Lois . . . thanks."

"No problem, Norman, really."

"No, I mean . . . thanks for the good times, all right?"

He turned and fled down the hallway, annoyed with himself for yielding to melodrama. That had sounded too much like an exit line for a suicide.

In case she was watching, he took the car for a several-block drive before doubling back to their street, where he parked in front of his own building. Loading the car with records, backpack, and clothing took no appreciable time and, as far as he could tell, went unobserved. Once inside the car again, he switched jackets between the eight records Lois had returned and the eight mundanes he had fetched. The mundane records, now in jackets claiming that they were rares, he put in the trunk of the car.

Walter, the collector who *appreciated* jazz rarities, had been able to acquire the cash Norman demanded. As Norman had expected, Walter accepted the jacket swapping and other skullduggery as a scheme to defraud Revenue Canada, and was quite happy to collaborate, as Walter's own tax position was chronically less than optimal. He actually drooled as he rummaged through the carton, establishing the identity and condition of each disc. His pudgy hands trembled as he gave Norman the suitcase full of used bills in low denominations—but only because the hands yearned to return to the records. Norman did not bother to open the case and count the money. He forestalled the attempts at conversation that Walter was really too excited to make, and left as soon as he decently could.

It was approaching four in the morning when he reached the hospital. His effortless success there had very little to do with luck. He knew the hospital layout intimately, knew where to park and where the few graveyard-shift personnel could be expected to be cooping and where spare uniforms could be had. And of course he had Lois's key ring. The late Aloysius Butt never had a chance. His absence, in fact, went unnoticed for several days, and when discovered was attributed to the notoriously twisted sense of humor of interns, so obviously was it an inside job.

By the time the sun was rising, Norman had succeeded in hitching the first in a series of rides, and was well content. He wanted to go west, and so he had hitched his first ride east. His hair was parted on the opposite side, and his hairline had receded a full inch. He wore entirely bogus eyeglasses that Lois had once given him as a birthday joke to make him look more "professorial." Cheek inserts subtly changed the shape of his face. His dress did not match his station in life, but looked at home on him. He was unshaven, and could not possibly have been mistaken for a dapper academic. He had a suitcase full of untraceable cash.

Behind him in Halifax, the local newspaper, famed for many years as not only the worst daily newspaper in Canada, but very likely the worst newspaper possible, was preparing to misinform its readers on at least one count for which, for a change, it could not reasonably be blamed. A story and photos on pages one and three alleged that a local English professor named Norman Kent had crashed his wife's car into an oil-storage tank at the foot of the hill by the waterfront, totally destroying the tank, the car, himself, and an extremely valuable rare-record collection whose ruins were discovered in the wreckage.

Norman was ready to hunt him some Jacques.

8 ≣

1999 There was one timeless frozen instant in which
I could close my eyes and murmur, "Oh, *shit*."

Then Karen and I were both in motion. We got the unconscious woman to a couch. We laid her out gently. Karen loos-
ened her uniform collar. It has been my experience that fainters
usually revive at this point, but she showed no signs of recovery
at all. Her color remained pale. The pulse in her throat fluttered.
Her breathing was shallow.

"Jesus, Joe," Karen said. "Jesus." Her eyes were wide.

There was too much in my head. I was dangerously close
to fainting myself, and dared not. "You sure can pick 'em." I
turned slowly round, looked at the room and everything in it.
"Oh, my, yes."

"Joe, she's—"

"—big trouble, right. No telling how big." I went to the
table and sat down. "Not until she wakes up—and before then
we have to decide which way to jump."

"I—what do you mean?"

I wanted to bark, kept my voice low with an effort. "We are engaged in a criminal conspiracy to wreck a billion-dollar industry. We require darkness and quiet. This client of yours has taken me for someone she knew and believed dead—someone who obviously meant a great deal to her."

"Her ex-husband, Norman. She talked about him a lot."

"Oh, fine. So as soon as she wakes up she is going to turn on all the searchlights and sound all the alarms. 'Oh, you're not my dead husband, Norman? Who are you, then? Can you prove it? What a terrific coincidence this is—I must get to know you better, there must be dozens of little nuances of irony here. I can't wait to tell all the girls down at the hospital.'" I frowned. "We need this like an extra bowel. You know what—"

"Joe!"

I trailed off.

"How do you know you're not Norman?"

My face must have turned bright red. I could feel my nostrils flair as I sucked in enough breath for a bellow. My teeth ached. It took all the strength I possessed to keep my vocal cords out of circuit while I exhaled. A shout might wake the sleeping nurse.

I gazed at her across the room.

Her uniform cap was askew. Her blonde hair was mussed. Now that she was unconscious, her face looked petulant. I scrutinized the face very carefully, and then the generous body. I was prepared to swear that I had never seen her before in my life.

Which meant nothing.

Or did it? It depended on which theory of amnesia you bought. Amnesia the way it is in the movies, or amnesia the way you think it really must be, or amnesia the way it really is.

Movie amnesia: if this blonde fem really was my wife once, I would unquestionably have remembered her at once, regaining my memory on the spot. Love is stronger than brain damage. Hate, too—since she was alleged to be an *ex*-wife.

Amnesia as one imagines it: no such pat, instant abreaction—but at least *some* few small bells should ring. A spouse becomes familiar on so many levels that you almost relate to them from your spinal column—the way a pianist will remember his way around his instrument, regardless of whether or not he can recall his name at the moment. This woman was a stranger. In odd hours I have tried to guess what kind of woman I would want, if I wanted women. As far as I could tell, this ex-wife was not even my type.

Amnesia as documented: in 1924, baker Benjamin Levy disappeared from his home in Brooklyn. Two years later a Catholic street sweeper named Frank Lloyd flatly refused to believe he had ever been a Jew, a baker, or named Levy— even when they proved it to him with fingerprints and handwriting analysis. He was quite suspicious, and only when other relatives were able to pick him out of a crowd did he decide there might be something to it. Reluctantly he moved back in with his wife and daughter in Brooklyn. He had to get to know them all over again, and to his dying day he claimed he had no recollection of his early life as Levy.

The mind is stranger than it can imagine.

I had myself back in control now. I looked up, saw Karen staring at me.

"What if I am?" I asked her calmly.

She started to explode.

I overrode her. "We are stalking some very dangerous game, and we are committed now. Maybe they know someone is angling for them, maybe they don't. We could be on borrowed time right now. Suppose this woman *does* hold the key to the missing half of my brain—is now the time to get into it? Either way it blows my cover, jerks me off the rails." I grimaced. "In fact, there's a mighty funny smell to the way she popped up just at this time in our lives. A nurse could be involved in wireheading . . ."

"But if she was sent here she wouldn't have fainted—and that faint is genuine."

"True . . ."

"You don't recognize her *at all?*"

I shook my head. "Proves nothing, though."

"Jesus Christ, Joe, aren't you curious?"

"Not half as much as I am scared. I want to defuse this one, fast. If there's anything to it, I can always come back to it when the job's done."

"You could die! You could die never knowing!"

"So what?" I snarled. "Maybe she was the whole world to me once—but right now she's a live grenade on my sofa. Let's try and get the pin back in." I got up from my chair. I took the headset off the phone and laid it down on the end table. I punched my New York number and put my portable terminal next to the headset. I told the computer to record audio from this location at maximum gain. I told it to transmit a constant dial tone to the phone's earpiece and filter it from both the recording and the extension phone in my bedroom here in Nova Scotia. I gave the computer a one-syllable audio-disconnect cue, which could wipe the whole circuit and all records save for the recording in its own impregnable memory. Then I switched off the terminal and put it away. The phone now looked and sounded as if it had been left off the hook for privacy, rather than for the opposite.

"I'm going into my room, so the shock of seeing me when she comes to doesn't start a loop. And so I can eavesdrop on the extension. When she comes around, convince her she made a mistake—and *pump* her for everything you can get on this Norman."

"She'll want to see you."

"And I won't want to upset her. But when she really insists, I'll have to come out and persuade her I'm not Norman. Which is why you have to get every drop of information you can *first*, so I can do a convincing job. Keep her talking."

"How do you keep someone talking?"

"Be fascinated. You can't fake it. Find her every vagrant thought interesting. Make small involuntary sounds of wonder and sympathy. Nod slightly from time to time. This fem could get us both killed, honey; be fascinated."

Karen took a deep breath. "I guess you're right. We play it your way." She shook her head slightly. "But I just don't know . . ."

"The most probable answer is coincidence. There's nothing unique about my face. Remember your last client in New York?

Lots of people, not enough faces to go around."

The reminder jarred her. "Yeah. All right—split. I think she's coming around."

I slipped into my room and closed the door.

I knew the beginnings of the conversation would be rather predictable and of no value to me. I found the Irish and poured a stiff one, and drank it down before I did anything else. My pulse was racing. I hoped the whiskey and the adrenalin would meet in my bloodstream and strike a bargain. That damned nurse bothered me, scared me. And the reasons I had given Karen were not the whole of it. I did not know the whole of it myself. I was only intellectually sure that I wanted to.

The whiskey helped. I picked up the phone.

Karen:—him a *long* time, honey. I'm telling you, this is the first time he's been north of Boston in his life.

Nurse: (pause) Then—(pause) God, how weird. I'd have—no, of course he isn't. He didn't know me—and Norman never could act worth a damn.

K: (laughing) That describes Joe, too.

N: Listen, I'm sorry for the way I—

K: No, no, that's cool—

N: Some prize customer I turn out to—

K: Really, it's all right.

N: Look, can I give you a little extra for your—

K: It's real nice of you to offer, no, thanks.

N: But I feel as though I—

K: Look, if you want to do something for me, help me kill my curiosity. How come you flipped?

N: I told you, he looks just like—

K: —a dead man, right. You told me about him before, you even told me what he looked like when you buried him. If I buried a burned roast and a few years later I saw a guy that looked just like him, I'd think, 'Gee, he looks just like my ex.' But what you said was, 'Norman—you *are* alive.' Like the idea wasn't new to you.

N: (long pause) Karen, can I trust you?

K: Look at me. I've hurt a few people in my time. Now watch my lips. I. Have. Never. Hurt anyone who didn't hurt me first. And you ain't hurt me. You made me feel good. Real good.

N: Do you have any pot? (sounds of a joint being lit, then a longer pause) I don't remember how much I told you. Eight or nine months after he threw me out, his sister, Madeleine, came home from Switzerland.

K: When was this?

N: Just as the '95 school year was starting, it was. She'd been working in Switzerland for years. A very beautiful woman. (long toke) Then a few weeks later she just...disappeared. All her things left behind, she just didn't come home one night. It was in all the papers and such, Norman did an excellent job of beating the bushes, but no trace of her was ever found. He took it badly. I went to talk to him one day, let myself in, and he...had a woman tied down on his bed, all naked and...he...he changed, you know? He turned cold to me, and he got strange.

K: You think he had something going with the sister?

N: Perhaps. I'm not sure. But her disappearance affected him deeply.

K: And then?

N: A few months later, during Semester Break, he knocked on my door, unannounced, at one o'clock in the morning. He woke me up. He wanted me to return some of his old jazz records.

K: What kind of records?

N: Oh, really old things. Charlie Parker. Jack Teagarden. Lester Young. Ray Charles Trio. Obscure people—King Pleasure, Lord Buckley, Jon Hendricks.

K: You gave them back?

N: There wasn't much else I could do. He wouldn't explain. Then he borrowed my car to transport them. The son of a bitch. A few hours later they called me up and told me he was dead. He and the car both burned to the frame. The ruins of the record collection were in the trunk.

K: They didn't burn?

N: Oh, there was plastic soup everywhere. But these were rare; Norman had sprayed the jackets with preservative, and it turned out to be fireproof. The jackets weren't entirely destroyed.

K: So why aren't you sure he's dead?

N: The last thing he ever said to me was, 'Thanks for all the good times,' and then he left. I thought it was a little odd at the time. Like an exit line in a movie. Norman Maine goes for a little swim. So when I heard he'd crashed I thought the bastard had decided to use my car to suicide in. I'll tell you the truth, my initial reaction, I wanted to kill him. He could just as easily have jumped off the roof of his building. That little Chrysler cost me six months of Neuro Ward.

K: What changed your mind?

N: Little things at first. That plastic soup in the trunk had scraps of charred labels floating in it—and I happened to notice that one of the labels was from a ghastly laser disc one of his students had given him, worthless from any standpoint. That stuck in my mind. Later that day I let myself into his apartment, and I looked for the jacket to that record. It was gone. Then I noticed that there were too many empty spaces on the shelves. He'd had about twenty other rare records, in addition to the eight I returned—and there were many more than that missing. Maybe twice as many. And the *other* missing records were utterly ordinary, of no value.

K: So you figured he swapped jackets and tried a switched-package con? And maybe it blew up in his face?

N: Actually, I did think something of the sort. You're very quick. I almost went to the police, but...I decided not to.

K: Sure.

N: Then a day or two later I went back to work and the rumor was that some crazy intern had swiped a pauper's body from the morgue. Things like that go on all the time. One time...anyway, we all waited for a few days for the other shoe to drop—for the corpse to turn up nude in the ladies' room, or in Maternity, or fully clothed with a magazine on its lap in the lobby. Nothing happened. After a few days, just as everyone else was beginning to forget it, I happened to remember that the key ring I'd lent Norman that night had held *all* my keys.

K: Oh.

N: He knew that hospital as well as anyone. Better than some. Once, just after we were married, we...used to meet down in the morgue, in the small hours, and make love. Anyway. So I accessed the coroner's report on Norman, and tried to compare it to his X-rays and things.

K: Yeah?

N: I couldn't be sure. Not enough data. It might have been Norman that burned. It might have not been him. And I couldn't get more data without giving a reason. You can picture that: "You say you think your dead ex did *what?* He had a set of keys? You *gave* them to him?" Dentals would have sewn it up, but there were none on file for the burnt corpse and I didn't have access to Norman's.

K: Wow. What did you do?

N: I thought it over, and I went to see a policeman I knew. A Sergeant Amesby at Missing Persons. I met him when Madeleine vanished, a very good-looking man in an odd sort of way. He impressed me a good deal, and I trusted him. I brought my suspicions to him.

K: How'd it turn out?

N: He heard me out, and then he slapped his forehead and said something about a wild-goose chase. He called the front desk and asked if Norman had been in looking for him on the day he died, and they said yes. He pulled the file on Madeleine and nothing was missing. He frowned and thought for a while. All of a sudden he jumped out of his chair and yelled and dove at the wastebasket. I thought he'd gone bug. He took a used-up IBM typewriter ribbon out of it and began unreeling the ribbon on the floor and squinting at it. After a while he growled and unreeled more slowly.

K: You mean—?

N: Norman had used Amesby's typewriter to copy off some information from Maddy's file. Information about a man she'd worked with named Jacques LeBlanc.

K: Worked with where? Here or in Switzerland?

N: Switzerland. Not in her firm, some related group. Uh, Psytronics International, I think. Did I say something wrong? No? Well, Norman decided, for some reason, apparently, that this LeBlanc character was involved in Madeleine's disappearance.

K: I don't get it. Norman thought this guy had his sister

snatched. So he switched some records, snatched a stiff, and died?

N: This LeBlanc is apparently a very wealthy man. If Norman decided to go after him, he'd need a new identity, and untraceable cash. And some way to account for his own disappearance.

K: Jesus. That's brilliant. You're really smart.

N: Well, Sergeant Amesby did most of the deduction.

K: After you got him started. Your subconscious was smarter than his conscious. Well? What happened?

N: Well, Amesby cautioned me to keep quiet, of course, and said he'd check into it. A few days later he called up and said we were wrong. He'd checked dental records, and it was definitely Norman I had buried. He'd investigated LeBlanc, and positively cleared the man.

K: You didn't believe him.

N: (long pause) I didn't know. I still don't. He was very convincing. He offered to show me the dentals.

K: But you couldn't help wondering if maybe a phone call came down from on high: lay off the rich guy.

N: Exactly. You *are* quick.

K: (slyly) Not as quick as you were . . . an hour ago.

N: Oh! (pause) A tribute to your talent, darling. And your beauty.

K: Why, you sweet thing! (rustling sounds) Come here.

N: But—I—

K: Come on. A friendly freebee, okay? I've been on my own time for the last half hour. And you could use some cuddling.

N: I—

K: Couldn't you?

(sounds of embrace, wet slow kissing, whispering fabric)

N: Wait.

K: Uh? Are you kidding?

N: Wait. Before we . . . God, I'm inhibited. Verbally, I mean. Before you suck me off and make me crazy again, I want to see him. Meet your Joe, I mean. Then maybe I can get all this tangled old kharma out of my mind. May I?

K: In the morning, maybe?

N: Please, darling. I'll be able to relax better. I'll make it worth your while. (gasp) Oh! Not with money, I mean—I mean—damn my primness! What I *mean* to say is, I believe I could make *you* crazy—once I get this out of my system.

(rustles)

K: (groaning) Oh, you naughty bitch. All right, you've convinced me. Just a second while I—(rustles, sigh) There. Don't take long on this, now, you've got me all hot.

N: I won't, darling—

K: Mmmm, yes.

N: Stop, now. Say—won't Joe object to a freebee, as you put it?

K: Naw. I told you, he's more of a friend than a pimp. In fact, *I* got *him* into the business. Joe's a sweetheart. HEY, JOE!

I answered her second call. "Just a sec," I yelled. I drank more whiskey from the bottle. I turned the TV on, yanked out the earplug so they could hear me turn the set off, and joined them.

The room smelled of pot and of girl. It made me edgy. "I'm terribly sorry I frightened you, Miss . . ."

"Mrs. Kent," she murmured automatically. "God, this is fantastic! Oh—forgive me. You didn't frighten me, Joe. I frightened myself. Excuse me, but would you mind stepping over here into the light?"

"Sure." I moved closer. She rose and approached me.

"Fantastic," she said again. "I can see the differences now, but—Joe, I mistook you for my ex-husband. He's been dead for almost five years now, and you look remarkably like him. The corpse I saw could have been anyone, it was that bad. I mean, it was just barely possible—"

I looked astonished. "No wonder you keeled over. Uh . . . how close is the resemblance? Now that you can see me better."

"Startlingly close. I can see now that you couldn't possibly be him, of course. For one thing, you're much more than five years older than he was when he died. But you could be his older brother. Could you bend your head down?"

I did so.

"Fantastic. You both have scars on your scalps. Yours are

in different places, of course. His were from an old war wound."

"Mine are from a less official war."

"Could I ask you a terribly personal question?"

"You can try."

"Well . . . are you circumcised?"

An impulse uncommon to me made me answer truthfully. "Yes."

She nodded. "That settles *that* forever. Norman wasn't. And not for any reason can I imagine him disguising his penis with a knife. Not that it wasn't settled already, Joe . . . I just meant—"

"Look, Miz Kent—"

"Call me Lois, please."

I grinned. "Lois Kent? Like Mrs. Superman?"

She burst out laughing. "Now *that* settles it. Norman always said if he heard that joke one more time he was going to end up on Neuro with hysterical deafness. Thanks, Joe—you've put even my subconscious at rest."

We laughed with her. I made my excuses and left.

There was a chance that Karen might get something more from her. I went to the phone again.

Lois:—to bring this up without asking you about it first, but . . . is there some way I could persuade Joe to join us? It would be so much like a fantasy I've had.

Karen: (startled) Wow. Hey, I see what you mean. Sorry, honey—Joe doesn't go for girls.

L: Damn. What a shame. Uh . . . (long pause, rustle of clothing) Karen? Couldn't he be persuaded . . . well, to just watch? That'd be almost as—

K: Sorry, honey. I don't think so.

L: I just don't understand monosexuals. It just isn't *natural*.

K: Well, there you go. (pause) And there you go. And there . . .

I put the phone down. The room was very hot. I undressed and sat naked on my bed. Something was wrong with my stomach. I took a long gulp of whiskey and sat on the bed clutching my knees and shivered. The world closed in around me and shimmered. It was very much like a bad drug experience, too much strychnine in the acid, and that made it a little less scary. I found that if I concentrated, I could make the world shimmer at the same cyclic rate as my shivering. Somehow that helped.

After a few hundred years the door opened and Karen slipped in. She looked and smelled well used. "She's gone," she murmured, and found my whiskey. I began to calm down.

"I think I convinced her to keep her mouth shut, Joe—"

"Great. She won't tell more than fifteen other fems. I probably won't hear the story in a bar any sooner than the day after tomorrow."

She frowned but said nothing.

"I'm sorry, Karen. You done good. Weird little fem—maybe she will keep her mouth shut. It must be tough to be a gay nurse—or she wouldn't have had to come to you in the first place. Hell, she's probably wishing she'd kept her mouth shut herself, right now. You pumped her good, Karen."

"That's an awful pun, friend."

"Well . . ." I scratched my bare thighs.

"You want to talk about it now or later?"

I sighed. "Now. You caught the name of the outfit this LeBlanc character worked for?"

"Catch it? I thought I'd shit."

"Psytronics International. Our target. I wonder why there's no Jacques LeBlanc on our hit list?" I reached out, got the phone, and asked the computer. We watched the readout on the terminal together. "Retired, huh? Shortly after this Norman Kent business. Hey, look! Lives in Nova Scotia, by God. Where the hell is Phinney's? Aha. Fundy Shore. Maybe a hundred miles from here. Hey!" Something struck me. "Remember that old army buddy I told you about that used to live in Nova Scotia? The Bear?"

"Sure. You tried to look him up when you got here."

"Yeah. No joy. Maybe he never came home from the jolly green jungle. But he used to live not far from where this LeBlanc is supposed to be." I scowled. "The more I pick at this, the more it bleeds. And the worse it smells."

"Joe? You *can't* be Norman, right? No bells ring at all? Different scars, no foreskin?"

"None of those things are conclusive. You disguise scalp

scars with a skin graft that leaves new scars. Circumcision's a simple operation. There are just too fucking many coincidences. I look enough like Norman to fool his wife in fairly bright light. We both took head wounds in the war. We both like vintage jazz. We're both tricky—that switched-bodies scam was a beaut." I scowled again. I was uncomfortable; I slipped into tailor's seat. "And in the end, we may have both met our ends by trying to tackle Psytronics." I finished my drink. "I don't like this. If I am . . . if I used to be Norman Kent, then this Jacques has something that scares me to death. The world's first genuinely effective method of washing brains."

Karen was staring at the wall. "I can't think of anything that's more obscene."

"Neither can I. Until half an hour ago I would have said that was a meaningless word. But if what happened to me . . . was . . . was *done* to me, by a human being—"

She turned to me, and gasped. "Joe!"

I looked at her, followed her gaze.

I had a powerful erection.

I stared at it for a long time. It did not seem, did not feel, like a true part of me. Then as I watched, it started to. I was fascinated, repelled. It swayed rhythmically with my pulse, like an old tree in gale winds. I had the idiot impulse to throw my hands up and cry, Don't shoot.

Out of the corner of my eye I saw Karen's hand gingerly approaching, fingers forming the ancient shape—

"Leave it!"

She started at the volume and jerked her hand back.

We sat in silence for a while, watching the phenomenon together. Gradually, but steadily, it subsided. Each pulse raised it less than the last, until it was only the familiar flaccid appendage. After a while she rose and went to the door.

"Karen?" I called after her.

She turned.

"We're going to kill that motherfucker. You and I."

Slowly she nodded. "Yes. We are. Get some sleep."

She left, to sleep in her work-bed.

I found it surprisingly easy to take her advice.

9 ≡

1995 Virtually every inch of the Fundy Shore, Nova Scotia's northern coast, is stunningly beautiful at any time of day or year, under any weather conditions. But to sit on a sun-warmed rock at the high-tide line beside a brook that chuckles as it covers the last few meters to the Bay of Fundy, on the first really nice day in weeks—at sunset—is pure Beethoven. Norman had come down to the water's edge for a few minutes only, to pay his respects to the Bay before going about his business—more than an hour ago. The sun was almost down now, but he knew the light-show in the sky had a good half hour yet to run. And then the stars! And the moon! To one on the Fundy Shore, the world is mostly sky; no grander canvas exists anywhere on the planet's surface. Norman had been living without sky for too long, and could not tear himself away.

Nova Scotia winter is savage and merciless, and every year the same thing happens: spring, heeding the frantic prayers of the cabinbound, comes forth to do battle with winter *much* too early—about the end of January or early February—and is utterly destroyed within a week or two. Thaw, as the period is called, is a pleasant time, but subsequent to it, winter returns with redoubled ferocity and remains until about mid-June, when it suddenly gives way to summer without transition. Norman could not be sure, but it felt as though this were one of the last days of Thaw. Good reason to get up and resume the hunt, before the hammer came down and made everything more complicated.

Yet he could not get up. Norman Kent had not felt good in quite some time, and right now he felt very good. He had self-worth. He felt fast and tricky and lucky and dangerous. He remembered flashes of a similar feeling from eight years ago, from his earliest days as a grunt in Africa. But this was different, was better. This time he understood what he was fighting for, knew his enemy to be genuinely evil, this time he was a volunteer! The old skills were coming back, he could feel it. All the mad activity of the last several months had formed a kind of Basic Training, leaning him down and toughening him up, and with the return of good physical condition came muscle-memories of deadly games once taught him by weary old professionals and by clever enemies. He expected to die on this venture—but he was certain that Jacques would predecease him. Norman was even fairly sure that he could manage to persuade Jacques to answer a number of questions before dying.

At last he had drunk his fill of the place. He rose as the sun's last gleam winked out, stretched carefully, and clambered up over vast white driftwood mounds to the marsh flats and the road beyond. He made his way with care, for he did not know this ground; although he was in a beautiful spot, he was not in Paradise.

Norman's own getaway cabin *was* in Paradise. Its postal address was Rural Route 2, Paradise, Nova Scotia—although in fact it was situated well up over the North Mountain from that sleepy and well named little Annapolis Valley community. The cabin could be reached by foot, four-wheel drive, or horseback. It was heated by wood, powered by Canadian Tire solar collector and wood-alcohol combustion, had neither telephone nor television. Norman never considered going anywhere near it. It is said around the Valley that if a man breaks wind on

the North Mountain, noses will wrinkle on the South Mountain.
Norman was entirely too well known around Paradise, and even
if he had reached the cabin unobserved he could not have hidden
his chimney smoke.

Phinney's Cove, his target area, lay about twenty kilometers
west of his cabin, just inside the radius within which Norman
could reasonably expect to meet someone he knew along the
road, and thus come to the attention of the jungle drums. So
instead of hitching the North Shore routes, Norman had followed the province's *southern* coast, then taken 8 North past
Kejimkujik National Park and crossed the North Mountain at
Annapolis Royal, some fifteen klicks *west* of Phinney's Cove—
avoiding the region where he was known, and approaching
Jacques from the opposite direction. He was now on a part of
the shore called Delap's Cove.

But the fact that he was not known here did not mean that
he did not know anyone here. Civilization on the North Mountain is spread thin, scattered so widely that anyone who has
lived there for any length of time comes to know at least a few
people who live many klicks from his home. Norman had once
needed water found, and so he had come to know old Bert
Manchette.

He crossed the Shore Road (only the Tourist Bureau called
it "The Fundy Trail" anymore) and entered the woods. The
ground rose steadily before him; he was now climbing the gentle
slope of the Mountain's north face. Fifty yards in from the
road, well out of sight of passing traffic (perhaps one car per
hour), he found a distinctive stand of white birch. He stopped,
took two balled-up green plastic garbage sacks from his backpack, and shook them out. He removed a few hundred dollars
from his suitcase of cash, sealed the case with a combination
lock, and double-bagged it tightly against moisture. Then he
rammed it beneath a rotting deadfall and concealed it with dead
leaves and bark. He had marked the spot where he had entered
the woods; nonetheless, knowing from experience how hard it
can be to locate a particular patch of forest again, he used the
woodsman's knife that now hung at his hip to blaze a few of
the surrounding birch—about a meter *above* eye level, where
the scores might go unnoticed by another.

He continued on uphill. The sun was well and truly down

now, and the moon not yet risen; yet the darkness was far from total. The sky was clear, the branches naked overhead, and a city dweller might be astonished by the amount of starlight to be found in a forest. And Norman could hardly have gotten lost. The directions to Bert's were simple: proceed uphill until you strike the old overgrown road, then follow it east until you reach the ruins of the mill. Straight uphill from there half a klick to Bert's Ridge, and holloa the house from just outside buckshot range.

The walk gave rise to thoughts about eternity and entropy. Once this whole forest had been settled and populated. The overgrown trail Norman walked had once been a busy road, bustling with carts and buggies and wagons and hitched oxen and running children. Then, more than sixty years ago, for reasons Norman still did not fully understand, the Mountain community had died back. The people had all . . . gone away. Houses fell in upon themselves. Cultivated fields vanished under the alders. Nature, which had been literally driven away with a pitchfork a century before, had returned as the Roman maxim prophesied.

The region was actually less spooky by night than by day. The bones did not show—the occasional glimpse of foundation and sills in the undergrowth, the odd bottle-and-can heap, every so often an orange axe head or fitting or fastening slowly oxidizing on the ground. All of these were invisible in the dark, and Norman was able to keep mortality from the surface of his thoughts for some time. The air was inexpressibly clear and good, the smell of woods had all the subtle nuances of flavor of a truly great dessert, the earth was springy beneath his feet. Rotted leaves and branches and occasional unmelted patches of snow crunched under his boots, and the quality of the sound told him the true size of the room within which he walked. He was aware of distant deer avoiding him, and caught a brief glimpse of a weasel silhouetted against the sky.

Then Norman heard the sound of the stream that meant he was approaching the ruined sawmill, and he was reminded of all the ghosts that lived along this road.

He forced the thought from his mind. He drank from the stream with cupped hands, and took time to enjoy the almost forgotten taste of unchlorinated water. Then he left the stream, which cut sharply east, and struck straight uphill—giving the sawmill a wide berth.

Norman had spent enough time in jungles and woods to know how to move without undue noise—quietly enough to sneak up on a city man, certainly—but he made no effort to use his skill as he neared the Ridge. There was no telling when old Bert might take a notion to go grocery shopping, and Norman was walking through Bert's pantry. He even went so far as to whistle, to remove the possibility of being mistaken for a moose. No moose had walked the North Mountain for twenty years or more—but there was no telling how good Bert's memory was these days. If he still lived, of which Norman was certain only intuitively, he was a hundred and four years old.

Norman had never, in the dozen or so times he had visited old Bert, met another guest on the Ridge, and he knew Bert seldom left it. Nonetheless the old man knew everything that happened on the North or South Mountains (he paid only slight attention to "doings" in the more civilized Valley—or indeed, anywhere else on the planet). Most every mountain dweller at least knew of him; he was a fixture, an area landmark. Most people believed him to be half crazy—but no one laughed at his dowsing rod. The cost of having a well drilled ran upwards of thirty dollars a meter these days, and a man fool enough to sink a well without consulting Bert might easily rack up three or four thirty-meter dry holes before getting lucky. Enough money can make even the most cynical superstitious.

Five years ago, Norman had heeded the earnest counsel of his friend Bear, and told the men to drill where Bert said to drill. He had seen the drill-boss's face change when he gave the order, and so he had been prepared when they struck sweet water at four and a half meters. The next day Norman had fetched a bottle of good Cointreau up to Bert's Ridge, and stayed long enough to annoy hell out of Lois.

He smiled now as he replayed for perhaps the hundredth time the memory-tape of that first visit. He had come upon old Bert, ninety-nine years old then, chainsawing logs into stove-length behind his house—with bedroom slippers on his feet.

Norman had been told, by several different locals, that Bert was "some strange," but this seemed to call for comment. "Hey, Bert," he had hollered over the yatter of the big old Stihl saw, "didn't you ever hear of steel-toe boots?"

Bert had let the saw finish its cut, then throttled back to idle, thumbing the oil feed to lube the chain. Idling, the ancient Stihl sounded like a motorcycle with no muffler, but Bert's voice had carried over it easily. "Yuh. Tried dem once." He smiled evilly. "Dull too many blades."

V-rrrroooooooom, back to cutting—and how the logs had danced!

The moon was coming up as Norman reached the Ridge. From here one could catch glimpses of the Bay through the spruce and pine. The sky was clear enough for him to make out the faint ribbon of light which was the province of New Brunswick on the horizon. The sight tempted him to stop and gawk, but he kept walking. He was pleased at how little winded he was by the climb just past, feeling his second wind strong in his chest, eager to be about his business. Bert would not mind being kept up late, but it would be impolite. Wind from the south, from the Valley—shit, that probably meant snow by morning. Oh, well.

He was still whistling softly when he first saw the lights of Bert's house. An instant later the whistle chopped off and he stopped in midstride. A woman crying out in pain . . .

He shrugged the backpack off his shoulders and held it by its straps in his left hand; his right pulled the knife he had bought on Route 8. He used all his woodcraft now, approached Bert's house rapidly but without ever exposing himself needlessly to fire from any direction. His awareness of the world expanded spherically. The cries came clearer as he neared the house. Sounds like upstairs. Sounds young. Sounds like someone's beating hell out of her. Sounds like . . .

All at once Norman grabbed a maple and stopped. His eyes widened. He dropped pack and knife, slapped both hands over his mouth, and quaked. He dropped to his knees, then fell over on his side.

The cries intensified, built to one wrenching terminal shriek. Norman curled up in a ball and bit the heel of one fist while the other pounded the outside of his thigh. Even so, he could not completely stifle the sounds he made—but he did a creditable job. No one more than three meters away could have heard him laughing.

The smothered laughter was some time in passing. When he had his breath back, Norman sat up against the maple and tried to light a cigarette, but the giggles kept returning and it took him three matches. He smoked it down, then leaned back against the tree with his hands laced behind his head, and waited.

Presently the door of Bert's house opened and alcohol light spilled out. A girl no older than fifteen emerged, wearing jeans and a garment more collar than coat. "Go on now," Bert's voice came after her. "Your mudder be mad if you late on a school night."

"Screw her," the girl said boldly.

"Not in twenny years, more's de pity."

She laughed, blew him a kiss, and left. Norman watched her disappear into the forest, shaking his head and grinning.

Bert was still alive, all right.

In 1755 the British kicked the French the hell out of Nova Scotia. The few Acadians who survived and stayed were herded together, on the French Shore, a godforsaken stretch of the Fundy coast between Yarmouth and Digby, some fifty to a hundred and fifty klicks west of Bert's Ridge. The region is one of the proudest and most fiercely self-sufficient in the world. Norman had only driven through the French Shore— few Anglophiles are at home there—and so Bert was the only Acadian he had ever met. Nothing could make the old man divulge the reason he had left the French Shore so long ago.

But once in a while Norman believed he could guess.

When he was sure the girl was beyond earshot, Norman stood and called out Bert's name, then approached the house slowly. Bert came to the door at once. Mountain folk do not greet each other with "Hello," or "Hi, how are you?" The preferred greeting is an insulting commentary on whatever the greetee happens to be doing.

"Don't you ever poke yourself, Bert?"

Bert showed no surprise at finding Norman at his door, betrayed his pleasure only by the faintest of smiles. "How you mean?"

"Getting the diapers back on 'em afterwards."

The smile widened. "By de Jesus, dat's true. Worth it, dough. Come on in and set."

Norman came in, took off his boots, and sat. There was a small but elegant tea ritual, involving both kinds of tea (Bert grew his own marijuana), and a sharing of the Cointreau that Norman had fetched in his pack. The next step then would have been a swapping of lies, regarding what had happened to each of them since their last meeting. But Bert broke tradition.

"You got troubles, man?"

Norman took a deep breath. "Yes, Bert. I do."

"Taught so, by Jesus."

Norman sipped Cointreau before speaking again. "No reason to burden you with them. But I need your help."

"Yah?"

"Phinney's Cove, Bert. Two men and a woman, a few months ago. She was probably quite ill. Uh...woods around the house—and a stream hard by, that isn't fit to drink. At least one of the men is there now: Jacques LeBlanc. *Pas Acadien*. A Swiss. The only way I have of locating them is to ask Wayne down to the Hampton post office—and I mustn't let him, or anyone, so much as know I'm in the area."

Bert nodded. "Shoor. You supposed to be dead."

Norman stared. Bert had no radio, no TV, and the only newspapers he ever saw were donated firestarter, months old. Norman's "death" had taken place less than twenty-four hours before. The old man was uncanny.

"If anyone can help me, you can, Bert."

"Shoor. De old DeMarco place. Just past Lester and Beth's, hard by de fisherman's markers, you know? One man dere now, maybe de woman too, I dunno. Big place, used to be painted red, dere's a wreck out back used to be a goat shed. You want to sneak up on dem, you go through Lester's woodlot to de bog, den go right downhill when you reach de bust-up tractor. Watch out for a 'lectric fence."

A wave of relief spread over Norman. "Bert, you're a god-send."

"Some say. What else?"

"I want your outlaw gun, the one that isn't registered. And all the dynamite you can spare. A meal—I've been on the road since sunup—and a place to crash, I guess." Bert nodded imperturbably at each request. "Down by the road, by the little stream, there's a stand of white birch with my mark about a meter above eye level. You remember my mark?"

"I know de birches."

"Right. There's a suitcase buried there, combination lock. You remember my birthday?"

"Shoor. First of January—you never had a birthday party in your life. Forget de year, dough."

"Sixty-five. Dial the numbers and take whatever you think is fair for the gun and dynamite. Stash the rest, I may need it fast."

Bert nodded. "You look at the Bay before you come up?"

Norman's heart sank. "Oh, hell. Tell me." Bert could glance at the Bay and, from its color alone (he claimed), give you a weather forecast for the next week, more accurate than satellite tracking.

"In two hours hit begin to snow like a fucker. Snow mebbe two, tree days."

"Damn. Skip the crash, then, and I'll need that gun and at least a little dynamite right away."

"Eat first. Straighten you head."

"I can't, old friend. I have to scout *now*, before I'll leave tracks. I may be back around dawn, I may not."

Bert frowned but did not argue. He got up from his ancient rocker and left the house, returning with an ancient but impeccably maintained M-1 and a satchel. "Dynamite, detonators, fuses, ammo for de gun. We ever get time for a proper drunk, you and me?"

Norman hesitated, then answered honestly. "I don't think so, Bert. I don't expect to live through this."

Bert frowned again. "Like I taught. De lady, she be your sister, eh?"

"I think so. I hope so." He took the gun and satchel, got his pack, and headed for the door. "Thanks, Bert. Thanks more than I can say. I should have come here months ago."

"No," Bert said surprisingly. "No, you wasn't ready den.

You ready now. You always was a good boy, Norman."

Norman found that his eyes stung. He reached the door and put his boots back on. "Hey, Bert," he said as he straightened. "I always heard that as a man gets older, his interest in the ladies kind of diminishes. They say sooner or later it goes away altogether. You think there's any truth in that?"

"Aw, shoor," Bert replied at once. "God's troot, by de Jesus." He relit his pipe full of homegrown. "You first notice it come on, oh . . ." He paused reflectively. ". . . oh, about ten minutes after dey lay you in de ground."

Norman laughed. "Thanks again, Bert." He shouldered his gear and left at once.

Bert called after him. "Hey, Norman—catch!" Norman saw something sail at him against the door light, stuck up his free hand, and caught it. It was a large hunk of ham. He smiled toward Bert's silhouette in the doorway, and chewed off a piece.

"Bon chance," the old man called. "Be careful, Norman."

Norman took the advice to heart. The gathering clouds over-head made him risk a hitch up to Phinney's Cove, but once in that region he stopped being in a hurry. He finished the ham, and drank from one of the many streams that seek the Bay. He took to the trees on foot, following Bert's directions, and moved as cautiously as he knew how. He spotted the electric fence in plenty of time, cleared it with practiced skill. Half a klick farther downhill he located, identified, and passed a sleeping guard. He was expecting an infrared scanner; he moved as a deer would move, walked where a deer would walk. He did it very well; he was actually in sight of the house before they bagged him.

Suddenly he was very very happy.

10 ≡

1999 Perhaps a cockroach cleared its throat. I woke up on my feet, in streetfighter's crouch, hands and feet prepared to kill the first thing that moved. A few seconds passed. I tried to laugh at myself, but the sound frightened me even more. I made myself sit on the floor and breathe deeply and slowly. Soon I was calm enough to notice how much my neck hurt. I decided that was all the improvement I could stand and left the bedroom.

The door to the medicine cabinet stood ajar. While I was urinating I caught sight of my face in the mirror. It didn't look any more familiar than ever. "Hi, Norman," I said to it. It said the same thing to me. Only one voice heard. Conclusion unmistakable. Shake it and flush, let's us both go have breakfast.

Karen was waiting for me. She had started the coffee. She knew better than to attempt breakfast herself. I mixed up things while the coffee finished dripping, drank some while I cooked.

She had the table ready when the food was. We ate. She was halfway through her cigarette when she broke the silence.

"Okay, let's break it down. What do we know for sure, what do we guess, what do we propose?"

I nodded approvingly. "Good. Okay, known for sure..." I paused. "Not much."

"We know you look like a man named—"

"No, we don't."

"But—oh. I see."

"Right. Who vouches for Lois Kent? What evidence did she offer?"

"Um. None at all."

"So known for sure is: we are in Halifax, drawing a bead on Psytronics Int. A woman has alleged that I look a lot, but not completely, like her ex-husband. In support of this proposition she offers a detailed circumstantial account that she says convinces her that I am not this gent, but which makes *us* suspect that I might be. Her story is checkable on several major points, so before we go any further, let's check it out. The whole story could be some kind of ploy by PsyInt, to set us up for something."

"Okay."

I suppose I could have used my terminal. But I was feeling paranoid; we took a bus to the library.

The newspaper morgue backed Lois Kent on the disappearance of her ex-sister-in-law and the spectacular fiery death of her ex-husband. There was a picture of the deceased English teacher. He looked like me—but like me ten or fifteen years younger than I looked now, rather than three or four. The sister had indeed worked for a company in Switzerland, and shortly before she left it, it had been absorbed by the Swiss wireheading outfit that I suspected of being secretly allied to Psytronics International. There was an extraordinary amount of followup for a missing-persons case, even a beautiful female one. Norman Kent must have been industrious.

What tore it were the photos of Madeleine Kent.

I knew her. That is, I had known her. She was the grownup version of the sister I dimly remembered from my childhood but could not name.

"She's different," I told Karen. "She looks like she grew up into a nicer person than I remember. But most kids do. That's my big sister."

"Does the name Madeleine—or Maddy—ring a bell?"

"Not at all. But I do have a vague recollection that my sister went away somewhere when I was in college, and I guess it could have been Switzerland. Let's see . . . assuming Norman's birthday is mine . . . yep, dates match."

"Let's get out of here."

"In a minute."

I found a sound-only pay phone and called the city police. I asked the desk man for Missing Persons. Shortly a voice said, "Missing Persons, Amesby."

"Never mind, Officer—he just came in the door. Bobby, *where* have you been?" I hung up. Another detail of the nurse's story confirmed: there was a Missing Persons cop named Amesby.

"*Now* let's get out of here."

We walked to Citadel Hill. It is an amazing monument to the thought processes of generals. I'd read the brochure while dealing dope there. The Citadel—the first Citadel—was built by the British Army in 1749, to protect settlers from Indian attack. Nineteen days after its completion, a group of woodcutters were attacked and killed by Indians under its guns. For some reason the settlers had refused to help in its construction. It was completely torn down and rebuilt three times in the next century, in response to the threats of the American Revolution, Napoleon, and the War of 1812, and each rebuilding was obsolete well before completion. There has never been a day on which it was not obsolete. No shot was ever fired in anger by or at any of the four Citadels. Haligonians are fiercely proud of this boondoggle, which cost hundreds of thousands of pounds. They say it was an important base for the subjugation of Quebec—but *was* Quebec subjugated? During World War I, it was a detention camp for radicals and other suspicious types. Leon Trotsky is said—falsely—to have done time there. It has been a tourist trap for over forty years. High-rises block its view of the harbor.

Perhaps I'm being harsh. Halifax is a splendid port, and no

invader ever so much as tried to take it. Was that *because* of the Citadel? You tell me.

But you can still see water and sky from there. The entire Halifax Peninsula is laid out around you, the best view in town. The obsolete fort, crumbling in the sun, whispers of entropy and Herculean labor wasted. It is a good spot for thinking.

Karen and I used it so.

That early on a workday, it was almost deserted. We walked around to the southeast section, closed off for repairs, and found that completely deserted. There was heavy construction equipment here and there, but a strike had kept all the workers home. By our standards it was chilly for August, but not intolerably. The breeze was surprisingly light for such an exposed location. Nonetheless, I shivered as I thought.

After ten minutes I was done thinking.

A deep trench encircles the Citadel. It is perhaps twenty feet deep and thirty across. It prevents access except by the gate on the east or harbor side, and provides a breastwork around the fort, which, like everything else, was obsolete before completion. We were sitting a few yards from the trench. On the far side an iron staircase gave access from the floor of the trench to a sally port in the side of the Citadel proper. I nudged Karen, got up, and went to the trench. Fifteen feet below me, a construction flatbed of some kind stood abandoned. I lay down on my stomach and swung my legs over the stone lip of the trench.

"Joe, what—"

I shushed her. I lowered myself in stages until I was hanging from the edge by my hands. There were footholds in the stone block wall that any spider would have found more than adequate. I glanced down, kicked slightly away from the wall, and let go. I landed well, and waved her to join me, holding a finger to my lips for silence.

Shaking her head, she followed my example. She also landed well. We got down from the flatbed and sat cross-legged on the ground facing each other.

"This strikes me as a hard spot to mike from a distance," I said.

"Oh. Good thinking. And we can go up those stairs to the inside and out the main gate."

"So let's talk."

"Joe—me first, okay?"

"Go ahead."

"I think we should go back to New York, right away."

"Karen—"

"Let me finish! The evidence says that you already took on this Jacques LeBlanc once—and lost. Pretty decisively. I can find something else to do with my life."

"The man who took on LeBlanc five years ago is dead. I am not him. And I carry none of the excess baggage—broken marriage, kidnapped sister—that he had." I chucked her under the chin. "Plus, he didn't have *you*. Or anybody."

"Then you think we may have a chance?"

"Not for a second. We're dead; question of when."

She didn't flinch. "Not even if we cut and run?"

"Much too late. *Think* about it, baby. Visualize the enemy. If he can erase specific memories, no *wonder* the power flow in the wireheading industry has no relation to the money flow! What the fuck would Jacques want with money? If he can scrub brains, suck memories, what is there that he cannot do? We are to him as bacilli to a whale."

"So maybe he'll overlook us."

"You're still not thinking. If I am—if I was once Norman Kent, *whose computer is that down in New York?*"

Now she flinched. "Oh, my sweet . . . and you recorded that whole scene with Lois . . ."

"Yeah. The really surprising thing is that we woke up this morning. And are breathing now. We're blown, baby."

"Maybe he's not monitoring—maybe we've got some time!"

"Unlikely. But it's hard to argue with the fact that we're alive. But we can't have *much* time."

"So what's our next move?"

"All-out attack. Crazed-wolverine style. Get out of here, clout a good car, run out to Phinney's Cove. Fake it from there. Maybe turn the car into a bomb and run it through his kitchen. Maybe stick up the nearest Mountie detachment for some automatic weapons. Christ, I wish I had an atom bomb. I wish I'd brought more ammo when I left the house this morning. I wish I hadn't paid the rent last week, I'm never going to see the place again. Well, let's—"

"Joe—something we ought to do first."

"Yeah?"

"Make a record of everything we know."

"What, for leverage on Jacques? To warn the world? Don't you und—"

"No, no, for *us*."

"Huh?"

"Look, the evidence says, anyway suggests, that Jacques doesn't kill. Doesn't kill bodies, I mean. He doesn't need to; he's the mindkiller. Suppose he follows his pattern: wipes our brains and turns us loose. And then we find a record we left for ourselves . . . get it? He can't steal all our memories if we stash a few. Maybe two or three tries from now we kill him."

"No."

"But—"

"One: no time. It'd take too long to write out even the basics, we're not holding enough cash for a tapedeck, and there's no time to steal one. Two: where would we leave the record? Three: when the mindkiller gets us, he opens up our brains and finds out where we left the record. Let's get moving."

"You're right. Maybe we'll get one clear shot before we go down."

Someone yanked the sun across the sky.

Shadows leaped, and froze where they landed. The breeze changed direction and speed radically. The temperature dropped a couple of Celsius degrees in an instant. Internal changes were subtler but no less perceptible. My folded legs were suddenly stiffer. My mouth tasted slightly different. An exhalation was suddenly an inhalation. My breakfast was slightly farther along my gut.

The oddest part was the absence of terror. A parallel example *should* have been an earthquake. Humans require constant sensory reassurance of reality. When the solid earth dances and a thousand dogs howl, when the evidence of your senses is suddenly placed in doubt, you experience primeval terror. I received, in a single instant, a number of sensory reports that were simply impossible—and the terror did not come. I seemed to be too exhausted to be terrified, as though all my strength had fled from me in that same instant. Karen was gaping at me, clearly as stunned as I.

"What—" I croaked.

And then I got it. It was as well that I was too exhausted for terror, or my heart might have exploded then.

There is an old Zen conundrum: if a tree falls and no one is there to hear it, does it make a sound? Here is a related question: if a man's brain is awake, but his memories are not allowed to form, is he conscious? Does he, in fact, exist?

My (hiatus)es usually averaged five to ten seconds in duration, with fuzzy edges, like a sloppy job of record-muting. This one had lasted at least ten minutes, and it was a clean splice. This one had not been preprogrammed. This one had come from the source. Jacques, or an agent of his, had shut off our minds from a distance.

"Joe, God oh God Joe, God—"

She was staring at the ground between us.

A folded piece of eight-and-a-half-by-eleven paper lay there. Excellent paper, a heavy linen parchment, cream-colored. The typing on it was executive face, quite neat and centered. It read:

I request the pleasure of your company this evening at my country retreat. Ask for the Old DeMarco Place. Dress informal; weapons optional. I promise to give you both at least temporary possession of any information you desire.

—J.

It was unsigned.

My hands went instinctively to my weapons. They were in place. I looked around, pulled the gun, confirmed that it was loaded and live, and put it away. We both got stiffly to our feet. I tucked the letter into my shirt pocket.

"Well," I said.

Karen could not speak. She trembled just perceptibly.

"Hoy," came a voice from above our heads.

I jumped a clear foot in the air, came down with one arm

around Karen. I never even tried to go for the gun. Just for her. We gaped upward together.

A uniformed security guard stood at the edge above, looking down at us with detached interest. I was glad I hadn't tried for my gun. All the Citadel guards are experienced war veterans. He seemed vaguely relieved. He looked quite tidy and dapper, and when he spoke his accent said that he was British by birth, of cultured origins, and had a sense of humor about his job. His left sleeve was pinned up to the shoulder.

"You two seem on friendly enough terms."

Instinct came to my rescue. Agree with the nice policeman. "We are."

"What was all that screaming about a minute ago, then? Two screams, one from each of you. Sounded like black murder being done; I heard you both all the way over in the North Ravelin. You haven't murdered anyone, have you?"

Lie. "Yes."

He raised an eyebrow. "Really?"

"My father. Well, actually, my primal rage at my father. You're familiar with Janov's work?"

"Can't say I think much of it. Particularly in urban areas." He turned his gaze to Karen. "I suppose *your* father—"

"—makes his look like the Easter Bunny," Karen said. Her voice sounded okay. It held the ring of sincerity.

"I suppose you know you're not permitted to be down there, primal screaming or otherwise?"

"We're just leaving," Karen said.

"Splendid. I'll just meet you round at the Main Gate and see you both safely on your way home."

He didn't buy our story for a minute, but there was little he could do. He checked our ID. I always buy good ID. It's worth the extra money. He arched his brow at me a few times, admired Karen's ass, and let us go.

There seemed no reason to go back to the apartment. At a supermarket I bought ammo, food, and common household items with which I could make a cottage-industry bomb capable of converting a cottage into splinters. I got lucky, stole a four-wheel-drive with real muscle and a rifle behind the seat. Neither of us was hungry, but we ate anyway, and then hit the highway.

It was sundown as we left the city behind.

About ten miles farther on, I pulled over at a place that was wall-to-wall forest. We walked a ways into the woods. We both sighted in the rifle and practiced with it a bit. Our unknown benefactor had bequeathed us two full boxes of slugs. The rifle was a thirty-oh-six with good action. It threw high and to the left. Karen, an indifferent pistol marksman, turned out to be damn good with a rifle. We got back in the truck and drove on.

Neither one of us had had a thing to say since we had left the Citadel, barring short functional sentences. There seemed nothing to say. As we were passing Wolfville, after an hour of silence, I thought of something, and said it.

"I'm sorry I got you into this, baby."

Karen jumped. "Christ!"

"What?" The truck swerved.

"That's *spooky*, man. I was just opening my mouth to say those identical words to you."

"To *me?*" I growled. "What—"

"Yeah," she snapped back. "To you. I'm sorry I got you into this."

"I was into this before I ever laid eyes on—"

"Well, if I hadn't dragged you into this wirehead scam—"

"If I hadn't spoiled a perfectly good suicide—"

"Dammit—"

She stopped, and I stopped, and there was a pause, and then we both broke up. I laughed so hard I had to pull over and put it in park. We held each other awkwardly in the cramped cab and laughed on each other's shoulders.

After an immeasurable time I heard her voice in my ear. "Don't be sorry, Joe."

"You either. I might have lived out my life in New York, never knowing the Mindkiller *existed*. I might have died never knowing what my mother called me. Now at least I'm going to get some answers before I die." ("Again," I did not add.)

"I'm satisfied too. I told you once I want it should be a shame that I died. Well, if I go down before I get to shoot that mother-fucker in the belly, it'll be the dirtiest shame I ever heard of."

"That it will."

"What do you suppose his game is?"

"Power. What else? As long as he can snip sections out of memory-tape, and keep a monopoly on the secret, he's God. And it looks like he can keep a monopoly on the secret. It's that kind of secret. It has to have something to do with wireheading; remember the joint that blew up just before we left New York, and the inductance patent that wasn't in the files?"

"Sure. Inductance—that means wireheading at a distance, right? Jacques—or his agent—used some kind of wirehead field to keep us docile while he picked our brains and left us his invitation. That's why that guard heard us screaming on Citadel Hill. I bet I screamed first. And loudest." She sat up and lit a cigarette. "Do you know," she said, dragging deeply, "that there is a part of me that can't wait to get to Phinney's Cove and get another dose of the juice? Even if I don't get to keep the memory?"

I shuddered slightly. I wanted to say something to break the silence, but nothing came. I listened to the engine idling in the cool evening. I rolled down the window to let her smoke out, and heard some kind of mournful bird call. I wondered if that was an owl.

"Karen? I . . ." It wouldn't come out right. "I'm—I'm glad I've known you."

She didn't react at once. She took two more drags on her smoke, then stubbed it out and turned to face me. "I love you too, Joe."

We embraced again.

"Maybe," she said a while later, "he'll turn us loose together . . ."

"No!" I said sharply, and disengaged.

"Huh?"

"Don't think that way. Don't let there be any favor he can do for us, any boon he can grant, any hold over us. I love you and in a couple of hours we're going to die and that's the end of it."

She thought. "Yeah. You're right. God, I wish I could make it with you just once."

I kept my voice even. "Karen, I accept the compliment, and

in theory I agree. But the thought makes me twitchy."

"That's cool," she said at once. "I . . . I think I kind of know exactly what you mean. I used to feel that way when I was with someone I loved."

"I think I could make *you* come."

"Yeah," she agreed. "But don't. Let's drive."

I put the van in gear.

We took the main highway all the way through the Annapolis Valley to Bridgetown, then drove up over an immense mountain. The road resembled headphone cable hanging from the ceiling, an endless upward zigzag. I was glad I'd stolen a good vehicle. Despite the extreme hairiness of the road, we were twice overtaken and passed on blind curves by farmers in battered pickups. Just after the second one yanked in front of us, a half-ton loaded to the gunwales with hardwood appeared round that blind curve, plunging downhill at terrifying speed. Its driver and the driver of the pickup waved to each other as they passed.

Eventually the road yanked around one last vicious bend and leveled out. It stayed level for a good two hundred yards, then began sloping down. About the time that the Bay of Fundy became visible below us in the moonlight, demanding our attention, the slope suddenly became drastic. I had my hands full there for a while. Then the road went into rollercoaster dips and rises for a bit before settling down to a last long downward plunge. There was a stop sign at the bottom of it. I never considered obeying it, but I was very disconcerted to learn that the road turned into gravel just past the stop sign. We damn near went into a ditch.

I got us heading west on the Fundy Trail. It was a lovely drive by moonlight and must have been stunning by day. I drank it in thirstily—and almost succumbed to the road's last crafty attempt to kill us, with a blind curve/vertical drop/vertical ascent/blind curve pattern that must have afforded the locals much amusement in the tourist season.

A brief flurry of relatively modern houses—say, twenty-five to forty years old—called Hampton, then almost at once we were in farmer and fisherman country. Big spreads, houses well over a hundred years old and widely spaced. Some were kept up, many were hulks. Some had as many as a couple of dozen junked cars scattered around them. All the ones that looked inhabited had a woodpile and a garden. I saw outhouses. Barns. Fishing nets and traps. Great fields of hay and corn. I nearly hit a deer. The Bay was never more than two hundred yards to our right, sometimes as close as a hundred feet. There was no other traffic, and no one walking the road. Most of the inhabitable homes had few or no lights showing—folks went to bed early hereabouts. I began to wonder how we would find the "Old DeMarco Place."

Just then the headlights picked up a pedestrian, walking in our direction. I pulled up past him and waited.

In the moonlight he looked two hundred years old. He wore a disreputable woodsman's cap and carried some kind of odd stick in his hand. Stick and hand were equally gnarled.

"Excuse me, sir," I said, and he came to the window.

"'Allo," he said. Up close his face had so many wrinkles as to preclude expression of any kind. He was two hundred and fifty if he was a day.

"We're looking for the old DeMarco Place."

"Oh, shoor," he said. His breath smelled of whiskey. "Hit be up the road some." He gestured with his stick, and I realized with faint amusement that it was a dowsing rod. "Mebbe two, tree k'lometer. You been dere before?"

"No. How'll I know it?"

"You got paper, I draw you a map."

"Are you going that far?" Karen asked.

"A little ways past."

"Can we give you a lift?"

"Shoor ting."

He was slow getting in on her side. In the sudden overhead light he looked two hundred and seventy-five. He studied Karen and me dispassionately, and showed us a smile comprising three teeth. We drove on.

"What're those?" Karen asked, pointing to what looked like three tall billboards, facing the Bay in a row, two to our left and one to our right. The two we could see had large, simple designs painted on them.

"Navigation markers for de fishermen. Line dem tree up, you know just where you are."

"What do they do when the fog rolls in?" I asked.

"Navigate by potato."

"Beg pardon?"

"You keep a bunch of potatoes on de bow. Every couple minutes, you t'row one over de bow. If you don't hear no splash—*turn*."

Karen and I chuckled politely.

"Dere," he said after some time, pointing. A mailbox with no name marked the beginning of a rude mud-rutted path that disappeared into the woods on the left. "You follow dat up a k'lometer or so, you be dere. Tanks for de ride." He got out.

As he walked on up the road, I turned to Karen. "This is it."

She nodded.

I drove just far enough up that trail to be out of sight of the road. I turned the vehicle around to face the road. I shut it down and arranged the ignition wires so that it could be jump-started again in a hurry.

We sat a moment in silence. My window was down. I smelled fresh sweet country smells I was too ignorant to identify. I heard night creatures I could not name, small things. A car went by on the road. Tall grasses and trees whispered. I felt a sensation I remembered from Africa. An eerie, unreasoning certainty. Someone or something had a dead bead on my head. It might be a sniper with nightscope, or a heat-seeking laser, or a small dark man with a blowgun, or an ICBM silo a hundred miles away, but I was standing on the spot marked X.

Karen lit a smoke. "We're targets, aren't we?"

"We're naked. Scanned, X-rayed, doppler ultrasounded, and the contents of our pockets inventoried. You feel it too?"

"Yeah. Was it like this in the war?"

"No. This is worse."

"I thought it was. Let's not bother with weapons. They're cumbersome."

"He said they were optional."

We got out of the van, leaving the firearms in it. I got out both of my knives and the sap and tossed them onto the front seat. Karen added items, then came around to my side.

We looked uphill. The road curved up into forest. She took my hand and we walked. After a few thousand yards the woods gave way to an immense cleared field, perhaps twenty acres, most of it waist-high in hay. At the far edge, where the land turned back into forest and began climbing again, stood a house. It was a big three-story with four chimneys, two of them in use. There were lights on in the ground floor, and a spotlight illuminating a yard on the right. A jeep, a four-wheel like ours, and a Jensen Interceptor were parked in the light. There were two outbuildings. A barn the size of my New York warehouse home stood to the right of the house, and a smaller building lay to the right of that. No people or defensive structures were in evidence anywhere, not so much as a chain-link fence.

The moon was high above the mountain. It made the scene as pretty as a postcard, and would make us tabletop targets all the way to the house. The hay had been cut back on either side of the path.

"Nice spot," Karen said, and we kept walking.

After a while we became aware of how much sky there was here. I could not remember the last time my world had held so much sky. I looked up, and stopped walking, momentarily stunned. Karen kept on a few paces, then turned and followed my gaze. *"Oh."*

I had forgotten God made so many stars.

We watched them for a few minutes together—until the temptation to lie down on our backs and watch them forever became acute. Then I dropped my eyes, and saw Karen drop hers. We looked at each other, sharing the wonder.

"Been a long time," she said softly.

I nodded. "First time I ever shared it."

I put my arm around her and we continued on.

The house looked a hundred years old and poorly kept up. It had no door facing the Bay, but several windows, one of them gigantic. We went around to the lighted side and found the door. It had a brass knocker. I used it. The door opened and the Fader smiled at me.

"Hi, Joe."

"Hello, Jacques. You remember my friend Karen."

"Enchanted, my dear. Please, both of you, come in and make yourselves comfortable."

11 ▦

1995 Norman Kent no longer wished he could die. He had stopped wishing that hours ago. What he wished now was that he could *have* died, many months previously.

Preferably at the moment when he had stood on the edge of the MacDonald Bridge, ready to jump. When his biggest problems had been a failed marriage and disgust for his chosen work. When his death would have meant no more than the end of his life.

That had been his last golden opportunity, and he had thrown it away for a hat. A half hour after that, Madeleine had come back, so briefly, into his life, and started him on the treadmill that led to this place and this time.

This time was late evening. This place was the most beautiful, luxurious, and comfortable cell imaginable.

The clock, for instance, which apprised him of the time,

was a world standard chronograph of Swiss-Japanese manufacture, simple, elegant, and utterly accurate. The light by which he saw both clock and room was artfully muted and placed so as to complement the room. The furnishings—chairs, desk, shelves, tables, bar, tape system—were quite expensive and exquisitely tasteful. (The bar had not functioned since his arrival; he was on limited fluid intake.) The books lining the shelves were, in his professional judgment, impeccable. So were the audio- and videotapes. The bed in which he reclined was a rich man's powered bed, a distant and highly evolved descendant of the hospital bed. The large bay window to his left offered a stupendous view of the Bay of Fundy and a cloud-strewn sky, the faint glow of distant New Brunswick serving to hold them apart.

It was very nearly the ideal room. Only two things were immediately apparent as odd about it. First, that such a triumph of wealth and leisure should exist in the most rural part of a rural province, on the third floor of a one-hundred-and-fifty-year-old house that seemed, from the outside, quite ramshackle. Second, that a room so carefully appointed should lack any telephone equipment whatsoever.

That omission, and the fact that the bay window was shatterproof, and the fact that the door would not open at Norman's will, made it a cell.

It contained means of suicide in abundance. But Norman could not bring himself to use them. He knew that his end was coming soon enough, and he knew that it would be more painful, and more horrible, than anything he could devise himself. It was interesting to learn that he was more afraid of pain than of horror. It was the latest in a series of unendurably interesting learnings, and he knew it was not—quite—the last.

The door slid open.

He lay motionless, head still turned toward the window, but he stopped seeing the Bay.

"It has been twenty-four hours, Norman. I must ask for your answer."

Norman turned his head slowly. He marveled again at the absolute nondescriptness of Jacques LeBlanc. The man could have been a fisherman or a night watchman or a bank teller or a member of Parliament. An actor would have killed for his face; he could play any part simply by dressing for it and altering his accent. On any street in the world, from the Bowery to Beverly Hills, from the Reeperbahn to the River Ganges, he could pass unnoticed unless he chose to draw attention to himself. For some reason the eye wanted to subtract him.

"Why ask," Norman said, "when you can fucking well *take* it?"

Jacques's face remained impassive. "Because I prefer to ask."

Norman considered lying. The lie could not survive longer than ten minutes—but it might not need to. If he could convince Jacques, just long enough to lull the man into a moment's unwariness, he might get a single chance to...

But Jacques understood that, and the object in his hand said that even the attempt would be pointless.

Norman answered honestly. "I'm against you. With my whole heart. I think you're the greatest madman the world has ever seen, and if I could kill you now I would, whatever it cost me."

Jacques nodded gravely. "I expected as much. I hope you are wrong. Goodbye, Norman."

And he activated the thing in his hand, and Norman Kent became ecstatic.

When Jacques turned on his heel and left the room, the ecstasy went with him, and Norman Kent followed it. Doggedly. Mindlessly. Urgently. And, since his legs were adequate to the task of keeping up with ecstasy, happily.

Jacques led him downstairs, and through a living room that made Norman's cell look like servants' quarters. Jacques activated an instrument board against one wall. "Make sure the area is not under observation," he muttered to himself, summoning up reports from various security installations. Shortly he needed both hands. He put the device that was the source of Norman's ecstasy down on an end table, then met Norman's eyes. "If you touch this," he said, "it will stop working."

Norman more than half believed that Jacques was lying. But he did not dare take the chance. He waited patiently while Jacques monitored the electromagnetic spectrum for Heisenbergian observers who might seek to interact with him by the process of observation.

None was apparent. Jacques cleared the screen and retrieved his ecstasy generator. He put on a coat, and made Norman put on his own. He opened the front door onto a combination woodshed/vestibule, which only a very discerning eye would have realized was also a serviceable airlock. He led Norman into it and thence to the world outside.

It was very cold now. Norman laughed and wept with joy at the sight of snow falling from the sky. He watched individual snowflakes as he followed Jacques, for he did not need eyes to follow the ecstasy. Then he tripped over a chopping block and roared with laughter. The laughter changed in an instant to a bleat of terror as he felt happiness slipping away, and from then on he used his eyes to help him follow his perfect master.

They walked past the larger of the two outbuildings, which seemed to be a barn, to the second one, which Norman had taken for some kind of workshop. The rustic, poorly hung door, which fastened with a piece of wood spinning around a nail in the jamb, revealed behind it a more substantial door with a Yale lock. Jacques used a key in that lock, then knocked two bars of "Take Five" and said, "Open." The door gave way and both men stepped through it.

They left their coats and snowy boots in an anteroom that Norman did not bother to examine. It gave onto a room that strongly resembled an operating theater. There were six fully equipped tables, but no surgeon or support team visible.

Jacques set down the ecstasy generator. Norman stopped in his tracks. "Sit down, please," Jacques said, pointing to a table. Norman complied at once, anxious that no thought or deed of his should offend the lord, from whom all blessings flowed. Jacques touched an intercom. "Come," he said.

Two people entered the room, gowned, gloved, and masked in white. Norman became slightly uneasy, but relaxed when he saw that they were as loyal to the master as he.

"Prepare him," Jacques said, and left the room. An air conditioner clicked on as the door closed.

The two undressed Norman with efficient skill. He experienced orgasm as they removed his trousers and shorts. The only reaction they displayed was to clean him carefully with disinfectant-impregnated toweling. They helped him to lie down, and arranged his head on a complicated cradle. He felt supremely comfortable, and grateful that his ending place had been so thoughtfully prepared for him. They strapped him down at ankles, thighs, waist, wrists, biceps, and head. The head straps were complex and kept his skull immobile. The shorter of the two attendants carefully shaved Norman's head to the scalp, then painted that with disinfectant. When this was done, the taller one caused the table to "kneel" at one end, so that Norman's cranium was raised to working height and conveniently deployed. The shorter one rolled a large, ungainly machine from the wall to a place near the table, and began separating and arraying a series of leads from the machine for easy access. On Norman's other side, the tall one prepared instruments of neurosurgery.

Visualizing his death in nuts-and-bolts detail for the first time, Norman came again. A catheter accepted his ejaculate.

Jacques reentered the room. He too was surgically clothed now. Without a word he took up a tool and laid open Norman's scalp.

It felt wonderful. It felt exciting and holy. The sensations of craniotomy were nuggets of joy, and when the living brain had been laid bare and the first probes inserted, Norman was slightly disappointed to learn that there was no such extra surge of pleasure; for the brain cannot feel.

The mind, however, can, and there was indeed some small place deep within Norman's gibbering mind that was horrified by everything that was being done to him, something that strove to fight ecstasy.

But the thrill of horror outweighed the horror; that small portion of his mind was like a single ensign in a battleship full of mutineers, trapped in the paint locker.

Then the first probe reached his medial forebrain bundle, and it was as if all the ecstasy *clicked* into focus for the first time. This was perfection, this was Nirvana. He orgasmed a third time. As an ejaculation it was insignificant, but subjectively it was the fiery birth of the macrocosmic universe; his consciousness fled at lightspeed in all directions at once.

From now on, his body would have an instinctive, mindless revulsion for ecstasy.

It was several hours before Jacques required him to be conscious. Bliss gave way to pleasure, then to simple euphoria and a dreamy, slow awareness of his surroundings. What a *nice* dream that had been. And how nice to find Jacques here upon awakening. It was going to be a *fine* day.

"Hi, Jacques."

"Hello. Listen to me. I must engage your subconscious mind as well, so listen to me. If you evade my questions, if you stop listening to my voice, I will take the pleasure away. Ah, I see that you understand. Good. Listen to my voice. What is your name?"

The ensign in the paint locker knew what would happen, watched hopelessly as it happened. Your magic carpet will perform flawlessly as long as you do not think of a blue camel. Norman Kent's name leaped into his mind, in response to the question—and vanished.

It was not simply the name itself that vanished. With it went the associations and mnemonics keyed to it in his memory. Jokes from childhood about Superman, jokes from adolescence about the Norman Conquest, jokes from the jungle about the Norman DeInvasion. An old Simon Templar novel he had read many years ago, and remembered all his life because it featured a hero named Norman Kent, who laid down his life for his friends. Certain times when the speaking of his name had been a memorable event. The sight of his dogtags. The nameplate on the desk in his office at the University. His face in the mirror.

If you take a hologram of the word "love" and try to read a page of print through it, you will see only a blur. But if the word "love" is printed anywhere on that page, in any typeface, you will see a very bright light at that spot on the page. In much the same way, one of the finest computers in the world riffled through the "pages" of Norman Kent's memory, scanning holographs with a reference standard consisting of the sound of his name. Each one that responded strongly was taken from him.

All this took place at computer speed. Without perceptible hesitation the man on the table answered honestly and happily, a puppy fetching a stick. "I don't know."

"Very good. What is your wife's name?"

"I don't know."

"What were your parents' names?"

"I don't know."

"Your sister's name?"

" . . ."

"What is your occupation?"

". . . I . . ."

"Where are we?"

" . . ."

"What is my name?"

"You are . . ."

"What did you do when you left the army?"

" . . ."

The questioning took several hours. It would be extremely difficult to pinpoint just where in there Norman Kent ceased to exist. But by the end of the interrogation he was unquestionably dead. As he had yearned to be since the long-gone jungle days. The prayer he had prayed so fervently then was retroactively answered at last: his memories now stopped there. The paint locker was empty.

He was happier than he had been in years.

He remained on that table, cocooned in ultimate peace, for an unmeasurable time, drifting in and out of sleep. Jacques visited him from time to time, always alone. As intelligence reports trickled in from Halifax and New York and Washington, Jacques would ask him additional questions, covering loopholes, sealing leaks. A microchip was wired into five of the ultrafine filaments that skewered his brain, and tucked up into a fissure in his skull. The whole assembly would escape detection by anything short of a *very* thorough CAT scan, and it would briefly scramble the recording circuits of his short-term and long-term memory systems if certain thoughts entered his mind. Any direct or associational clue that might help him deduce his former identity would trigger a (hiatus). Thoughtfully, Jacques had added a fail-safe: if someone else ever suggested to this man that he had once been called Norman Kent, the microchip would self-destruct, allowing him to consider the idea dispassionately without going into suspicious fits of paralysis.

The man on the table experienced all this through a haze of bliss. But his memory-recording circuitry was in "erase" mode; none of the experience was retained. His consciousness had a duration of perhaps four seconds total. He simply marinated in pleasure, for what seemed like forever. His body achieved orgasm every time it was capable. At the end of a week he developed a prepuce infection necessitating circumcision. He never knew it; it transpired in his sleep.

There came a time when he slept and did not wake. His dreams were confused and painful, but he could not wake. He dreamed of plugs being drawn from tight sockets in his head, phone-jack plugs and DIN plugs and little RCA phono plugs. He dreamed that a man without a face was stirring his brains with a spatula, as though they were scrambled eggs that must not stick to the pan. He dreamed that a woman with blonde hair was holding him by one hand over a harbor he could not recognize, from a bridge he could not name. He dreamed that a bear and a mouse were calling a name that he ought to recognize, but did not. He dreamed that he was in his mother's womb, and refused to leave. He dreamed that he was a burglar, that a dry voice on audiotape was acquainting him with details of a burglar's trade, and when he had mastered the lessons the voice began to teach him the rudiments of high-level computer programming.

None of these memories recorded in his conscious mind. They were groundwork only: they would give a false "echo" of familiarity when his conscious mind "relearned" them.

At some point in his sleep the ecstasy began to fade, so gradually that he never experienced a distinct "crash" state. Eventually it was completely gone. And completely forgotten.

He woke with a hell of a headache in a strange place—a very strange place.

"It's good to see your eyes open," said a man he did not know. "You've been out for a long time; for a while there I was sure you'd bought it. I got the son of a bitch, by the way."

He knew his response was silly even as he said it. "What son of a bitch? It was a mine, a Bouncing Betty."

Then his eyes took in the room around him and he knew that he was somehow no longer in Africa.

12 ▰

1999 Jacques led us through the woodshed into the house proper.

"Sit down," he said, smiling warmly. "Can I offer you refreshment?"

"Nothing for me," Karen said.

"Thank you. Coffee for me."

"I have some twelve-year-old Irish whiskey—"

"Perhaps another time?"

That made his smile sharpen at the corners. "Well phrased. Please—make yourselves comfortable. I'll be back in a moment."

I was bemused by my host. He was unquestionably the man I had known as Fader Takhalous in New York. But his whole manner was different. He no longer had a Bronx accent. His speech was accentless now, newscaster's English, but somehow he was unmistakably a European. The Fader had been a tired old cynic; this man was a vigorous fiftyish with sparkling eyes. He was, I could sense, smarter and faster than the man I had been subconsciously expecting to meet.

If he was leaving us alone in the room, there was no point in searching it. It was large enough to have two distinct groupings of furniture. The set to our left faced a splendid bay window, now opaqued. The second, to our right, faced a large stone fireplace in which a fire was crackling. To the left of the hearth was a powered chair, the equal of my own in New York; to the right was a small sofa facing the chair. Between them a much larger couch and a second powered chair faced the fireplace, but we never considered sitting there. To do so would present our backs to both the front door and the door by which Jacques had left the room. Karen took the sofa; I sat down in the chair and swiveled it to face the room. I noticed that she moved the sofa slightly before sitting on it. It was a good idea, but my chair was bolted down.

Jacques returned almost at once, with nothing in his hands but a remote terminal. A table followed him. At his direction it rolled itself up to the fireplace, between Karen and me, and knelt, like a New York bus, to coffee-table height.

"Slick," I said. "How does it corner?"

He was surprised for a second. He had forgotten that the table was worthy of comment. He grinned then. "Poorly. But the mileage is good."

The table contained coffee, cups, spoons, sugar, honey, and cream. The cream was at least twenty-percent butterfat. The honey was local. The sugar was unrefined. The cups were lightweight plastic, double-walled with vacuum between—they would keep coffee drinking temperature for half an hour. The coffeepot too was thermal. A trigger in its handle operated the pour spout; there was no way to make it disgorge all its contents at once. Into someone's face, say. The cups had half-lids, open just enough to admit a spoon. You could pour out their contents, but not fling them. Jacques poured all three cups, adulterated his own to taste, and sat in the powered chair.

I sipped my own coffee. As I had expected, it was fresh brewed Blue Mountain, with just a trace of an excellent cinnamon. I usually take coffee black, but I added a little sugar.

Jacques waited politely for us to comment on the coffee.

"Why are we here?" I asked.

"To judge me."

"To *judge*—"

"—*you?*" Karen finished.

"Yes."

"Guilty," she said at once. "Die."

Jacques smiled sadly. "I will require you to go through the formality of a trial first. An old American tradition: allowing the accused to speak his piece before you hang him."

"Do you seriously suggest," I asked, "that there can be any justification for the things you have done? That would persuade *us?*"

"It is precisely because I cannot answer that question that you arc both still alive. Consider this question: How is the most powerful man in the world to know whether he is sane or not? For *certain?*"

It was a good question.

"Why would he care?" Karen asked.

That was another.

"That is a good question," Jacques said. "I will give you an honest answer, and if it sounds melodramatic, I am sorry." His voice changed. For the first time he sounded like the Fader I had known. "If I am mad, the human race has had it."

"I am afraid," I said slowly, "that I agree with you. But again, why should you care?"

He sighed. "All humans with enough imagination to understand that they will die have an intolerable problem. They must reconcile themselves to extinction, or else work at something larger than themselves, something that will survive them. Their children, most often. The identity relationship between parent and child is direct, demonstrable, basic. Some are imaginative enough to see that their children are as ephemeral as they themselves, as susceptible to chance destruction. So they transfer allegiance and identity to something more than human. To a nation, or a notion, or a religion, or a school of art."

I was almost beginning to enjoy this. This was the Fader I knew. We'd had a dozen of these raps together. It was from him that I had picked up the habit of arguing in precise, formal language, like a lecturing professor. I found that it clarified thought.

Or *had* I picked it up from him? Apparently I had once *been* a professor.

"A few," he went on, "a very few, are afflicted with the insight that all those things too are mortal. For these few there is no alternative but to love their entire *species* above all else, to love the idea of sentient life." He paused and drank coffee. "I am thus accursed. I have thought it through. I will sacrifice anything to preserve the human race. Your lives. My life. Those I love. Anything. Nothing else that I know, not planets or stars or the universe itself, has as good a chance of living forever. It's the only game in town."

I let a few seconds of silence go by. "The argument has been made before," I said. "The classic reply is, 'Who appointed *you* preserver of the human race?'"

He nodded. "I call it random chance. My lover says it was God. You might split the difference and say, 'Fate.'"

"You, in other words."

The one time I had ever beaten him at chess, I saw him smile just like that. "Yes. I chose not to duck."

"Standard answer. But if I understand you correctly, you doubt your fitness for the job?"

"That is correct."

"Now that is something new." I turned to Karen. "Which would you say is worse, honey? A confident megalomaniac, or an insecure one? Generally speaking, I mean?"

"Shut up, Joe. I'm starting to like his vibes. Listen, Jacques— I assume we're formally introduced, yes?—if I understand you, you're telling us that you did not seek the power you've got. It's kind of something that happened to you?"

He looked sad. "I'd like to say yes, but that's not strictly true. I . . . saw that the power would come into existence, would come to *someone*. Once I knew that, I was obligated. I fought the idea for almost a decade, hoping that someone else would emerge more worthy of the power. No one did, and my hand was forced. I live for the day I can put down the burden. But I took it voluntarily and wield it ruthlessly."

"You know," I said, "I'd like to believe that. I have always felt that the best candidate for a position of power should be the one who wants it least. But you have, however reluctantly, wielded that power for at least five years now—"

"More like ten."

"—and what little I personally know of the accomplishments of your administration smells rancid. You have made money from the deaths of thousands, perhaps hundreds of thousands, of wireheads. Like my friend Karen. You have learned how to make involuntary wireheads, and used that ability to make sure it stays exclusively yours. You blew up a shock doc and his shop in New York, suborned the Patent Office—"

"You scooped out Joe's brains, and put back the pieces that suited you," Karen cut in. "You kidnapped his sister—"

"What did happen to her, Jacques?"

Karen saw my face. "Easy, Joe."

"She is upstairs."

I blinked.

"She was not certain whether or not she wished to meet you. I don't believe she was certain that she even wished to monitor the video feed from this room. She was holding back tears when I left her." He saw my expression and made that pained smile again. "She is the lover I mentioned, who thinks that God did this to me."

I thought that over for a measureless time. "Why isn't her opinion of your sanity good enough for you?"

"She loves me. You two hate me."

"Huh." I burned my tongue, having forgotten about the thermal cup. "Tell me something. That shock doc in New York—that *was* your doing, yes?"

"The bombing on the lower West Side? Yes. Pure chance you were passing by. But it was *not* luck that you were not hurt. My agent had orders to wait until he was certain there was no one else in the blast zone."

That was true. "Okay. Now tell me: why a bombing? Wouldn't it have been simpler and less risky to mindwipe him?"

He was shocked. "I have had to make my own rules. One of the most important is this: I never mindwipe a man if I can accomplish my purpose by merely killing him."

I looked him square in the eye. "That is a very good answer."

He relaxed and smiled. "For a moment I thought you were serious. The thought that I might have so seriously misjudged you scared me badly."

"Yeah. You know all about me. I want to know about you."

He nodded. "And the most important things I say will be the ones I hadn't planned to say. Keep prodding."

"Why do you sell the wire?" Karen asked. She got out cigarettes and lighter, and he watched her hands carefully while replying.

"For cover, and for money."

"Cover?"

"It gave me a plausible and legitimate reason for research into brain-reward, which is the key to memory—and it gave me a plausible and legitimate reason for keeping the results of that research secret."

"With mindwipe, what do you need with money?" I asked.

"I have had mindwipe for a little over four years. It was very expensive. Projects now on the drawing boards will be so immensely expensive that I will need every little billion."

"All right. We now know at least a smattering of your means. Next topic: What are the ends that you contend justify those means?"

He nodded. "Now we are getting somewhere. Let me refill your cup. This will take some time." He busied himself with the pot. "I must start from the beginning."

I accepted more coffee, and Karen took a cup. Maximum alertness here.

"I was born into the midst of planetary war. Literally the midst, for Switzerland is bounded by France, Germany, Austria, and Italy. It was the eye of the storm, and by the time I was old enough to truly understand the danger, it was past. When I was six, my father attempted to explain to me something of the significance of the atom bomb, which had just annihilated Hiroshima and Nagasaki. He was a director of what was then Switzerland's fourth largest banking firm, located in Basel. I'm sure he made an effort to soften the horror of it, he was not trying to scare me. But when I understood that *one* bomb had destroyed a city the size of Zurich, I was appalled. I had been taken there twice, and believed it to be the largest city on earth.

But my father told me that the bomb meant the end of war. He said now the whole world would have to be as smart as Switzerland, would have to learn to live together in peace, because the weapons were now so terrible that it was too dangerous to start a fight. 'What if they're not?' I asked. As smart as Switzerland." He paused a moment in thought. "Strange. One of the things I admire the most about my country is that nothing is done without consensus. To raise taxes requires a national referendum and a constitutional amendment. We did not enfranchise women until I was thirty-two years old and my mother, a neurosurgeon, was dead. A coalition of major parties has ruled for nearly half a century, talking every issue to death before anything is done. And now I, a Swiss, am acting as unilaterally as any tyrant in history. On a scale that Genghis Khan could not have dreamed of."

"God is an iron," I said.

"Eh? Oh, yes, I remember the conceit. A person who commits irony is an iron. God knows, cold and hot iron have figured prominently in His ironies. Yes, God is an iron. Switzerland produced me. And my Uncle Albert. Not really my uncle. A friend of my mother's, a chemist who worked in the big laboratory across town."

A jigsaw piece clicked into place. "Jesus. Basel. Sandoz Laboratories. Dr. Albert Hofmann."

"It was the day after my fourth birthday. Uncle Albert ingested what he thought was an infinitesimal amount of LSD-25, climbed onto his bicycle to pedal home, and took the world's first trip. The day was beautiful; I was playing outside with my new toys when he pedaled past. Even at four years old I was aware that something extraordinary was going on with him. He seemed to shine. He saw me and he smiled at me as he rode past. He did not wave or call out; he only looked at me, turning his head as he went by, and smiled. You can think of the contact-high phenomenon if it suits you. I say that for those few seconds time stopped and we were telepathic. I remember today the exhilaration . . ." He frowned down at his coffee and drank of it.

"My," Karen murmured.

"Never, even with my parents, had I felt so close to another human being, adult or child. There was a bond between us. Eighteen years later to the day, the day after my twenty-first birthday, he gave me my first dose of lysergic acid diethylamide under controlled conditions. It had been decided before my birth, possibly before my conception, that I was to be a doctor. It was Uncle Albert who suggested I go into neuroanatomy. At that time there were less than a dozen neuroanatomists on this planet, and they were some of the most eccentric men alive. I fit right in. I was something of an odd duck."

"I can imagine."

"By this time, you see, I was already deeply interested in the interface between the brain and the mind. Next to nothing was known about the brain, and I felt that better maps might be the key. It was a wide-open field, an exciting puzzle with the answers seemingly *just* out of reach, possible of attainment.

"The year I began my medical training, I read an article in *Scientific American* about the work of two men, James Olds and Peter Milner, at McGill University in Canada. They had discovered that if you placed an electrode in a certain part of the brain of a rat—"

"We know about Olds," Karen interrupted. Her voice was harsh.

"Of course you do. Forgive me. I worked with Olds, later, and with others who followed him. Lilly, Routtenberg, Collier, Penfield. After a time I worked only with myself. Routtenberg had put me onto the connection between the brain-reward system and memory formation, and I was absolutely fascinated by memory. I had decided that life is the business of making happy memories—and I was offended as a neurophysiologist to be completely ignorant of the process by which this most basic task was accomplished.

"But I had no intention of publishing my results in *Scientific American*. Or anywhere else. I had learned from John Lilly's experiences with the CIA involving brain-reward research, and Uncle Albert's experiences with the same group and others like it, that the kinds of answers I was looking for were dangerous answers."

"Tell me about your personal life during all of this," Karen said.

He sighed and sipped coffee. He got up and poked the fire with an andiron, then put on more wood. "While I was acquiring an M.D. and becoming a neuroanatomist, there was of course not much personal life to talk about. I received my doctorate at twenty-six. I had friends. I had lovers, but only the friends lasted. I don't think there was enough of me left from my work to satisfy a lover, to give to her. When I was thirty-two I met Elsa. She was as stable as I was wild. She calmed me, housebroke me. She was a cyberneticist; she could make a computer do anything, and she was deeply interested in holography. We learned from each other. We were married and had six wonderful years. Then—"

He finished his coffee and put the cup down with infinite care and attention. Then the words came out a little faster than before.

"Then a piece of equipment exploded in her laboratory. Below and to the side; a fragment evaded anything vital and entered the skull. The hippocampus and several associated structures in both temporal lobes were virtually destroyed. She lived. With anterograde amnesia."

He was silent for a few moments.

"The skills and knowledge she had acquired up until that time remained largely intact. She seemed able to register limited amounts of new information. But she could no longer retain it. Her short-term memory system and her long-term storage had been disconnected. She never again learned to recognize anyone she had not known before the accident, not even the specialists who worked with her daily. Each time she met them was the first time. Her memory had a span of perhaps ten minutes. She lived another five years, perpetually puzzled by the fact that the date always seemed to be later than it could possibly be. She never got more than ten minutes past 1978, and it seemed to confuse her a little, the way the world went on ahead without her. But she was fairly happy in general.

"I was familiar with the syndrome from correspondence with Milner. I lived with it with her until she died, working ferociously to understand her condition so that I could alleviate it. I failed. When she died I gave myself to my work entirely, as a kind of memorial. If that word is not too ironic.

"She had given me many tools, many leads. She had taught me more about computers than any university could have. She had taught me much about holography. By the time of her death, it was well established that memory storage takes place in a manner analogous to holography."

Karen frowned. "I don't think I follow."

He seemed to come back from a far place, to recall that he had listeners and a reason for speaking. "If you cut the corner off a hologram transparency, you do *not* take a corner off the image it yields. Both it *and* the cut-off corner will produce the complete, uncut image. The former will be very slightly fuzzier than before the mutilation; the latter will be quite fuzzy, but still complete. Similarly, you cannot remove a given memory by removing a specific portion of the brain. Each memory is stored *all over* the brain, in the form of a multiple redundant *pattern*. Each neuron thus represents many potential bits of information—and there are as many neurons in a brain as there are stars in the galaxy."

"So the question," I said, "is how are the memories encoded and how are they retrieved?"

"Precisely. Computer theory was essential. And my hunch was right: brain-reward was the key to the puzzle. The brain-reward aspect of memory formation was the only one I knew how to detect, and to measure and track accurately. The task was rather like a space explorer studying purely economic data for a planet, then trying to deduce or infer the body of its inhabitants' psychology. But I knew where I was going, I had known for years, and I was determined to be the first one there. By that time I had transferred my personal allegiance to the human race. The last few decades have not been such as to encourage ethical behavior by scientists, and a relatively large number of people were chasing the secrets I sought. A psychologist stood up at a Triple-A-S meeting in the mid-seventies and declared that the information-storage code of the human brain would be cracked within ten years. That frightened me. While pursuing my own researches, I did my best to cripple the work of others by feeding false data into the literature. Red herrings, blind alleys, false trails. I succeeded. By the late 1980s, I was the only one still digging at the spot marked X,

unnoticed by the crowd over at the other end of the field. Simple
surgery and brain/computer interface were the last tools I needed.
By 1989 I had a rudimentary and cumbersome, but fairly effective, version of mindwipe. It was of some help to me in
capturing the wirehead industry, and concealing the extent of
my own involvement in it."

"You run the whole thing?" Karen exploded.

"I am and plan to remain the whole thing. I assure you that
no one now living can prove that statement—although you,
Joe, guessed or learned more than I would have thought possible. But the whole industry is and has been my personal
monopoly."

"How *could* you—" she began, and ran out of words. She
had begun to like him, and could not swallow the new information.

"Most of the basic patents are mine, under an assortment
of names. If I did not do it, someone else would. Once it
became possible, it became inevitable. I accepted the responsibility, destroyed all would-be competitors, and kept the industry just as small and stunted as possible. Do you remember
anything of how *fast* marijuana and LSD spread in the sixties
and seventies, when organized crime realized their economic
potential? Has the growth of the wirehead industry been anything like that?"

No. It had not. It got a lot of talk in the media, but the
numbers said it was nothing like the social problem alcohol or
cocaine posed. That had always struck me as odd. People dumb
enough to flirt with *heroin* would not touch the wire; it was
strictly for born losers. Could that be because the wire was
simply not being marketed aggressively?

"Those who seek pleasure at any cost are those to whom
ethics matter least. I have been weeding the human race of its
most selfish and self-indulgent."

"I'm selfish and self-indulgent," Karen said darkly.

He smiled. "Is that what brings you to Nova Scotia?"

She got her knee out of the way in time; the spilt coffee
landed on the rug.

"Of *course* you were obsessed with ecstasy, having been
denied it all your life. Once you tasted it in full, you established

normal relations with it—one of your customers reports to me—and turned your attention to other things. To an ethical task."

She frowned, but said nothing.

"And you, Joe. I supplied you with the most comfortable and carefree existence that modern society affords, no taxes, no mortgage, no bills, and what did you do? You dumped it all for a crusade. Or did you ever seriously expect to survive this?"

"No," I said. "Not once, even from the beginning. But I had a responsibility to Karen."

"To Karen? Why?"

"I meddled in her life, spoiled a perfectly good and painless suicide. I had to accept the con—"

"Bullshit," Karen snapped.

"She is right, Joe. Paramedics spoil suicides every day, then punch out and go home. You *perceived* a responsibility. Because it suited you. Underneath it is something else. You saw the horror of Karen's experience. In your heart, you believe her cause is just. You believe, like her, that every man's death diminishes you. Don't you?"

I said nothing.

"I could be wrong, of course. It could simply be emotional involvement—"

My voice was bleak. "You, of all people, should know that I am unable to love."

This smile reached his eyes. "I don't know any such thing."

The sentence hit me like a surprise slap in the face that bewilders, hurts, and angers. "The hell you don't!" I shouted.

"Your sex drive is disconnected, yes. But these days sex and love don't even write to each other much. I think your love for Karen is very much like the love your sister has for me. And Karen's love for you is much like mine for Madeleine."

I tried to gain control of my emotions. "Perhaps I do agree with Karen about wireheading. In any case, I believe I'm ready now to render the judgment you asked for."

"Be patient. I've given you the background. I have yet to present my defense."

I had to admire his nerve.

"Proceed," Karen said after a while. She struck another cigarette.

"Thank you. As to wireheading, you must admit that the way I set up the industry, it is something that can only happen by choice. The subject has to assist in the placement of the wire. Inductance—wireheading without consent, from outside the skull—is a childishly simple refinement. I have made it my business to kill any entrepreneur who tries to introduce it.

"Should I manufacture automobiles instead, and kill more people than wireheading does *without* the element of choice?

"What you dislike about wireheading is not the wire itself. There were wirehead personalities *long* before the wire existed. What it is that horrifies you is what it displays: the component of human nature that *wants* the wire, that wants pushbutton pleasure badly enough to pay any price, that is so blind and afraid that it will suicide with a smile. You would like, rightly, to eliminate that part of human nature. I tell you that *you cannot do that by eliminating the wire.*

"My first mindwipe technique was a very clumsy and primitive thing. I could *not* erase a memory pattern, but I could, in a sense, erase its retrieval code. The memory remained in the skull, but the mind could not access it. I redoubled my efforts, because I wanted direct access to memory itself."

"True mindwipe," I said.

"If you will," he agreed. "But recall this: the same man, Heinrich Dreser, discovered both heroin and aspirin. Consider an analogy, shall we? You are an aborigine genius. Someone gives you a good reel-to-reel tape recorder. He explains electronic theory in some detail, and you are so bright you follow most of it. Then he rips out the heads and all their circuitry, destroys them, and departs—leaving behind tapes containing directions to a buried fortune. The tape transport still functions, but the heads are gone.

"Now suppose, against all odds, you somehow manage to make that tape recorder functional again. Perhaps it only takes you a few hundred years and requires a complete reorganization of your tribe. Forget all that. *Which will you succeed in reinventing first: the record head or the erase head?*"

Answering the question took a split second; it was seconds later before the implications registered. Then I was startled speechless.

"The erase head, of course," he said. "It is a much simpler device—a single blanket signal that disrupts any and all frequencies. It is an infinitely simpler task to destroy information than to encode it in the first place. Which is easier to do: create a book, or burn it?"

"My God," Karen cried. "You weren't after mindwipe. You wanted—"

"Mind*fill,*" he said quietly, and the room seemed to rock around me as my beliefs began rearranging themselves.

"To continue the analogy," he went on, "I have recently learned how to build both record and playback heads. Neither process will ever be as elegant and simple as the erasure process." Suddenly there was a weapon in his hand, so suddenly that neither Karen nor I jumped. It looked like a water pistol. "With this I could remove twenty-four hours from your mind, and put your memory on hold. You experienced a taste of the latter this afternoon. To dub off a copy of those twenty-four hours' worth of memories would require much more equipment, power, and time. To play my memories into your skull would take nearly twice as much of all three. *But I could do both of those things.*

"Understand me: to copy your memories from last night to *this* moment, I would have to wait several hours, until the information has had time to soak into long-term storage. And any information that your mind's metaprogrammer elected not to store would be lost."

"Then you haven't got a handle on short-term memory?" I said, watching the water pistol.

"I know only how to erase it. Record and playback heads for it will take about fifteen years to develop . . . if all goes well."

"And then you'll have true telepathy," Karen breathed.

"That is correct. And I have devoted my life to ensuring that no individual, group, or government will gain exclusive control of these developments. At present, I have a monopoly.

I live for the day when I can responsibly abdicate. My secrets must belong to all mankind—or to no one."

He fell silent then. He put the weapon away. I didn't even see where. He let us have about five minutes of silence, to think it through.

The first, and least important, implication was that the deadly threat of mindwipe could be at least partially mitigated. By the record head. If there is a memory you especially want to ensure against theft, make a recording of it and put it in a safe place. If someone wants to steal your memory of this moment, right now, you have several hours to try and escape him—though that may be difficult if he has a water pistol that destroys your short-term memory as it forms, holds you mindless and happy.

But the second implication! The playback head . . .

Suppose you could give a Hindu peasant the memories of, say, a scientific farmer? Not an *account* of those memories, translated into words and retranslated into print and retranslated into Hindi—but an actual, experiential memory. What soil *looks* like and *smells* like when it is most fruitful. The sound of a correctly tuned engine. The difference between hand-tight and wrench-tight. The smell of disease. Principles of health care. They say experience is not just the best, but the *only* teacher. What if it were willing to travel?

Suppose you could give a student the memories of a professor. Log tables. Tensor calculus. Conversational Russian. The extraordinary thing about Kemal Ataturk. Pages of Shakespeare. The Periodic Table.

Suppose you could give a child the memories of an adult—of several adults.

Suppose you could give an adult the memories of a child, fresh and vivid.

Suppose you could show a Ku Klux Klanner what it is really like to be black.

Suppose you could give a blind man memories of sight. Give music to the deaf. Give entrechats to a paraplegic. Orgasms to the impotent.

Suppose the desire to know everything about your lover could be satisfied.

Suppose your need to share your own life completely with

your lover could be satisfied.

Suppose a historian had access to the memories of Alger Hiss, or Richard Nixon.

Suppose politicians were required to submit to periodic memory audit.

Suppose accountants were.

Suppose you were.

Suppose a doctor could determine incontrovertibly, in a matter of hours, your innocence of a crime.

Or your guilt.

Suppose all these things became the exclusive monopoly of anyone. Like Jacques's monopoly on wireheading . . .

I opened my mouth to ask Jacques a question. I don't remember what it would have been. A board lit up on the wall across the room, over his terminal, and he gave it instant, total attention. Almost at once he relaxed slightly, but got up from the chair nonetheless and walked to the board.

"No reason to be alarmed," he said. He punched a few buttons, studied a readout, and nodded. "Perfectly all right. For a moment I thought we had uninvited guests, but it is only an animal. No sentience-signature in the brain waves." He frowned. "Big animal, though. I thought—" Suddenly his voice was urgent. "*Fast* animal!" He punched more buttons in a great hurry, and fire erupted in the night outside through the big bay window. Laser come a-hunting. He half turned toward the window and it exploded into the room in a spray of glass, letting in fire and smoke and sudden thunder. A man came headfirst through the hole it left, rolled when he hit the floor, and came up on his feet. His gun covered all three of us, settled on Jacques.

Karen and I sat very still, sudden breeze fanning our hair.

13 ≣

1999 His eyes were brown. Black pants, turtleneck, and boots. Nightsight goggles pushed up onto his forehead. An odd headgear covered everything but his eyes. He seemed to have taken five yards of heavy-duty metal foil, painted it black, crumpled it until it was all over wrinkles, and then molded it around his head like a ski mask, in multiple layers. It distorted the shape and contours of his head. All at once I understood it.

Jacques broke the silence. "My guards?"

"I got them both."

Jacques looked very sad. I liked his sadness. "Why are you here?"

His voice from under the foil was vaguely familiar. "I'm here to kill you, LeBlanc. And steal your magic."

"What do you know of my magic?"

"I know everything about you. For instance, you have a

weapon. Give it to me very carefully. Very slowly."

Jacques complied.

"I've been tracking you for five years. And you know nothing about me."

"On the contrary, Sergeant Amesby. I know you to be one of the finest policemen in the world."

Amesby. The cop who had handled Maddy's case. My mind went into passing gear.

Being recognized rocked him a little; he tried not to show it. "I've put five years in on you, all by myself, without letting anyone else know what I was doing, because I had some kind of notion of how important you'd turn out to be. But I've left records where they'll be found in the event of my untimely death, so you daren't kill me even if you could. And you can't brainwipe me as long as I'm wearing this helmet. And it isn't coming off until one of us is dead. I know all about you, LeBlanc."

"Who am I, then?"

"You are the first genuine ruler of the world. And I'm your successor."

Jacques burst our laughing. *"You* will replace *me?"*

"Why not? As of tonight, *everything you know belongs to me."*

Jacques's laughter chopped off short.

"Why did you happen to pick tonight?" he said at last.

"Kent, here."

I blinked. Me, he meant.

"He's how I got into this—him and his sister—and he's the only part of it I never understood. What the *hell* he does for you that was worth all the trouble you took, I can't for the life of me figure out, and that makes me uneasy. I did a lot of sniffing around in this neighborhood, times you were off in Switzerland and Washington and places. Mapping your security perimeters, testing the helmet, asking questions of the locals. There's an old fart west of here used to know Kent. He was the last person to see Kent before he disappeared. He called me tonight, said he saw Kent and a woman come here, and he said Kent acted like he didn't know him anymore. That puzzled me. I remembered a phone call I got this morning, a voice that sounded familiar but I couldn't place it. It just didn't add up. I had Kent figured for dead. I've been thinking about making my move for a couple of months now. I decided if I did it tonight I might get the only answers I haven't got yet."

He turned to Karen and me.

The gun was a Yamaha Disruptor, with solenoid trigger and twenty-five-round capacity. A sneezing cat makes more noise. A slingshot has more recoil. The M-40 I used in the jungle has about the same stopping power. Two guards lay dead outside, presumably good guards. He had dodged a tracking laser. I feared him.

While he was looking at us, Jacques was situated at the extreme limit of his peripheral vision. Jacques shifted his stance very slightly—experimentally? hard to say—and Amesby, without moving his eyes a millimeter, produced a second Disruptor from a back-pocket holster and drew a dead bead on Jacques's nose.

Oh, my mind scrabbled around in my skull like a trapped rat.

Jacques had been right. This hick cop was *good*, was seriously dangerous. And he wanted answers I did not have and he was going to kill me if he didn't get them. Probably even if he did. I sensed that Jacques was worried, though he hid it well, and that realization nearly panicked me. If *he* had no ace up his sleeve, no rabbit in the hat—

Oh, God. He did have a rabbit—he was worried that the rabbit might be foolhardy enough to take on the fox. Maddy. Something about a video feed from this room . . .

"All right, Norman, talk to me. How do you figure in this business? Just where the hell do you fit?"

Now, there was a question—and the clock running out. I yearned for the comfort and security of a burglar's life.

I could see Jacques looking at me, wondering how I would play it. This was the first moment that day that I had not been under threat of instant death from Jacques, and we both knew that. If I could convince Amesby of that, maybe we could deal. I might convince him, too; I was sure he had scouted our four-wheel and seen the weapons we'd abandoned.

I think what decided me was the grief that had splashed

across Jacques's features when he heard that his two guards were dead. I knew that he was one of the best actors alive— but the sadness had been too spontaneous to be faked. He cared when his employees died.

I took my face out of neutral. I gave Amesby mild, sour amusement. A very small smile, a slight shake of the head, a suggestion of a sigh. Then I turned away from him, powering the chair around thirty degrees to face Jacques. Because of Amesby's solenoid trigger, I wanted to do it very slowly. So I mashed the button down and whipped the chair around just as fast as it could go. Both my hands remained in sight; Amesby flinched but held fire.

"Sometimes being half smart is worse than being stupid." I smiled wickedly at Jacques. "Who'd know better than you, eh?"

Without waiting for his reaction, I whipped the chair back to face Amesby again. His flinch was not visible this time, but I knew that was twice he had decided not to kill me. A habit to encourage. He was now conditioned to permit sudden movements in front of his eyes.

I said, "I own you or I kill you, sonny, there's no third way. Make up your mind."

"You own—?"

I sighed. *"Look at me,* jerk."

He frowned and looked closer. The timing was important. In the split second *before* he got it I said, very softly, "Am I Norman Kent?"

"Jesus." He stared. "By Jesus, you're not! But who—"

I kept my eyes on his, held out my left hand toward Karen. "Cigarette, please," I murmured. And bless her, she was with me, she said "Yes, sir" quite smartly, struck a cigarette, and placed it between my spread fingers as smoothly as if she were accustomed to it. It is much easier to put across aristocratic superiority if you have a cigarette to work with. It is not necessary to smoke it.

As this business ended, Amesby got his first question formulated in words and drew breath to ask it. "Shut up," I said, with absolutely no whip-of-command in my voice. He obeyed. "You don't know *what's* going on, do you? You actually thought Le Blank here was the top man. You really thought I was

Kent." I shook my head. "I don't know that you're bright enough to be worth keeping. How long did you say you'd been working on this? Five *years?*"

He was good. He was very good. His mind must have been racing at a thousand miles an hour, but his face gave away nothing at all. I glanced at the knuckles of his gun hand and saw that he was wondering, But why can't I just pull this trigger?

There were two places my sister could be. She could be upstairs with the video switched off, crying at the thought of her crippled baby brother down in the parlor. If so, she was safe. If not, she was standing about fifteen feet away, trying frantically to think of something. Only one door led from this room into the rest of the house. It lay well within Amesby's field of vision. I had been observant when Jacques had come through it with his coffee cart. It opened on a long hallway, not much wider than the doorway. The doorknob was on the right. From Madeleine's perspective it would be on the left, and the door would open toward her. She was right-handed. She could pull the door open with her left hand, wait for it to get out of her way, and fire backhand. Or she could pull the door with her right hand and try a left-handed shot. Neither was very good, against a man with one gun on her lover and another on her brother. Could I sucker his gaze away from the door? No, his instincts were too good, it would be pushing him too hard.

I knew she was there. I could feel her there. I could hear her pleading with me to come up with something. I was running out of seconds.

"*I'm* a layer or two from the top, sonny, and Le Blank here jumps when I say frog. If he's all you've come up with after five years, I don't think the firm will be interested in your services." I raised my voice. "Madeleine, dear, come in here, will you?"

Everyone turned to the door, and it opened, not too fast and not too slow, and Madeleine Kent walked into the room with both hands prominently empty. Her bearing was regal. Her eyes swept the room, dismissed everything but me. I did not recognize her.

"Yes, sir?"

"Radio the ship. Tell them there will be three bodies to be picked up for disposal. Oh, and tomorrow evening I want you to order a new bay window from Halifax, and arrange for something local until it arrives." I dropped my cigarette on Jacques's expensive rug and trod it out. "I think that's all."

"Very good, sir." She turned to go.

"Hold it right there," Amesby snapped, his voice cracking on the last word. One of his guns tracked her, trembling just perceptibly.

She came to a gradual stop, turned slowly, and stared at him as though he were something distasteful written on a wall. His gun did not even rate a glance. "Are you speaking to me?"

I had run this bluff just about as far as I could. I had him off balance, paranoid. I had kept him on the trembling verge of pressing that trigger for so long that his finger had to be tired. One disadvantage of a solenoid trigger. I had managed to introduce a fourth person into the room without provoking shots. Now he had four threats to cover with two guns. It takes an extraordinary mind to handle more than three of anything without time-sharing.

But he had an extraordinary mind. And in my scale of evaluations, the most expendable person in the room was me. I wanted insurance.

"What I'm doing, lady," he said, his voice dismayingly strong, "is promising to shoot you in the belly if you take a step or move some way I don't like."

"Do you know why you're still alive, Amesby?" I asked. "It's a matter of probabilities. I settled it to my satisfaction in Africa, a long time ago. Even if you put a nice heavy high-velocity load right on the money, just punch a couple of vertebrae right out and bounce the skull off the ceiling, there'll still be about a ten-to-fifteen-percent chance that the corpse's trigger finger will clench. Spasmodic nerve action, like a headless chicken. Ten to fifteen percent. I'll take those odds if I have to, if you even *look* like actually pressing a trigger. But frankly, I would rather negotiate."

He grinned. "Who's going to shoot me? Her?"

"Did you happen to catch Le Blank's face when you told him 'both' his guards were dead? How it took him a second to get a sad face on? You clown, *you missed the point man.*"

He did *not* turn to, or even glance toward, the shattered bay window to his right. I had never expected him to. Whether he bought the bluff or not, there was no point in turning to see. But he bought it, I could see him buy it in his heart. I had softened him up enough, hit him from enough different directions in a short enough time frame to give him the feeling that he had stumbled into a threshing machine. Now he had five things to keep track of.

"So I've got a ten-to-fifteen-percent chance of negotiating a mutually satisfactory settlement," he said at last. "Until we do, the first one of you that moves is catfood."

In that moment I respected him enormously. I was glad, because I knew he was going to kill me.

"The rest of you *sit still,*" I ordered. "I refuse to be killed by a headless clown, if it can be avoided." I hoped they would keep backing my play and follow orders. "All right, Amesby, what have you got to trade with?"

"I told you: I left evidence behind, in enough different places that even you can't find them all. Kill me and you're blown."

I smiled politely. "I don't think I'll lose much sleep over the Halifax Police Department—once you're retired from it."

"Yeah? How about Interpol and the—" He shut up and looked properly disgusted at himself for giving away information. "Believe me, you'll never find all the stashes I left. You'll blow LeBlanc, and that's got to be at least a large part of your organization."

I frowned and tried to look like I was not worried. Casually, I put my right foot up on the chair and rested an elbow on my knee. Now I had one foot under me. At last I nodded. The good executive makes decisions without wasting time.

"All right. We'll make a place in the firm for you. You can be one of the lesser gods—but you'll wear a belly bomb just like the rest of us and you'll take orders." I raised my voice two notches. "If he puts up his guns, let him live."

He took a full ten seconds making up his mind. Then, slowly and deliberately, he pointed both guns at the ceiling and waited to see if he was going to be shot by my imaginary assassin.

Pointing at the ceiling wasn't good enough. He was too far

away. I glanced toward the window, widened my eyes, and roared, "Dammit, *no!*"

I had to assume that this time he would go for it. As he began to pivot, I rocked forward and launched myself. I expected him to check in midstream and kill me, but I thought I could immobilize one or both of the guns long enough for Karen or one of the others to find a weapon and use it. I was so full of adrenalin the seconds were passing by like clouds.

There is a bit of movie film I will carry around in my skull forever. It is a silent movie, no soundtrack at all. I am partway to Amesby, in midair and in ultraslow motion, arms coming up. One of the Yamahas is arcing around toward me, almost there, while the rest of him continues to spin toward the window. Suddenly a hole appears in the neck of his helmet, under his Adam's Apple, the size of a Mason jar lid. I continue to drift toward him a few more inches, and see two vertebrae leave the back of his neck, one atop the other in stately procession, attended by gobbets of meat and larynx. A moment later his body begins to travel backward and his head starts to come forward. The body wins the uneven argument, but as it drifts back out of my way I see his nose hit his chest. The coffeepot, thrown by Karen, passes through the space his head used to occupy, trailing drops of the world's best coffee. I note with approval that his hands have reflexively *opened;* both guns are airborne. The sound of the shot arrives. I am still a few feet from the point at which we would have met if he had kept the appointment, beginning to think about my landing, when Madeleine slams into his shins from the side. Her intent is to knock his feet out from under him, but the slug that killed him has already made a pretty good start on that. One of his feet swings high and wide, impacts solidly on my left temple. There is a sudden jump-cut and I am on the floor on my belly, all the wind knocked out of me.

God, what a team! I though as reality returned to real-time. We *all* got him! But where did Jacques have that holdout hidden? I got one elbow under me, craned my head around, and took inventory. Amesby down. Madeleine getting up. Karen bending to retrieve one of Amesby's guns. Jacques right where

I had left him, his mouth a comical O, his hands empty at his sides. His gun had fallen to the floor, then. No, it hadn't. But there wasn't anywhere *on* him to conceal a gun capable of blowing a spinal column in two.

The voice came from the window. "Corporal, that was the *busiest* fucking sixty seconds in the history of the world."

I recognized the voice and I recognized the words. Subjectively, I had last heard both five years ago, in a damp trench full of fresh corpses on the Tamburure Plains.

"Bear!"

I rolled and looked and indeed it was him, face darkened with mud. He stood just outside the ruined window with weapon still extended. It was an Atcheson Assault Twelve—a twelve-gauge shotgun with a twenty-round drum and automatic or semiautomatic fire. He was ten years older than I remembered him. "Sergeant Bear, if you please." His eyes went to Jacques. "I assume Joe passes the exam?"

Jacques blinked, drew a deep breath, and nodded. "I would say so, yes."

He lowered the Atcheson then, and stepped gingerly in the window.

"Joe," Karen called. "You know this guy?"

"Bear Withbert. He saved my ass in Africa once. I told you about him." I smelled eucalyptus just seeing him. You crush the leaves and rub them on your hide for insect protection in the jungle. "If he's with Jacques, I am."

"Honest to Christ, Corporal, you damn near gave me fits for a while there. First you blow Madeleine's cover, and then you like to blow my own. And you know perfectly well there ain't more than a five-percent chance of a spinal shot going wrong. I couldn't figure out *how* the hell you wanted me to play it. How did you know I was out there?"

I got to my feet and worked my shoulders. For the first time in a very long while, I felt very good. "I didn't. I was just trying to divide up his attention too many ways."

He stared. "You were bluffing?" He turned to Jacques again. "Sign this one up, boss." He safetied the shotgun and set it down against the wall. He walked across the room, pulling out a handkerchief. He picked up Amesby's vertebrae in it. He rolled it up and tucked it into Amesby's pants pocket. He lifted Amesby's shoulders; the head dangled by the sterno-mastoid muscles. The metal foil made a crinkling sound. The features were deformed by hydrostatic pressure, eyes burst. "I'm afraid this rug is shot." He stripped off his black rainproof poncho and used it to wrap the upper portion of the body. He picked it up in his big arms and headed for the outside door. Madeleine held it open for him, then got the outer door. She closed and sealed both behind him.

"Madeleine," Jacques said, with just the right amount of irony, "please radio the ship and tell them there'll be three for disposal. And would you order a new window tomorrow?"

Karen glared at me.

"I was bluffing, I tell you," I said weakly. "It just seemed the logical way to handle the ones you use up."

"Jacques, stop teasing him," Madeleine said. "He was brilliant. I almost believed him myself." She came close to me, stopped, and looked me over carefully. She nodded slightly to herself. There were pain and guilt in her eyes, but there was courage there too. The pain was not crippling, the guilt not shameful. She was sorry, but unrepentant. "Thank you for saving Jacques. For saving everything. You did a good thing, Joe."

It was odd. With that last sentence she reminded me for the first time of the childhood sister I recalled; she had said that to me a hundred times while I was growing up. But she said "Joe," not "Norman." With that one sentence it was as though she were offering to transfer her sisterhood from Norman Kent to Joe, uh, Templeton. She saw that register on me, and waited for my response. I noticed that she had stopped breathing. Jacques too was watching me intently.

"My pleasure, sis."

She exhaled and her whole face lit up. Jacques relaxed. Karen got up and put an arm around me and kissed me on the cheek. I put an arm around her too. "So we're bright enough to be offered jobs, eh? Both of us?"

"I knew I wanted you both before I invited you here. The question was, did you want me? Yes, you're both in, and you won't be 'like gods,' but you won't wear belly bombs either.

You probably will die unpleasantly, like Reese and Cutter outside, but you'll do it voluntarily."

"I knew that," I said. "I had to make the pitch plausible to Amesby's kind of man. Tell me something: how come I pass now? Why did I fail four and a half years ago?"

"I offered you the choice then. Join my conspiracy or be mindwiped. You chose the latter. I've never been sure why."

It was hard to get a handle on. "Can mindwipe change personality that much?"

"Personality is built with memories."

"Joe, let me try," Madeleine said. "When I got to Nova Scotia from Switzerland, you were in *rotten* shape. The war had shattered you, busted your philosophy of life apart. You made a superficial adjustment, and in a few years it started to go sour. It all came apart on you. Your work, your marriage, your self-respect. You were suicidal when I arrived. I was confused myself. We leaned on each other. We became close. And so you were set up for the coup de grace.

"I had left Switzerland because I discovered, accidentally, that the man I had come to love was someone I did not know at all. I knew almost nothing—hints, little things that didn't add up—just enough to know that Jacques was something more than what he claimed to be. I presumed this to be sinister. International espionage, drugs, I suspected one of those. I left him without telling him I was leaving. I came to Canada, where I thought he could not find me, to think things through. And I smuggled a present for you through customs. A phonograph record. Lambert, Hendricks, and Ross, mint condition. It got past customs, but an agent of Jacques scanned my luggage more thoroughly and reported the package to him. He had to assume it was a floppy disc full of damaging computer data that I was planning to use against him."

"It hurt to think that," Jacques said. "I had her watched very carefully for a few weeks. She did nothing alarming, but finally I decided I could not afford to leave the situation unresolved. I ordered her kidnapped and taken into the country. I planned to come at once and interrogate her, but I was delayed."

"An assassination attempt," Maddy said drily. "He was a week recovering in hospital. Then he came here and told me who and what he was, and . . . well, we've been together ever since.

"But by that time it was too late to undo my 'kidnapping.' There was no explanation I could give you or the police, and besides, I could be of more use by remaining underground. I *had* to leave you in the dark; you were in no shape to handle anything like this.

"So you had the last pillar knocked out from under you. After a while, all that sustained you was fury at whoever had taken me from you. You kept digging until you found Jacques, and you came after him with a gun. Much like Amesby did tonight. Except that you were out for vengeance rather than gain."

"You weren't as good as Amesby then, Joe," Jacques said. "You never got close. I must say you did a much better job of stalking me the second time."

"I had more information this time. So you bagged me."

"By then," Maddy continued, "you had too much invested in hating Jacques. You couldn't shift gears. You didn't want to. You knew mindwipe was a kind of death, and you'd been wanting to die for some time."

"Jacques, why didn't you just kill me? I would have."

"I begged him not to," Maddy said, her voice firm and strong. "I argued that if you were taken back to the war years, and allowed to start all over again, you might just take a different path from there."

I grimaced. "So I spent four years doing nothing whatsoever and then became a crusader."

"Not so," Maddy insisted. "You spent four years coming to terms with the war."

"War can be exhilarating, exciting," Jacques said. "That is its dirty secret. A life-threatening situation is stimulating. If you know that, it is because you are the one that survived. So, if you are an introspective, sensitive man, you may mistakenly decide that it is killing that excites you—when in fact the exciting part is almost-being-killed. To encourage you to stay underground, I gave you enough illicit computer power to plunder banks at will—yet you chose to become a burglar. To put yourself on the line, to give your victims, and the police, a fair crack at you. You used the computer only to give you an edge. In that four years you had some very narrow squeaks, and you acquired some interesting scars, and you never killed anyone. Look at you: that little dance you just did with Amesby got you high, didn't it? The crucial element that was missing in the war, and that has been present in your life since I set you down in New York, is ethical confidence. You *believe* in the causes you fight for now. Or else you don't fight. I know I can trust your commitment, because you fought for me."

"How did the Bear come to work for you?"

Madeleine answered. "He and his wife, Minnie, moved to Toronto shortly after you moved up here. They came back to visit you before you dropped out of sight. You told them the whole story, and so when you did disappear, Bear and Minnie decided that Jacques had had you killed. It bothered them both—they both loved Norman Kent—but there was nothing they could do. They couldn't go off commandoing like you, they had responsibilities. Minnie was tied to her job, and Bear was inhibited by Minnie's being pregnant. Then, four months later, she was killed in an auto accident. When he was over his grief, Bear decided it would be good therapy to go look up Jacques. He went through much the same thing you have to-day—without the floor show. He's been with us ever since."

There was no way to take this all in; I filed it for later. Bear married, and widowered. I wondered if I had liked this Minnie, if Norman would have mourned her. "Everything has ripples, doesn't it?" I had a sudden alarming thought. "Hey! How badly is Amesby's planted evidence going to mess us up?"

Jacques smiled. "Not too badly, I think. You pumped him well; I believe he left leads only with the RCMP and Interpol, and we have both of them under control. It may even be possible to recover the evidence before his death is known."

"So where do we go from here?"

His smile widened. "Lots of places, Joe. Lots of places. I intend to loose mindfill on the world, for good or ill, in a little more than five years. We will be busy."

I was shocked. "Five *years?*"

"That soon?" Karen gasped.

"I'd like it to be longer. But I can't keep the lid on forever, even with mindwipe to help. The leaks keep getting harder to patch, and the assassins keep getting better. As it is, I don't know if I'll live to see even the first-order results of what I have done."

"But how can you get the world ready for a trauma like that in five years?" Karen shook her head. "Sounds to me like World War Three and a new Stone Age. You read the papers. The world ain't *ready*."

Jacques nodded in agreement. "It will be necessary," he said in a perfectly normal, conversational tone of voice, "to conquer the United States, the Soviet Union, the People's Republic of China, and the Union of Africa, without letting anyone know."

"Oh," she said weakly. "Well, as long as you've got it worked out, okay."

"Jacques," Madeleine said reprovingly, "you are an awful tease. Karen, honey, come here." She led Karen to the couch and sat them both down. "Who is the most powerful man in the United States?"

She gestured with her head toward Jacques. "Besides him?"

Madeleine smiled. "Yes, hon. Besides him."

"The President."

Madeleine kept smiling while she shook her head. "No. It's the man who pulls the President's strings, dear. For decades now, it has been impossible for a man suited to that power to be elected. Stevenson was the last to try. The rest of them accepted the inevitable and worked through electable figureheads. There hasn't been a president since Johnson who wasn't a ventriloquist's dummy. Some of them never knew it. The present incumbent, as a matter of fact, has no idea that he is owned and operated by a mathematician from Butler, Missouri. They've never been introduced. But *we* know—so we needn't waste time and energy trying to get past the Secret Service."

"I'm beginning to see how I can be of help to you," Karen said.

"You're very quick."

They smiled at each other. They were going to be friends.

I had reached that state of mind in which nothing can surprise. If Amesby had walked back into the room, on fire, I'd have offered him coffee. "So we conquer the world..."

"A necessary first step," Jacques agreed. "Then it gets harder." He laughed suddenly. "Listen to me, eh, Madeleine? All my life I have thought of myself as a rational anarchist. Albert Einstein said once, 'God punished me for my contempt for authority by making me an authority.'"

"Darling," my sister said, "lay out the Grand Plan later. Right now Joe has a choice to make."

He blinked. "Yes, my dear. Quite right."

Choice to make? Sure, anything, go on, ask me anything.

"Joe, would you like your memories back?"

I stopped moving. I stopped breathing. I stopped seeing. I stopped thinking. I kept hearing.

"You received the most primitive form of mindwipe. I spoke of it before. The memories themselves were not actually erased. They...they were hidden from your mind's metaprogrammer. The access codes were removed from the files. And placed, as carefully as the state of the art allowed, in *my* files. I can put them back now if you want."

He waited in vain for a response. He went on, his voice strained, "Some damage will always remain. If I restore your access to those memories, they will..." He reached for words. "Joe, one day soon I will play into your head a tape of my memories of the last thirty years. It will take a few hours. When I'm done, you will have access to everything I've done and seen and thought. You will be able to recall it all, experience it through the eyes of the viewpoint character. But you will not confuse those memories with your own experiences. The *identity* factor will be attenuated. The memories will have a kind of 'third person' feel—the experiences of someone not-you. Ego knows its own work.

"Memory is a living process—continually shuffling and rearranging itself. By fencing off some of your memories for so many years, I weakened them, blurred them slightly. The gestalt they were part of no longer—quite—exists. Those years I stole from you will, at best, always seem like something that happened to someone else. But they are not necessarily completely lost to you."

He stopped talking again for a time. Then: "It is the only

restitution I can offer for what I have done to you. If you refuse, I will understand."

Then he shut up completely.

I sat down on something. Hot wetness occurred in my mouth. Coffee the way I like it. I swallowed. My vision cleared and I saw Karen staring into my eyes from a foot away. "Thanks," I said, and took the cup from her.

She turned to Jacques, her expression angry. "Will it make him whole again? Or mess him up more?"

Madeleine answered. "Karen, listen to me. I have in my skull the memories of more than a hundred people, in whole or in part. Jacques has nearly three times that many. Between us we know more about human psychology than anyone now alive. This will make him whole if anything can. It will be up to him. It always is."

I put down the cup. I got up and went to Madeleine. She was standing near the fire. It was only coals now, but still quite warm. I put my hands on her shoulders.

"Were there any good times in there at all, Maddy?"

I recognized her now. The expression on her face I had seen often in childhood. When I broke my tooth. When I failed Social Studies. When I got mugged. When my first love left me.

"Yes, little brother. A few, at least, that I know of; I've never audited your tapes. Not many, I won't lie to you. Those were not your best years, Norm—Joe. A man sets a mine that very nearly kills you, to further a cause that he believes in, and your mind can find no good excuse to hate him and your heart can't help it. That's hard to integrate. It got worse from there, steadily. But yes, there were good times. Just not enough. We got to know each other, at least, at last, and I loved you."

"Did I love you?"

"You needed me."

I turned to Jacques. "Do it. Tonight. Now."

They took me to a white sterile place like a cross between an operating theater and the bridge of the Space Commando's starship. They laid me down on a very comfortable table. They spoke soothingly to me. They placed under my head and neck

what felt like a leather pillow. It was comfortable. They folded
parts of it over across my forehead and secured them. My heart
was racing.

Karen's face appeared over mine. Her voice was the only
one that didn't seem to be coming from underwater.

"Joe? Remember how I'd forgotten most of that stuff about
my father? And then after I told you about it, I could handle
it? You're a brave son of a bitch, Joe, and someday I want to
swap memories with you, if you're willing."

My mouth was very dry. "I love you too."

She kissed me, and her face withdrew. A tear landed on
my chin. I tried to wipe it, but my arms seemed to be restrained.

"*Now,* Jacques!"

Like two decks of cards being shuffled together.

First, large cuts, thick stacks.

I fought in the jungle burgled apartments taught English
befriended pimps and thieves bungled a marriage found Karen
in the living room found Maddy in the living room hunted the
man behind her death tracked him to Nova Scotia to Phinney's
Cove died killed.

Then individual cards.

The hoarse panting breath of the mugger beside him on the
MacDonald Bridge. The terrible smile on Karen's face as I
cleared the doorway. Weeping in Maddy's arms, the top of his
head bruised and sore. The smell of Karen's cigarettes. Naked
at the door and Lois grinning at him from the hallway. The
sound Karen made when she came the first time. Minnie in
his arms, calling his name. "— coward, what's he doing?" The
nurse calling me "Norman" and fainting. The Bay of Fundy
as the sun goes down, magnificent and indifferent and I know
I'm going to die soon. She's sorry she got me into this, and
the sky is so full of stars! That luxurious cell, Jacques will be
here soon for my decision. The flat, anechoic sound of the shot
that killed Amesby. My God, what if Maddy's never *coming*
back? The bitch broke my nose. God damn it, Sarge, the poor
bastard's dead *we've got to bug out now!* He has to be the

spitting image of her old man, oh, Christ. It's not really you I'm screwing, Mrs. MacLeod, it's your husband. The shock dock has the emptiest eyes I've ever seen. I'm gonna find that son of a bitch and kill him twice. This one's my size, no relatives, he'll do just fine. It's *his computer*, Karen, we're blown. We can really change the world. I love you too, Karen. Heinrich Dreser gave us both heroin and aspirin. God is an iron.

This is my memory record of how I came to join the conspiracy. Since it is the third record you have audited, you will probably understand why I have ordered it as I have. I want you to see the two paths I took, and the choices they led to. It will shed some light on why, of two very similar people, one will opt to join our conspiracy and one will not. Later records will be even more instructive in this regard.

One of the very best things about pooling memories is that it allows us to learn from each other's mistakes. And from our own.

If we have not already met, I love you for the choice you have made. We will prevail!

Tomorrow's record will be that of my wife, Karen.

AWARD-WINNING
Science Fiction!

The following titles are winners of the prestigious Nebula or Hugo Award for excellence in Science Fiction. A must for lovers of good science fiction everywhere!

☐ 47809-3	**THE LEFT HAND OF DARKNESS,** Ursula K. LeGuin	$2.95
☐ 79179-4	**SWORDS AND DEVILTRY,** Fritz Leiber	$2.75
☐ 06223-7	**THE BIG TIME,** Fritz Leiber	$2.50
☐ 16651-2	**THE DRAGON MASTERS,** Jack Vance	$1.95
☐ 16706-3	**THE DREAM MASTER,** Roger Zelazny	$2.25
☐ 24905-1	**FOUR FOR TOMORROW,** Roger Zelazny	$2.25
☐ 80697-X	**THIS IMMORTAL,** Roger Zelazny	$2.50